NURSING HOME NINJAS

NURSING HOME NINJAS

AL STEVENS

FIVE STAR
A part of Gale, Cengage Learning

GALE
CENGAGE Learning®

Detroit • New York • San Francisco • New Haven, Conn • Waterville, Maine • London

GALE
CENGAGE Learning

LIBRARY OF CONGRESS CATALOGING-IN-PUBLICATION DATA

Stevens, Al, 1940–
   Nursing home ninjas / Al Stevens. — 1st ed.
    p. cm.
   ISBN 978-1-4328-2694-9 (hardcover) — ISBN 1-4328-2694-8 (hardcover)
   1. Nursing home patients—Fiction. 2. Nursing homes—Employees—Fiction. 3. Conspiracies—Fiction. 4. Murder—Fiction. I. Title.
PS3619.T47876N87 2013
813'.6—dc23   2012037287

First Edition. First Printing: February 2013
Find us on Facebook– https://www.facebook.com/FiveStarCengage
Visit our website– http://www.gale.cengage.com/fivestar/
Contact Five Star™ Publishing at FiveStar@cengage.com

Printed in Mexico
1 2 3 4 5 6 7 17 16 15 14 13

To the memory of Jim and Mary Stauffer

ACKNOWLEDGMENTS

Thanks to Dea Kristensen for her patient and thorough review of this story and to Nick Chirico for his advice and assistance with research. And a special thanks to the many health care workers throughout the world who attend tirelessly to the care and needs of our elderly citizens, the residents of *Heaven's waiting rooms.*

CHAPTER 1

Marvin Bradley stepped along more quickly than usual this New Year's Eve. He walked down the stark white corridors that led from his small room in the assisted-living wing to the dining hall. Low temperatures in the nursing home hastened his pace, but there was urgency in his step, too. He had work to do, a mystery to solve. Somebody was abusing the old people, and Marvin did not know who or why.

His slippers and cane echoed off the bare floor and high ceilings. *Swoosh, click, swoosh, swoosh, click, swoosh.* Overhead fluorescent tubes flooded the hallways with a sterile bath of light and lit his way along checkerboard tile floors and colorless plaster walls.

"Nothing like it used to be," he said to himself. The institutionalized aura of the nursing home stood in stark contrast to his memories of what had once been a palatial mansion and home to the town's richest family.

Soon he was at the wide double entranceway into the dining hall. He pulled his robe around him to keep the chill off his neck and chest, ambled over to his breakfast table, hung his cane on the back of the chair, and plopped down across from Mike Charles, his best friend and frequent companion. They grunted their usual good morning greetings.

A server brought Marvin a cup of coffee. He picked up the cup, blew on the coffee, and sipped from the edge. A minute later she returned with his plate of breakfast, dropped it in front of him with a clatter, and walked off. He tucked his napkin under his chin and pushed the food around on the hard plastic plate with the stainless steel fork, trying to work up an appetite. Breakfast was the usual: powdered eggs, hash browns, and bacon strips. The bacon was burned, the hash browns were greasy, and the eggs did not resemble eggs in the slightest.

He waved for the server to come over. She looked his way and ignored him while she served other residents. Finally, after longer than it should have taken, she walked over.

"What?" she asked.

"Any chance I could get oatmeal and fruit?"

"Nope," she said with a laugh and walked away.

"There goes your tip," Mike called after her. Then to Marvin, "Every time you ask they just laugh at you."

"Doesn't hurt to ask. Nothing to lose."

A frosty glaze covered the tall undraped windows, which looked out over the lawn and out to the distant mountain range. The ground had no snow cover this morning, but the wind was up, the clouds threatened, and the wind chill factor shaved about fifteen degrees off the thermometer's already below-freezing reading.

Their breakfasts together usually sparkled with conversation about anything and nothing, the latest news, the weather, how they planned to spend their day, and sprinkles of gossip about the staff and the other residents. But today both men sat solemn and quiet.

The silence troubled Marvin, made him feel self-conscious. He wanted to say what was on his mind but couldn't bring himself to speak the words. He shifted around and fooled with his food, pushing it around on his plate.

Then Mike said, "Marvin, there's some bad stuff going on around here."

"What kind?"

"I think somebody's beating the crap out of the old people."

Marvin blew on his coffee again, not to cool it, but out of habit. It had cooled while they sat in silence. He was glad someone else had said the unthinkable before he had to. "You noticed it, too? I was hoping it was my imagination. What have you seen?"

"Bruises," Mike said. "Somebody's hitting them."

Hearing it said out loud, having it brought to the fore and acknowledged, somehow made it more real. No more believable, but more real.

"When did you start seeing it?" Marvin asked.

"A couple weeks ago. I figured it was from falls and such. The usual stuff. But it's getting worse. More and more every day."

Marvin sighed and said, "That's what I see, too. Do you know who's doing it? I sure don't."

"No. I asked Nurse Norma, and she said it was my imagination. 'Old people bruise easily.' But that's a bunch of horse hockey. Mr. Dalton never cried before, and he was sitting in the hallway this morning bawling like a baby. With a fresh black eye. I asked what happened, but he didn't even try to answer."

"But she didn't believe you?"

Mike pulled out his handkerchief, blew his nose with a loud honk, and rubbed it back and forth with a clean part of the white cloth. Then he looked at the handkerchief to see what he had produced. Marvin leaned on his elbows and waited.

"I couldn't tell." Mike folded the handkerchief to cover its contents and stuffed it back into his pocket. "She sure didn't want to talk about it."

"Have you told anybody else?"

"Carrie."

"What does she think?"

"She noticed it, too, same as us."

Carrie, a resident in her eighties, was the third member of Marvin's circle of friends.

"Where is she?"

"Her daughter picked her up to go shopping. I helped her get in her daughter's van. She's a heavy load. It was all me and her daughter could do to hoist her into the front seat. They ought to get a wheelchair lift."

"How'd you manage that with your walker?"

"It wasn't easy. Her daughter did most of it."

"You should have called. I'd have helped. Where were the orderlies?"

"Where they always are when you need them. Nowhere to be found. We managed. Anyway, she'll have breakfast and lunch in town. Maybe supper, too."

"Can't blame her for that." Marvin looked again at his plate. He ate slowly and wondered whether eating this kind of food would be as bad for him as not eating.

"I wish they'd turn up the heat," Mike said.

"And hire a decent cook."

"Dream on."

Marvin felt his age today. The brisk morning walk had taken a lot out of him. He pushed back his remaining wisps of white hair, put his elbows on the table and his chin in his hands, and watched his friend devour the slop that passed for breakfast in this godforsaken nursing home.

"Why are we putting up with this?" he asked.

"What choice do we have?" Mike looked glum.

The talk was bringing them both down, and that wasn't good. Marvin tried to show a cheerful face for his friend, forcing his trademark toothy smile. His eyes, though, usually a sparkling bright blue, betrayed his small charade with their sadness, evident to anyone who knew him. And no one knew him better than Mike, who ignored the phony smile and kept eating.

"Tastes like cardboard," he said. Then he shrugged his shoulders. "But not bad for cardboard," and he kept shoveling it in.

Marvin took off his glasses and rubbed his eyes. He pushed on the old hearing aid with his fingers to firmly seat it in his ear and shoved his plate with its half-eaten breakfast into the center of the table.

"What's the matter, old man, you don't like the food?" Mike asked. "It's good for you. Make you grow."

"I'm tall enough."

"You lost a couple inches in the last several years, I bet you did. We all do."

"That's because I'm bent over. Measure me with a tape measure, not a yardstick, and I am as tall as I ever was."

"I wasn't always this short, either. I used to work for the National Football League. Before then I was taller than you."

"Here we go again. How did working for the NFL make you shorter?"

"I was a human growth hormone donor."

That made Marvin smile, this time not a forced one. Once again, Mike's sense of humor had kicked in and lightened an otherwise depressing conversation. He looked at his pal with affection. Mike Charles had seen eighty-five years go by. He was short and skinny with no hair and a frizzy salt-and-pepper mustache that stuck straight out from under his round bump of a nose, which was red today from its encounters with the handkerchief.

"You're in the wheelchair this morning," Marvin said. "Where's the walker?"

"In my room. The chair's faster when I'm in a hurry."

"What hurry? Why would you be in a hurry around here?"

"I got places to go and people to see."

Marvin leaned back, clasped his hands behind his head, and

studied his pal, the mysterious Mike Charles. No one knew much about him except that his was a checkered past about which he spoke only in fragments, no details. Whenever someone asked Mike what he did before he retired, he'd say, "Odd jobs."

"What kind of odd jobs?" they'd ask.

"Odd ones."

By now the cafeteria had filled with residents. The servers hustled between the tables and service counter. They carried trays of food and the coffeepot to the newcomers, and bussed the tables of those who had finished early. The clatter of dishes and tableware combined with the chatter of the residents to fill the room with a typical mealtime drone.

Marvin pushed again on his hearing aid and leaned closer to Mike. "Heard any jokes?" he asked, still trying to lighten the mood.

"Yeah," Mike said. "My son told me this one. You know what's thirty feet long and smells like urine?"

"No. What?"

"Line dancing at the old folks home."

"That's pretty good."

They sat a while longer, not talking. Marvin looked first at his watch, then at his food, then at Mike, then back at his watch. Routine, boring, same old, same old, day in and day out. No more. He had needed something new to challenge him, to get him out of his pajamas every day and into street clothes, with a purpose, a mission, a reason to stay alive. He wished he'd found a more pleasant diversion, but with the help of his friends, this could be just the ticket.

CHAPTER 2

Every morning on his way back to his room, Marvin stopped in to greet and visit some of the old people. Marvin and Mike had daily rounds of such visits, Marvin in the mornings and Mike in the afternoons. They agreed that these visits benefited not only the old people, but themselves, too. They were doing something besides just getting older, something of value, something of service to their neighbors.

The name "old people" was what they used to distinguish the less capable residents from the high-functioning ones. It signified condition, not age. Old people had severe mobility and communications impairments, most stayed in their rooms, and many suffered from one form of dementia or another. Dementia was common at nursing homes, and Orchard Hills was no exception.

Marvin poked his head into the room of Mrs. Arnold, a lady at least five years his senior who lay in bed half-covered and shivering.

"Hello, Mrs. Arnold. How are we this morning?"

She didn't answer with her usual cheerful smile and wave. She just stared then rolled over in her bed. Tears streamed down her face, and she turned away from him. The sight saddened him. He went in to pull the covers up over her. Her arm had a big bruise above the elbow.

"How did you hurt your arm, Mrs. Arnold?" She wouldn't answer. Many of the old people couldn't speak coherently.

He sat with her a while and read to her from one of her magazines. She didn't react, so he left her room quietly, walked down the hallway a few steps, and looked in on the fellow next door, who was sitting in a chair next to the window.

"Good morning, Mr. Partlow. Looks like another cold one."

The old man looked around, grumped a response, and turned back to the window. Partlow usually welcomed him with a big grin. Not today. Marvin stood a while until his eyes grew accustomed to the dark. Mr. Partlow turned to look at him again. He had a black eye.

"What's this? Did you run into a door?"

Again, no response.

Marvin walked closer to the old man and sniffed. Partlow needed to have his diaper changed. Marvin picked up the remote intercom, pressed the button for Orderly, and waited. After a time, a male voice answered.

"What?"

"Mr. Partlow needs to be changed," Marvin said into the intercom.

"He ain't going anywhere," came the abrupt reply. "We'll get there when we can."

Marvin shook his head. Time was there'd be somebody there right away. He considered answering with an angry retort, but that would come back on him when he needed something. He put down the intercom and left the room to continue his rounds.

The scene was repeated at many of his stops. Instead of cheerful greetings, he was met with cowering and tears, bruises and welts. He didn't know who was responsible, and he didn't know why, but he had to do something about it. Nobody else noticed. Nobody else seemed to care. He felt a wave of determination. He'd need help. It would be up to him and his small circle of friends.

He hobbled along toward the hallway where he and Mike

lived and considered what they could do. First he'd need to know who the abuser was and why. He stopped in Mike's room. Mike was already there, sitting in his chair reading the newspaper.

Marvin sat in the chair next to Mike's desk. "It's getting worse, Mike. I'm seeing a lot more. Not only abuse, but neglect, too. What can we do?"

Mike put down the newspaper. "I'm not sure, but somebody's got to do something."

"Maybe it's just some sick-o that likes beating up old people. A loser without a life, so he takes it out on helpless folks. Is it anyone besides the old people?"

"Not that I've seen," Mike said. "I'd like to get my hands on whoever's doing it."

Marvin hit his fist on the desk. Then he shook his hand and looked at it to make sure he hadn't hurt it. "Something's got to be done."

"Let's find out who it is and get him fired."

"Or arrested. When's Carrie due back?"

"Not sure. Tonight or after breakfast tomorrow."

"Well, the three of us ought to be able to come up with a plan."

Mike went to the refrigerator and pulled out a can of beer. He pulled the tab up with a pop and took a gulp of the froth that bubbled up from the opening.

"Want a beer?"

"No, it's too early." Marvin hesitated. "Wait a minute. Are we supposed to have beer in our rooms?"

"No." Mike took another pull, and the beer ran down his chin.

"I won't ask."

"Don't tell, either. Do you want to know how I get it?"

"No. If I had beer, I'd only drink it."

"Uh, I think that's the idea." Another slurp.

Marvin went to his own room and plopped down in his recliner. He reached over and pulled his quilt from the bed and across his knees and chest to block out the cold. He thumbed through the latest edition of *Reader's Digest,* read a couple of articles and all the jokes, but it didn't cheer him up. His mind kept returning to the problem at hand.

He got up and paced around the small room. He used the furniture instead of his cane to keep from falling. From the chair to the desk, then to the bookcase, then the bed and to the window and back to the chair, moving slowly, deep in thought.

The abuse and what to do about it had him going. He wasn't sure what three impaired octogenarians could do against an unknown younger, stronger enemy, but he was sure going to give it a run. He tried watching TV to take his mind off of the problem, but, as usual, no matter how loud he set the volume control, he couldn't understand what most of the people were saying, so he turned it off. One thing was sure; to cope with this situation, he'd need more information.

Information. Information is power, he'd heard. Documentation. Proof that would indicate why someone was hurting the old people. Where could he find it? What would it be?

When noon rolled around, he got up and headed for the dining hall. He settled in at the lunch table with Mike and looked down at the bologna and cheese sandwich and half-warm tomato soup. He stirred the soup to get the sediment mixed in and said, "I think I'll do some research this afternoon if I can get on the computer."

"What can the computer tell you?"

"Online newspapers. I'll search for articles about resident abuse in other nursing homes."

"Better get there early. If the solitaire queen gets in there ahead of you, you'll wait all day."

"Solitaire queen? Who's that?"

Mike leaned over and whispered, "Elsie Collins." He tilted his head in the direction of a thin old woman eating her lunch alone at a nearby table. "She plays solitaire all day long. They should get a computer just for her."

Marvin hurried to finish his lunch and leave before Elsie was done eating. He went straight to the dayroom. No one was using the computer, so he sat in front of it and logged onto his account. Several months before, the nursing home had sponsored a class for residents to learn how to use the computer. He'd learned how to navigate to various websites.

He visited the sites of newspapers in neighboring communities and searched the archives for references to "nursing homes" and "abuse." The dayroom computer did not have a printer, so he sent the matching articles across the network to the printer at the nursing station.

Engrossed in his research, Marvin didn't hear anyone come in. But the aroma of stale, sweet-smelling perfume surrounded him, and a squeaky voice from behind said, "Are you going to be long?"

Elsie Collins stood behind him with her hands on the back of the chair. She leaned over his shoulder and looked at the screen as if to see what he was doing.

"Hi, Elsie. I didn't hear you come in."

"With all this jewelry clanging? How could you miss it?" She giggled and twiddled her hoop earrings and shook her bracelet-adorned arms.

Marvin tapped his hearing aid and said, "With these ears I can't hear a lot of things."

He took in the comical vision that was Elsie. A thin woman with a face like a peach pit and a figure like a scarecrow, her multicolored, polka-dotted outfit brought to mind a Raggedy Ann doll. Her perfume turned his stomach. He hoped she wouldn't wait right there next to him.

"I'll be here a while, Elsie. Why don't you come back later?"

"Hmph. Well don't stay there all day. I have work to do," and she clanged across the room, sat at the reading table, and picked up a magazine.

He grinned and turned back to the computer. He expanded his search to include statewide newspapers and then national ones, printing the articles that were relevant.

Then he logged off. Elsie was in the chair almost before he was up from it.

He walked down to the nursing station to get his printouts. Nurse Norma, the nursing supervisor, was behind the counter seated at the desk, leafing through and poring over forms on a clipboard.

"Hi, Nurse Norma. I need to pick up my printouts."

She put the clipboard on the desk. "Well, somebody sure does. I had to put more paper in the printer. What's going on? What are you printing so much of?"

"Newspaper articles. Research."

She got up from her chair and went to the printer. She took the pages from the printer's tray, got a manila envelope from a storage cabinet, put the pages in the envelope, and handed it across the counter to him.

"Don't let management know I did this. They don't mind a page every now and then, but they'd pitch a fit if they knew you were using this much paper. Costs money, you know." She clucked her tongue and looked sideways at Marvin with a grin.

"Thanks. I'll see you later."

Marvin took the envelope to his room, sat at his desk, and began reading articles. One by one he read them and stacked the pages in piles, each pile representing a category of information. He drew on his experience as an accountant to organize the data. A pattern was emerging among nursing homes in the surrounding areas. In several cases, an article would report incidents of resident abuse at a nursing home. Then a later edition would report that the home was closing, always with a reference back to the abuse. Marvin didn't know what to make of it.

His studies consumed his attention, and suppertime snuck up on him. He looked at the alarm clock on the nightstand. He'd be late if he didn't hurry.

Once again, sitting across from Mike at suppertime, Marvin described the newspaper articles and what they suggested.

"There are some similarities in what's been happening in other nursing homes, but it isn't clear yet and I can't tell whether it applies here. When Carrie gets back, we can kick it around."

"Three heads are better than one."

Marvin hurried back to his room after supper, the articles on his mind. He organized and reorganized the pages according to content and made notes in a tablet. Gradually, he refined his research to support some kind of conclusion, but he didn't know yet where it would lead. He sat up until midnight and worked on his project.

That night he didn't sleep well. He ran through the few things they had been seeing and tried to find a reasonable explanation, a reason it might have happened that did not involve abuse. The articles indicated that similar things had happened at other nursing homes. He didn't want to believe the obvious explanation, but what else could it be? He'd doze off and dream about it, wake up and dwell on it. He moved from his bed to the chair during the night with the quilt comforter pulled up to his chin to ward off the cold. He didn't cough as much when he slept sitting up. And maybe he'd get to sleep sooner.

CHAPTER 3

Sunday morning. Marvin pulled himself out of his chair, put aside the comforter, and put on his slippers and robe over his pajamas.

The room was a small but comfortable efficiency in the assisted-living wing. Bed, dresser, desk, recliner, coffee table. A floor lamp stood next to the recliner and pictures hung on the walls. The nightstand next to the bed had a reading lamp and a small book rack. Necessary furnishings for an old person to have. Nothing fancy, nothing extra. Only the essentials. The kitchen consisted of a half-sized refrigerator with a microwave oven on top and a cabinet for dishes and cookware. The closet was in the bathroom. Most assisted-living resident rooms had the same floor plan but with their furniture arranged according to their occupants' preferences.

"Where did I put my cane?" he said to himself. He looked high and low and finally found it under the bed. "How did it get there? Must've kicked it under when I was reading. Where are my glasses? Oh, yeah, over there. At least I don't have to worry about car keys any more."

He could hear Miss Jessie. "You'd lose your nose if God hadn't glued it on."

Marvin missed his wife, gone these four years. He had called her Miss Jessie since they were first married. He didn't remember why he began calling her that, but he did and it stuck.

He stood in the middle of the room propped on his cane. He had a busy day ahead of him. He turned toward his bathroom, said to no one, "Because I have to go in here, is why," and went in for his morning routine.

"If I had teeth, they'd be chattering," he told his reflection. He didn't like how he looked without his teeth. His mouth was all shrunk up with his lips drawn in and wrinkles etching paths from his cheeks, nose, and chin into his mouth.

"Anymore, I look in the mirror and I'm shaving my father."

He looked at his teeth in the glass of drugstore solution on the sink where they spent their nights while he slept. "Teeth, why aren't you chattering?"

He washed up, squirted deodorant and splashed aftershave lotion, put his teeth in, and looked in the mirror to assess his appearance.

He pushed his hair down and said, "That's the best I can do with what I have to work with."

He went to his closet and looked at the few outfits hanging there.

"Sunday. Got to dress up."

He dressed in slacks, a nice open-collar shirt, and a sports jacket. Then he put in his hearing aid, clipped the receiver to his belt, and left his room. He headed for the dining hall for breakfast with his cane to stay his course and steady his balance.

Today he was a little more wobbly than the day before. His joints were stiff from the cold and from sleeping in the chair, and he didn't step quite as lively.

He talked to himself. "Wonder what we'll have for breakfast today. Oh, yeah. Same thing we had yesterday. Same thing we'll have tomorrow."

He walked into the dining hall and looked around. Mike was seated at their usual table. He went over and sat in the chair across from Mike, and the server brought him a cup of hot coffee, the only part of breakfast he enjoyed. He got settled in and poked his gnarly index finger through the cup handle. His hand shook and the coffee splashed out. He blew on the liquid so it wouldn't burn his mouth and took a few sips.

Mike said, "Got dressed today?"

"Yep."

"I was getting used to the pajamas and robe."

Marvin reached down and smoothed his trousers. "I decided I should dress on Sundays."

"How come?"

"For the visitors."

"What visitors? You don't get visitors."

"My grandson sometimes, but, other than that, not very often. Every now and then I get surprised. So I'll dress just in case. And to look nice for folks who visit the others." He traced a swirl on the tabletop with his finger. "But most days it's pajamas and robe. If it's good enough for Hugh Hefner, it's good enough for me. We're the same age."

"Does Hugh Hefner get dressed on Sundays?"

"I don't know. Does he get visitors?"

The server brought their plates, and they ate their breakfast in silence.

Mike blew on his hands and rubbed them together to warm them up. He broke the silence. "Brr. It sure is cold in here. I wish they'd turn the heat up."

"Not likely. Fuel oil costs money. The new regime is pinching pennies at every turn."

"Even so, a fellow could catch his death in here. I bet it's at most fifty, fifty-five degrees."

"Be glad we're in here. Look at those trees out there."

Marvin gestured toward the west window, which looked out across the grounds and into the mountains. There was no snow, but the wind was up, and the branches of the trees stretched and waved steadily against the sky and horizon. Mike followed Marvin's gaze.

"The 'wind fill tractor' must have it down around zero," Mike said.

Marvin chuckled at his friend's spoonerism. Mike always called it the "wind fill tractor." Marvin didn't know whether Mike knew any better but Marvin wasn't going to correct him. The spoonerism was too funny.

"Where's Carrie?" Marvin asked.

"She called. She spent the night at her daughter's. Said she was going to early morning services. She'll be here sometime today."

"We can talk it over with her then."

"What? The weather?"

"No, Mike. The abuse."

They waited while the waitress poured coffee refills. After she left, Mike said, "There's more."

"More what?"

"More of what we talked about yesterday. More besides the abuse."

"I thought we were going to wait for Carrie." Marvin didn't want to proceed without Carrie's level head to keep them from going overboard. He was sure Mike felt the same way.

"Yeah, but there's more I haven't told you about."

"What else?"

"Somebody's stealing from the old people, too."

"Stealing? What are they stealing?"

"Jewelry, money, snacks, small stuff mostly. Anything valuable. Or edible."

"I'm not missing anything," Marvin said. "Are you?"

"No. I don't think they'd steal from us high-functioning ones. We'd tell on them, and they know it."

"How do you know about the stealing?"

Mike looked around the room as if to see whether anyone was listening. "From my daily visits. I help the old people with their mail and where they keep their things."

"I didn't know you did that much. That's the staff's job."

Mike sniffed and made a scoffing grunt. "Yeah, right. Half the old people here are lucky to get a bath once a week much less their mail read to them. I always keep a kind of mental inventory of their stuff, too. Lately things have been going missing."

"How lately?"

"In the past few months or so."

"You never mentioned it."

"None of my business. It's not a real big deal, a few cuff links, cookies, a couple bucks. I figure you can't control the small stuff. There's always going to be some dirtbag stealing whatever's laying around. But now with this abuse going on . . ."

Marvin folded his arms, pushed back in his chair, and pursed his lips. "I wish we could prove it. Catch them in the act."

Mike leaned forward and lowered his voice. "Maybe we can, Marvin, maybe we can. Think about it. We can do some spy work."

"You mean like go undercover?" Marvin was interested in Mike's ideas.

"Not exactly. Just be ourselves. They see us hanging around, and they don't pay us a bit of mind. Just old people wandering up and down the halls, slobbering and messing our pants. That's all they'll see, and I bet we can pick up a lot of information like that just by keeping our eyes and ears open and our mouths shut."

"You could be on to something, Mike. I've been wondering how we could find out who's doing it. That might be just the ticket. We'll have to run it by Carrie."

"Carrie will know what to do. She'll pull out one of her lists and start reading off items to consider and people, and it'll get us thinking."

"Yeah. I'm counting on that. We need Carrie in on this."

"Of course," Mike said, "in the interests of maintaining our cover, we'll have to actually slobber and mess our pants."

"I can't wait to tell Carrie."

Mike gazed out the window at the mountains. "This'll be a lot like the old days," he said almost to himself.

"What old days?"

"Oh, nothing. Just thinking out loud."

They were interrupted by a loud cry coming from somewhere outside the dining hall. There were often moans and groans, but this was different, louder, more desperate. Someone was in trouble.

"What was that?" Marvin said. He tapped on his hearing aid receiver.

"That's Whitley. He never hollers. We better get down there."

CHAPTER 4

Marvin and Mike hurried along out of the dining hall and down the corridor to Bill Whitley's room. Whitley had come to the home about a month before, and they didn't know him very well, so an occasional yell might not be serious. When they got to his room, they found him standing at his open window, bending over and looking out down toward the ground. He was crying.

"What's wrong, Mr. Whitley?" Marvin asked. "Why did you yell?"

Whitley stood and faced them, tears running down his cheeks. A nurse poked her head in and said, "Everything okay in here?"

"We're not sure, ma'am," Marvin said. "Mr. Whitley gave out with a yell, and he hasn't done that before."

She came in and felt Whitley's pulse and listened to his chest with her stethoscope.

She said, "Why is that window open?"

"We'll get it," Marvin said, and she walked out.

Whitley gestured for them to look and pointed out the window down toward the ground. Marvin and Mike went over and looked out. Whitley's gray and white cat lay in the dirt, motionless.

The cat was dead. Marvin felt a dread come over him. He didn't want to consider what this might mean. He was certain, given that the window was open in the dead of winter, that someone had killed the cat.

Whitley went over and sat on his bed. He put his head in his hands and wept.

"He loved that cat," Marvin said to Mike. "Not many know this, but they didn't want to let him have it here. He told me his family paid extra so he could keep it. I think he comes from money."

Mike sat next to Whitley and held his hand. "He told you? He can't talk. How did he tell you?"

"He writes notes." Marvin pointed to a notepad and pencil on the nightstand. "We've been talking the last couple of days. Nobody else knows he can do it. He was mad that his family had to pay extra for his cat, and that they complained about it, so he doesn't want to talk to any of them or the staff. Isn't that right, Mr. Whitley?"

Whitley nodded.

"I don't blame him. How much did they pay?"

"Five thousand. They called it an endowment. He calls it extortion."

"Man," Mike said. "Five Gs. For a cat. And now the cat's dead. I'm going to go look at it. That's not much of a fall to kill a cat."

"Well, go get your coat. And maybe take your walker. The terrain's rough for a wheelchair."

Mike wheeled out of the room and headed down the hall toward his room. Marvin sat on the bed next to Whitley and said, "Mr. Whitley, is there anything I can do?"

Whitley shook his head, turned to one side, and laid down. He buried his face in the pillow and sobbed into it. This was senseless. Why would anyone kill a man's cat?

He went to the window and looked out. Mike stood there leaning on his walker and holding the dead cat in his arms. He called up to Marvin, "Its neck is broken. Somebody killed it, for sure. I can't imagine why. Who'd do something like this?"

"The same one who's beating them up, I'll wager."

Mike looked down at the cat in his hands. Then he laid it on the grass underneath the window. "I'll get a shovel and bury it out beyond the garden. Get him in the ground before he goes stiff."

Whitley sat up, grabbed the pencil and notepad, and scribbled:

Bury Toby here.

"He wants him buried right there under the window," Marvin told Mike.

"Okay. Makes sense. I'll get a shovel from the tool shed." He left to make his way, walker style, across the lawn and around back to the service area.

Marvin called after him, "Button up your coat."

Mike waved him off with one hand and kept plodding forward.

"Mr. Whitley," Marvin said, "do you know who did this?"

Whitley shook his head. Then he wrote:

Went to bathroom. Toby OK then.

"How long ago?"

Whitley tapped the face of his watch and then held up both hands. He extended five fingers on each hand. Then he made fists and extended five fingers from his right hand only.

"Fifteen minutes ago?"

Whitley nodded. Then he wrote:

Couldn't find Toby. Somebody opened window.

His hand traced the pencil across the notepad.

Looked out. Toby dead.

He handed the note to Marvin and began to sob again.

"And that's when you cried out?"

Whitley nodded. Then he lay down and closed his eyes. Marvin went to the window and waited for Mike to come back with the shovel. Mike moved slowly across the lawn, juggling the shovel and gripping his walker. The sight was almost comical. Mike would put the point of the shovel into the ground and hold its handle under his arm while he took a couple of steps with the walker. Then he'd bring the shovel forward, stick it in the ground again, and repeat the procedure. Every couple of steps he'd reach up and tighten his cap on his head to keep the wind from blowing it away. He made slow but steady progress and inched his way across the lawn toward the window.

Marvin called out, "Mike, I could have done that."

"You'd freeze to death. I'm used to the cold. I used to work at a ski resort."

When he got to the window, he was breathing hard and his breath made wisps of visible moisture that blew away with the wind. "I don't mind doing it. But it is cold out here."

"I didn't know you worked at a ski resort. What was your job?"

"It was a summer job," he said. He poked the shovel into the frozen ground. "Groundskeeper. I mowed the lawn, trimmed the bushes."

"Then how did that get you used to . . . oh, never mind."

The earth was hard from the frost, and Marvin watched Mike struggle to dig the grave. He'd dig for a while, then he'd stop to rest and get his breath so he could dig some more. When he had dug deep enough, he gently laid the cat in the hole and began shoveling dirt over it. Whitley got up and came over for a last look.

Marvin touched Whitley on the arm. "Mr. Whitley, somebody is abusing the old people. Stealing from them, too. Keep an eye out. They think you can't communicate like the others. Maybe they killed your cat so they don't have to buy cat food and litter."

Whitley grabbed the notepad and wrote:

They didn't like cleaning litter box, too.

"Yeah. It figures," Marvin said. "Who usually cleans the litter box?"

Whitley wrote:

Leroy.

"Who's Leroy?"

Whitley tore the page off the pad, crumpled it, and threw it in the trash can. Then he scribbled on a new page:

Tall white guy. Red hair. Pock marks. Maintenance man.

"Oh, yeah," Marvin said. "I've seen him around. Not a pleasant fellow, it seems. Anyway, don't let any of them know we talk to one another this way. Or even that you can. I don't know what they'd do if they thought you could rat them out."

Whitley nodded and went back to his bed.

Mike called in through the window, "Yeah, but if they think he can't talk, he's a prime candidate for their abuse. You can't win."

Just then Carrie Fenway wheeled up to the door. "What's going on?" Carrie was a heavy lady with one leg missing who traveled in a wheelchair. She rolled into the room and surveyed the situation.

"Why do you have the window open, Mr. Whitley?" she asked.

"Somebody killed Mr. Whitley's cat," Marvin said.

"Oh, my stars. Who did that?"

"Probably one of the staff. We don't know yet. They've been stealing stuff, too. From the old people."

"Stealing? My god, Marvin. I know somebody's been knocking them around. Isn't there anything we can do?"

"I don't know. Let's you, me, and Mike get together and talk about it in private. How about my room in a couple hours? Until we know who's doing all this, we have to be careful."

"Where's Mike?" she asked.

"He's out there, burying the cat."

Carrie wheeled over to the window and looked out at Mike.

"Do you know what you're doing out there?"

"Sure," Mike said. "I used to work for an undertaker."

"Really?" she said.

"Yep," he said and kept shoveling. "I did shaves, haircuts, cosmetics."

"Yuck. Anyway, isn't it cold for that kind of activity? Especially at our age?"

"No, it was always warm in the mortuary."

"I mean now, Mike, out there."

"It isn't as cold as it feels. Wind fill tractor."

"Why do you call it that?" Carrie asked with a grin.

"I used to work for the weather service," Mike said. He continued to fill dirt in over the cat. "I know all the meteorological terms."

"What was your job there?"

"Mailroom."

"Mike," Marvin called out. "My room in two hours. You, me, and Carrie. Okay?"

Mike nodded and tamped flat the mound of dirt with the shovel.

Marvin turned to Carrie. "Why don't you stay with Mr. Whitley a while? Maybe he can get some sleep. He has a bum ticker and should rest. If anything happens, call the nurse. I have to go get ready for our meeting."

"Take a nap, you mean," Carrie said, laughing. "I'll see you in a while. Poor Mr. Whitley, bless his heart." She turned her attention to the old man, asleep now, his face still damp from the tears. She wiped his cheeks with a tissue. Then she wheeled over to the window, closed it, and drew the shade.

CHAPTER 5

Marvin sat in a rocking chair on the veranda that stretched across the front of the nursing home, his pipe clamped between his teeth. The temperature was in the thirties this Sunday morning, but he couldn't smoke inside, so he donned his overcoat and a cap, sat in a rocking chair, and smoked outside.

The episode with Mr. Whitley's cat troubled him. Out here he could get his mind off of it. He looked down across the valley at his town. The fields and mountains surrounding the town were barren, brown and gray in the depths of winter, no snow on the ground, no leaves on the trees, only the needles of evergreens to supply any color at all, the dark brownish green of winter.

Marvin tended to drift off into the past whenever he sat here alone. Some of his memories were good, some not so good. Among the not-so-good were those from a distant past when he was an infantry foot soldier in France and Germany. He had tried without much success to put that time behind him. The horrors he had experienced in combat made him want more than anything a normal, quiet life. It had taken years for the nightmares to stop.

He liked the small-town atmosphere of his hometown with row houses, shops, churches, a bar on most every block, a feed and grain mill, a factory, and a brewery. Down-to-earth people, traditional values, neighbors who helped one another, doors never locked.

He recalled those Sunday afternoons when he and Miss Jessie would leave church and drive throughout the region, stopping at small churches so she could pore over tombstones in the small cemeteries, looking for ancestors for her genealogy research. They'd stop at a small Amish store out in the country to buy scrapple, homemade jellies, and natural grain cereals. They bought their milk, cheese, and butter from a local dairy farm and their eggs and vegetables from the "egg man," an itinerant peddler, a local truck farmer who made weekly rounds from house to house in a beat-up old blue van.

The big wooden rocker groaned under his weight as his thoughts returned to the present. Sundays at the nursing home saw a lot of activity. Many of the residents got dressed up and rode the shuttle bus to and from church. They were at the far end of the veranda now lined up waiting for the bus. But Marvin never joined them. Not that he didn't believe in anything. Marvin and Miss Jessie had been members and regular attendees at the Lutheran church in town for over fifty years, but no more. He hadn't lost his faith; he just hadn't forgiven God for taking her. His mind wandered back again.

He never forgave himself either for leaving her alone to die that way. While he was in the kitchen making toast, Miss Jessie had reached out for him, and he wasn't there. That was difficult for him to deal with, and whenever he thought about it, tears welled up. So he tried not to think about it and never talked about it.

Now, when the weather allowed, Marvin sat in the rocking chair, looking down over the hill at the town, its rooftops on either side of Main Street, smoke trailing up from chimneys, traffic going both ways, stopping and going at the light at the Center Street intersection.

He lifted his binoculars and focused on the roof of his own row house, all that he could see of it among a cluster of roofs. It sat vacant now, waiting for him to come home. He'd like to see the old house again.

"Don't live in the past, Dad," his children would tell him.

"Why not?" he'd respond. "The present is dismal, and I have no future."

He watched the seasons change from the veranda's view of the valley and the mountains. He spent most of his solitary hours in this rocking chair, smoking his pipe, reading, or just gazing at the horizon, watching the sky change colors, the sun make its daily voyage across the valley, the clouds coming and going in random patterns. He watched long wisps of clouds stretching the width of the horizon, the orange-glow sunsets in the southwest, and the moon rise in the southeast over the mountain range. Pink, white, and blue blossoms dotted the scenery in the springtime when trees were in bloom; wildflowers, corn, wheat, and bean fields defined the landscape in the summer; a spectacular wash of colors painted the forests when autumn was at her peak; and postcard-perfect snowfalls blanketed everything, fields, mountains, and the town, in the winter. He could see all these things from the veranda, and it gave him pleasure and comfort.

Marvin rocked back and forth and thought about the past and how time had changed him. His once-sturdy physique had given way to the years and his bad habits.

"You need to quit smoking those cigarettes," Miss Jessie had said. "And you drink too much beer. It can't be good for you."

Eventually he quit both, but not before the years of cigarettes and beer had taken their toll, conspiring with the aging process to erode his body and surrender it to time. He still allowed himself a bottle of beer every now and then and the luxury of his pipe, smoked on the veranda where the wind carried its aroma off to where it did not bother the other residents.

His doctor disapproved of the pipe.

"What? You worried I won't live to a ripe old age?" Marvin would say with a chuckle.

Marvin had his own physician in town. The bus made a twice-weekly trip to the mall for residents to go shopping, and Marvin scheduled his appointments to coincide with those trips.

"Why do you come all the way into town for a simple checkup?" the doctor had asked. "The doctors up there could do it."

"Been coming to you for how long now? No reason to change to some young whelp that doesn't know me. Besides, it's how I keep up on current events. I read the news magazines in the waiting room." Then he would let a moment pass before saying, "Did you know that Nixon resigned?"

That one got the doctor and his nurse laughing. These exchanges were a traditional part of every checkup, and the doctor seemed to enjoy it as much as Marvin did.

"How's that hearing aid working?" the doctor would ask. "It's getting kind of old, isn't it?"

Marvin's hearing aid was the old style, a round amplifier stuck in his ear and a wire going down to a receiver clipped to his belt.

"It was old when I got it. Paid five dollars for it at a yard sale."

"Five dollars? What kind is it?"

He'd look at his watch and say, "About two o'clock."

They would both laugh when he told that joke, and the doctor would always say, "I kind of stepped right into that one, didn't I?"

Marvin enjoyed reflecting on the good parts of his past and of the present, too. Friends, the town, his doctor. Then he snapped out of his reverie, startled when the large wooden and etched glass front door opened.

CHAPTER 6

Marvin turned to see who was coming out. Carrie pushed her way through the door onto the veranda, using the wheels of her wheelchair as a wedge to hold the door open while she inched her way out. She was bundled in her topcoat and a knit cap and had two quilts folded in her lap.

He was glad to see her. He hardly ever got to talk to her alone, and they couldn't talk about anything serious or stay on point with Mike there. Even though he'd known Carrie and Mike for about a year, he didn't know much about either one of them.

"Want me to get the door?" Marvin called out over his shoulder.

"No, I can do it. Stay where you are."

The wind had died down. She wheeled out to where Marvin was sitting and pulled up alongside him. She draped a quilt across his shoulders, tucked it in, and wrapped the other one around herself.

He squirmed around in the rocking chair to get the quilt adjusted.

"This is a nice quilt. Is it new?"

"I've had it a while. My quilting club made it for me when I came here. This other one, too."

"Did you make a lot of quilts before?"

Carrie laughed the jolly laugh that endeared her to her friends. "I'll say. After my daughter married and moved away, I was alone, retired, with nothing to do. Quilting took over my life. I went to all the meetings, watched all the daytime TV shows about sewing and quilting, went to the classes and conventions. I spent hours in quilt shops looking for fabrics and patterns."

"With all that going on, how did you find time to make quilts?"

Now they both laughed.

"Where are all the quilts you made?"

"We made them for the children's hospital, for the homeless shelter, for the troops in Afghanistan, all over the place."

While they talked, Marvin's pipe went out. He rummaged in his pockets for matches to get it going again. The rocking chair gave out with complaining squeaks whenever he shifted his position.

"Whatever happened to your husband?"

"I don't know. He's probably dead by now given the way he lived. We lost touch when we split up. Ann doesn't know where he is either. Or care."

"Did you raise her alone?"

"Since she was about six. It was rough going there for a while, but when she started school I got a job at the A&P. Stayed there until I retired. Produce manager."

The wind picked up and she pulled the quilt tighter around her shoulders.

"Did you have a good time yesterday?"

"Oh, yes. Ann picked me up and took me out."

"That's what Mike said."

She began laughing. "You should have seen the three of us trying to get me in her minivan. Her pulling on me from inside and Mike pushing on me from outside. Me grunting and groaning. Them laughing. We were a sight."

"How did you manage in town without Mike to help?"

39

"Ann's husband met us in town and he's big and strong, so it wasn't a problem after that."

They sat quietly for a while. The wind swung the hanging light fixture above them back and forth, and it made a rhythmic creaking sound.

"Do you see your daughter often?" Marvin asked.

"She visits at least once a week. I see her more often now than I did before I came here. She got married and moved away about fifteen years ago. After I lost my leg she talked me into coming here."

Marvin wondered whether he should ask. "How did you lose your leg?"

"Diabetes. After they took it off, I couldn't get up and down the stairs, reach anything in an overhead cabinet, nothing." She looked up and down the veranda. "Most times getting on the pot resulted in an accident. Or I'd fall and have to call someone. Thank God for cell phones. When we realized I couldn't make it alone, I sold the old house and came here."

"Does Ann live nearby?"

"Not far. St. Clair."

"You're lucky to have Ann, what with her coming to see you so often and taking you out. You couldn't be more blessed." Marvin was thinking about his children and how seldom they visited.

"Only one thing would make it better," she said.

"What's that?"

Her voice took on a wistful tone. "Grandchildren. I wish she'd have kids. Before the clock runs out."

"I'm sure she knows about the clock," Marvin said. "It's really up to her and her husband."

"Well, she's almost forty. I was about that age when I had her. There's still time. If she hurries."

"There's always time when you're young. Then you're not

and there isn't."

Carried reached over and patted his hand. "Don't go getting all philosophical on me, Marvin."

"I was just thinking about my grandson. He's the only one who ever visits me."

"Well, at least you have that. Some never get visitors."

"Can't blame the kids. We remind them of their future. Depressing."

He looked out again at the mountains on the horizon. The sky was cloudy and suggesting snow.

"What are you doing out here, anyway?" she asked. "Trying to catch pneumonia?"

He pulled the quilt around him tighter. "Enjoying the view, taking my mind off things."

She looked across the valley into the town. "You never get tired of it, do you?"

"No. This is one of my favorite spots. I've been coming up here to this place for years. I used to do the books for Abel Simpson and did his income taxes, too, back when he and Portia lived in this place before it became a nursing home. This was a fine mansion back then. Abel and I used to sit here on the porch and enjoy a pipe and brandy in the evenings after we finished work."

Marvin's pipe went out again. He lit a match to the bowl and pulled on the pipe stem to get the tobacco burning again. The smoke billowed from the sides of his mouth and rose in plumes above his head and the sweet aroma filled the air.

"Were you in the war?" Carrie asked.

"France and Germany. I signed up in forty-two and got out when the war ended. Not the best time of my life."

"I bet you saw some awful things."

"I was there when we liberated Buchenwald in forty-five. You've seen those films on TV? It was worse than what they show." The memory was depressing him, and he didn't want to be any more depressed than he already was. "Let's talk about something else."

They sat without speaking for a while. Then Carrie asked, "When did they convert this place to a nursing home?"

"Oh, about ten years ago. The Simpsons were getting along in years and going to need full-time care, and what better place to get it than at your own nursing home? He added the resident wings and upgraded the kitchen. He and Portia moved upstairs to a suite. She still lives there. I hear it's nice, but I've never been up there."

"How come?"

"No reason to go up. I don't really know her."

"Maybe she could use some company," Carrie said.

"Heck, she has her own staff. Nurses, maid, all that. She has enough company. And two daughters, as I recall."

"Who, I'm sure, visit her all the time." Carrie paused before adding, "Just like your kids do."

"Yeah, right." Today was Sunday, and Marvin was sure he'd get no visitors today. Just like most other Sundays.

"What was the house like before?"

"Well, let's see." Marvin's hands raised and spread far apart as if to convey grandeur. "I think you'd call it palatial. Oak paneling, stained glass, antique furniture, and chandeliers. A brass ceiling overhead and thick pile carpeting. Lots of antiques. Big country kitchen. It was grand."

"What happened to all those posh appointments?"

"Sold at auction. Every antique dealer and decorator on the east coast was here. Abel told me the proceeds paid for most of the conversion."

The wind dropped off and Carrie let her quilt slip down off her shoulders.

"How did Mrs. Simpson like selling all her antiques?"

"I don't know. I never got to know her. We moved in different circles. Abel was more down-to-earth. He died not long after the nursing home opened, and Portia is full owner last I heard. She leased the operation to the new regime sometime since I moved in. I don't know the details."

"Do you like living here?"

Marvin shook his head. "I didn't at first." Then he nodded. "But I came to like it. Until the new regime took over, that is. It was a lot better than what I expected. I have friends here, you and Mike and a few others."

"Was it difficult agreeing to come here? I had lots of doubts even though I knew it was for my own good."

"Carrie, there is a sense of finality associated with the day you decide or at least agree to live in a nursing home," Marvin said. He sat forward and was enjoying his moment of reflection. "It's as if you have begun to write the final chapter of a book. The book of your life. A surrender to the inevitable. You have chosen your place to die, you have come to that place, and now you wait patiently for your time to come."

"You are the poet, Marvin Bradley. But I guess that's why they call nursing homes, 'Heaven's waiting room.' "

"Indeed. I always looked up the hill at this place and thought it would be a good place for an old fellow to live out his last years. I just never thought that I'd be that old fellow. But it isn't all that bad. Until lately."

He took another pull on his pipe and expelled the smoke into the cool air.

"The new regime," Carrie said.

"Too many changes and cost-cutting. All new staff. Hardly anybody left that we knew. Word is they did it because the new workers work longer hours for lower wages."

"There were a lot of tearful goodbyes when the old staff left on their last day."

43

"I can imagine. I didn't have time to get to know many of them. The new staff is smaller, too. Downsizing, they call it. Less money for fewer people."

"Have you met Director Bates?"

"Yeah, I've met him. Mike calls him 'Ollie.' He says Oliver Bates reminds him of Oliver Hardy. I can see the resemblance."

"I've seen him, but I've never met him. What kind of fellow is he?"

"Hard to say. Distant. All business."

Marvin's pipe went out again. He tapped it on the side of the rocking chair and stood, folding the blanket under his arm. "Let's go in, Carrie. The wind's picking up. It's getting cold out here."

He folded the quilt, too, and placed it on her lap, then walked over and held the door while she wheeled her way in.

"I'm going in for a nap before our meeting," he said. "See you then."

CHAPTER 7

A knock on the door startled Marvin from his nap. He looked at the clock. They'd have to go to lunch soon. His door was standing wide open, and the hallway was brighter than the room. He squinted his eyes to accustom them to the light and rubbed them with his fists. Mike stood in the doorway leaning on his walker.

"Ready for our meeting?" Mike said. "Carrie will be right along. She's making sure Whitley's okay."

"Come on in and sit down, Mike." Marvin gestured to the recliner. He pulled himself up, got off the bed, and sat at the desk. He stretched and yawned.

"Sure is harder moving from place to place," he said.

"Get used to it. It gets worse."

"You know, all these aches and pains, we weren't designed to live this long."

Mike dropped down into the chair.

"What do you mean, not designed?"

"Homo sapiens didn't start out at the top of the food chain, Mike. We were meant to be eaten by stronger, faster predators."

"Eaten? Meant to be eaten?" Mike made a face and shook his head.

"We were food for the lions and tigers. The confluence of our intelligence and ingenuity changed all that, and we prevailed with our traps and weapons, and cured most of our diseases. So now, once you get too tough to taste good and can't reproduce and add to the edible population, you are obsolete in the grander scheme of things. Time to check out and make way for the younger generation."

"That's really depressing. And I don't agree. You're only as old as you feel," Mike said, bobbing his head to punctuate each word.

"That old? I thought I was only eighty-seven."

They laughed.

"You never told me what brought you here, Marvin. You seem able to take care of yourself."

"Had a stroke. I lay on the kitchen floor for two days. Almost died. My neighbor found me after I didn't answer the phone or doorbell. Saved my life."

"You must have been in bad shape."

"Dehydrated something awful. The worst part was I was hungry. Pulled myself over to the floor cabinets, and all I found was a can of drain cleaner."

"What did it taste like?"

"Drain cleaner."

They laughed again.

"Yeah, I was a mess. I lay in that hospital hooked up to a bunch of tubes for weeks. Then I came here."

"I guess your kids couldn't take care of you."

Marvin couldn't count the times he'd considered that. "Nah. They have jobs and busy lives and families to worry about. I didn't mind."

"You wanted to come here?" Mike waved his hand around the room as if to point out the minimum surroundings.

"It's not about what I wanted. It's what I didn't want. I didn't want to be in their way, worrying I might move something to where it shouldn't be, use something I shouldn't use, or break something. I didn't want the women-folk bathing me, feeding me, changing my diapers and my soiled bedclothes. I didn't want that at all."

"You didn't want to be resented."

"That's about it. You know, kids swear they'll never put their parents in a nursing home. How many times have you heard people say that?"

Mike got a faraway look. "That's what my son said."

"Then I bet you became a handful. All of a sudden the good intentions cave in to convenience. Happens every time when you can't take care of yourself any more."

"You get around okay now."

"Took a lot of therapy. I have this cane now. But I still have balance problems. I can't put my pants on without falling down."

"I sit on the bed to put my pants on. Problem solved."

"I've been putting my pants on standing up ever since I started wearing pants. I just forget to sit down. Then I lift a leg and fall down. Oh, well."

"Well, nobody can say you aren't trying. That's how you'll be remembered, pal. You're a fighter."

"Remembered. Yeah. You know, Mike, all you take to the grave are your good name and a suit of clothes, and nobody remembers the suit of clothes."

"You're starting to depress me again."

They sat in silence for a while longer. Marvin leafed through his printouts, and Mike read the ads in a copy of *Popular Mechanics.*

Marvin stood the pages on end and tapped them up and down to straighten them. Then he put them on the desk and said, "You never told us why you're here, Mike."

"Spinal injury."

"How'd you hurt your back?"

"At work."

"And you need special assistance?"

"So they tell me."

As usual, Mike didn't offer any details and Marvin didn't push it.

Carrie stuck her head in the door. "Private fight or can anybody join in?"

"Come in and sit down," Mike said.

"I am sitting down," she said and wheeled herself into the small room.

"How's Mr. Whitley?" Marvin asked.

"Sleeping. This is really a sad thing for him. All we can do is stand by him until he's himself again."

"Yeah," said Marvin. "And find out who the dirty rat is who did it."

"I'm going to check out this place," Mike said. He walked around the room feeling under the edges of the tables, looking at the window casements, the door frame, behind picture frames.

"What are you looking for?" Carrie asked.

"Bugs."

"Bugs? What do you mean?"

"Surveillance devices. Microphones, cameras, that kind of stuff."

Carrie seemed incredulous. "You think somebody's eavesdropping on us?"

"Better safe than sorry."

"That's really dumb, Mike," Carrie said. "Why would they care what we talk about?"

Marvin said, "I can understand Mike's concern. They need to worry about us high-functioning ones seeing what's going on around here. There are only a few of us, and I can see where they'd worry about what we talk about in private."

"Would you know a bug if you found it?" Carrie asked Mike.

"Yeah, they're crawly little things with wings and a bunch of legs. Bzzzt." He wiggled his fingers in Carrie's face. She pushed his arm aside.

"Okay," she said, laughing. "Enough. Where do we start? I'll make a list." She got out her notepad and pencil and turned to a fresh page.

"Let's get right down to brass tacks," Marvin said. "We know that someone is abusing the old people. And stealing. We should do something about it. But I'm at a loss as to what to do. Who can we tell? How do we know who all is in on it and who to trust?"

They were quiet for a spell. Then Mike spoke up. "Has to be a freakin' lunatic."

"I don't know," Marvin answered. "We have to think about whether there's anything they have to gain. We've had cutbacks, budget cuts, staff reductions, and God knows the meals aren't near what they used to be. These people are definitely in it for the money. The income from what we pay to be here stays the same, but they're cutting expenses right and left."

Mike said, "Like the guy in the movie said, 'Show me the money.' "

"Didn't he say, 'Follow the money'?" Carrie asked.

"Different movie. Anyway it's all about the money."

"Yeah," Carrie said. "Getting rid of Whitley's cat improved the cash flow. They don't have to buy cat food and litter. I'll write that down under 'motives.' "

"It's worse than that," Mike said. "Tell her, Marvin."

"Whitley's family paid the nursing home five grand to let him have his cat."

"Oh, my stars. And then they killed it? That's awful. What can we do?"

"Well," Marvin said, "first we have to find out who's doing it. Based on what Mr. Whitley told me, our main suspect is Leroy Parker, the maintenance man."

"The one with a face like Craters of the Moon?" Mike asked.

"How do you know about Craters of the Moon?" Carrie asked.

"I used to work for the Forest Service."

"I should have known."

"He looks like he used to be goalie in a dart game," Mike said.

Carrie made a face and shook her head.

"That's the guy," Marvin said. "Once we determine that he's the one, if he is, we have to find out whether he's doing it on his own, or if he's acting on orders coming down from the top."

Mike said, "We better be careful. If we expose him too soon, whoever's giving him the orders will throw him under the bus, so to speak, and cover their own behinds."

Carrie looked from one to the other. "From the top? Orders? You guys think this is a conspiracy?" she asked.

"It's starting to look that way," Marvin said, "and it makes my blood curl. It might be top management, not just here, but corporate. I hate to think it, but for some reason someone is trying to make living here a less than ideal experience. Like they want us to leave. Or worse."

"So," Mike said, "we can't let anybody know we might be on to them."

"Right. Especially somebody with a big mouth. Don't show our cards yet. After we know who the bad guys are, we can deal with it. Let's snoop around. One of them will tip their hand before long. Maybe more than one. But one is all we need. If we can build a solid case, a phone call to the newspaper will blow the lid off."

"What's a solid case?" Carrie asked.

"More than just eyewitness evidence." There was an edge to Marvin's voice that the others had never heard. "I want documentation. And I want it before anybody gets hurt any worse."

"Do we have anything to go on?" Carrie asked.

Marvin went to his desk, picked up the handful of printouts, shook them in the air, and said, "I have this pile of newspaper articles about nursing homes going back a couple of years. I've been reading and correlating them. There's a pattern of abuse followed by closings."

"Closings?" Carrie said. "Why?"

"Because the resident population goes down to nothing."

"Wouldn't you expect that?" Carrie asked. "Who wants to live in a place where they'll be mistreated?"

Marvin said, "You'd expect them to fire the abuser and sweep it under the rug, and then back to business as usual. But that hasn't happened."

"What has happened?"

"I can't find where they ever found out who was doing it. Usually just accusations from family, then the papers report it as a big story, then interest dies out, and a few months later, the nursing home closes its doors."

Mike's cell phone rang. He answered it. "Yeah," he said, "I'll be right there. Marvin, would you come with me? I might need help."

"Sure, what's up?"

"It's lunch. Carrie, you can come, too."

They followed Mike out the door and down the hallway to the reception area. A young man was there at the counter. He wore a Pizza Jubilee hat and held a thermal pizza bag. Loretta, the director's assistant, was glowering at him from behind the counter.

"Hi," said Mike. "Is that for me?"

"Mr. Charles?" the delivery boy asked.

"That's me. How much?" Mike was fishing money out of his wallet.

"Mr. Charles," Loretta said. "What's the big idea?"

"I ordered in a pizza."

"What? You can't do that. It's against the rules."

"I just did. We're having a meeting. We need nourishment."

"What kind of meeting?"

"Prom committee. Do you have a date? Marvin's available."

"You people are on strict diets. And Mrs. Fenway, you're a diabetic. This goes against policy. Young man, you'll have to take that out of here right now."

"No can do, ma'am. I have to be paid for this pizza. Otherwise I pay for it myself."

Mike said, "Loretta, why don't you just look the other way?"

"I could lose my job letting you bring that thing in here." Her voice softened, and she looked at the pizza box. "But it sure smells good."

"We won't tell," Marvin said, taking the boxed pizza from the delivery man.

Mike gave the boy some money. "Keep the change, son."

"Wait, you three," Loretta said. "You can't take that pizza to your room."

"Watch us," Marvin said. He put the box in Carrie's lap and said. "Head for my room, Carrie. We'll hold her off." He laughed. "Now, Loretta, don't make trouble. I'll put the box in the Dumpster tomorrow morning. Nobody will know."

"Oh, I guess so. Just make sure you eat it all."

"Sneak away in a while and come have a slice," Mike said. "Do you like anchovies?"

"No."

"Me, neither. I hate 'em. I didn't get anchovies. Come on down later."

"I wish I could. Get out of here you three before I change my mind."

"I'll meet you there," Mike said to Marvin and Carrie.

They went to Marvin's room and waited for Mike. He walked

in carrying a six-pack of beer.

"Where'd you get that?" Carrie asked.

"My refrigerator."

"How'd you get it in?"

"I bribed the housemaid. I can get anything you want."

They sat around eating pizza, drinking beer, and talking more about the problem.

Marvin said, "This is great, Mike. Thanks."

After a while, Loretta pushed her head in the door. "Any left?" she asked.

"We saved one for you," Mike said. He gave her a slice on a napkin. She looked around to make sure no one was watching and headed back to her station.

"Hey, wait!" Mike called. She stopped and turned. "Want a beer?" he said, holding out a bottle.

"Mr. Charles, I didn't hear that." She left them to their party.

After more chat and when the pizza was gone, Carrie and Mike left to return to their rooms. Marvin closed his door and lay on the bed to think. He burped from the pizza and beer. His mind was on the problem. Who could help that they could trust? Loretta? No, she was with the new regime. Bribing her with pizza might not be enough. Maybe Nurse Norma. She'd been there a long time, and she and her staff were well-liked. He burped again.

A scratching noise came from his door. Then the door opened. Arnie Peters stood there waving his white cane back and forth.

"Am I in the wrong room again, Mr. Bradley?"

"Two doors down, Mr. Peters. To your right."

Peters tapped the wall with his white cane. He often went in the wrong room these days. It had become a joke around the nursing home.

"How did you know it was me?" Marvin asked.

"Everybody burps different."

"I didn't know that."

"Not many do. To us blind folks, what you sound like is as distinctive as a fingerprint. Sorry for the intrusion, Mr. Bradley. I can't get used to not having Bruno."

"Are they going to get you another dog?"

"They said no. Too much trouble getting it arranged, they said. And I ain't got no money to pay for it. I guess I'll have to get by on my own. Sure do miss old Bruno, though."

Given what had happened to Whitley's cat, Marvin wondered now about Bruno. The dog had died right after Leroy Parker came on board. Peters woke up one morning and found Bruno on the bathroom floor. They said he had died of old age. But Marvin wondered whether Leroy had a hand in it.

CHAPTER 8

Late afternoon on New Year's Day, Marvin headed for the nursing station to discuss the problem with Nurse Norma. She was the head nurse and couldn't have missed the increase in injuries among the old people, and he couldn't imagine her letting it continue without speaking up. The only way to find out was to ask her. Maybe she'd have ideas about what they could do about it. He left his room and headed for the nursing station.

Nurse Norma sat at her desk preparing the evening's medications when Marvin limped up and leaned on the counter. She had a small television set on her desk and was listening to one of the Bowl games while she worked.

A short lady in her early fifties with a wide frame and a neat bundle of gray hair pinned up and topped by a white nurse's cap, Norma Fellows was liked by all the residents.

"How come you're working on New Year's Day? And a Sunday, too?"

She looked up at him. "I traded off with the other supervisor. She has company. I can watch the game here while I work."

"You know, Nurse Norma, I've seen you do that so many times, I bet I could do it myself."

She put the medicine tray and clipboard down on her desk, got up, and walked over to the counter. "It just looks routine, Marvin. But it changes all the time."

He often hung out at the nursing station. Watching Nurse Norma was one of life's diversions, and she seemed to like having him there, liked having the company. She was from the old regime, and Marvin enjoyed their friendship.

"How long have you been at this?" he asked.

She looked at the clock. "I started a half hour ago like I always do."

"No. I mean nursing. How long have you been a nurse?"

She rested her elbow in one hand, touched her other hand to her cheek, and looked up toward the ceiling. "Most of my life. I came out of nurse's training about twenty-five years ago and went to work in a hospital. I came here about four years ago after both my parents died. They died within a month of one another."

"One goes and the other isn't far behind. I can understand it. After my wife died, I didn't want to go on."

Nurse Norma looked at Marvin with a warm smile that said she understood and wanted to reassure him. "But you did go on."

"I'm still here, that's for sure. And so are you. Working here, I mean. And the other nurses. I was wondering, how did you gals survive the new regime's hatchet job? So many others were laid off and replaced."

"They can't downsize medical staff. State regulations control how many doctors and nurses they need, and we were already down to the minimum."

Marvin was getting tired standing. He pulled a stool over from the wall and leaned his cane against the counter.

"But word is all the new staff is working for lower pay. None of my business, but didn't you get a pay cut?"

"Nope. Our salaries are fixed by the union. Thank God for the union."

"Lucky you."

"I don't know, Marvin," she said, shaking her head. "This new management has everyone worried. The budget cuts are beginning to hit us, too. We run low on stuff all the time."

"What kind of stuff?"

She gestured toward the storage cabinets on the wall behind the counter. "Bandages, gauze, splints, aspirin, ointments, all the non-prescription items, you name it, we run out of it. And when we need to replenish, the procedures for getting things are complex and time-consuming. Forms to fill out, approvals to get signed, logs to keep."

"Wasn't that always the way? I mean, you always had forms and procedures."

"Not like this." Nurse Norma looked around to make sure no one was listening in, then leaned closer. "The gals have a saying. 'Takes a mile of red tape to get a yard of adhesive tape.' "

Marvin laughed, grateful for the comic relief.

"As head nurse I ought to be able to order things directly. Now it takes approvals from the doctor and the director in triplicate to get a bottle of aspirin or a box of band-aids. Half the time we don't have what we need and have to improvise."

She turned and walked over to her desk, then turned back and faced him. "But never mind all that. What brings you here today other than just my winning personality? Do you need treatment for something?"

"No. I need to talk with you privately. When's a good time?"

"How about now? The gals are on rounds."

"Okay. First, can I trust you?"

Nurse Norma looked surprised. "Why would you not trust me?"

"Sorry, I didn't mean it that way. What I mean is, if I get into some sensitive areas, does it stay here or will management hear about it?"

She tilted her head and looked directly at him. "It stays here, Marvin. What's this all about?"

"Have you noticed an increase in the number of injuries

among the old people?"

She relaxed. "Oh. That. Is this that same thing that Mike Charles was talking about? I told him it was his imagination. I'll tell you the same."

"Well, no disrespect, Nurse Norma, but you're wrong. Mike and I are seeing it, and so is Carrie Fenway. I'm serious. Something bad is going on around here. And we've got to do something about it. We've got to. We're seeing bruises, injuries, like that. It's abuse. I'm sure of it."

"Marvin, patients with dementia often hurt themselves. And each other. Bruises don't mean abuse. Bruising is common in nursing homes."

"But we're seeing an emerging pattern." He was getting frustrated. He couldn't convince her. "Old people who never showed injuries before are lining up with bruised arms, black eyes, and such. Is it normal to start happening on a grand scale all at the same time?"

She gestured toward the printer. "Is this what all your research was about? All those articles you printed out?"

"I'm trying to see if other homes have similar problems."

"What did you find out?"

"I'm still studying it."

"I'll be interested in what you learn."

"But there's not only bruises. Somebody killed Bill Whitley's cat."

"I heard. That's terrible. That cat was everything to Mr. Whitley." She went back to the desk and sat in her chair. "Toby was in his lap all day, slept in the bed with him. Really good company. And such a friendly cat. That's so sad. Are you sure somebody killed it? That cat was kind of old as I remember."

Marvin leaned forward and pushed against the counter. Nurse Norma was trying to talk him out of the obvious, as if to patronize an old man. He raised his hands palms up and moved his arms up and down to emphasize the point he was trying to make.

"No!" he said. "The cat fell from a first-story window. A five-foot drop at the most. A cat lands on its feet. And why was the window open this time of year? And the cat's neck is broken."

"Okay, okay, settle down. You're getting all red in the face."

Marvin didn't want to settle down. "But there's more. Somebody is stealing from the old people, too. Stuff is going missing all over the place. And now, with all the rest, the cat makes me wonder about Mr. Peters's guide dog."

Nurse Norma got up and came over to the counter. She took Marvin's hands into hers, looked at the rugged old hands dotted with liver spots and blue veins popping up, and gently stroked the backs of them with her stubby thumbs.

She said, "Marvin, I don't know what I can do about the animals. Or the stealing. It's true, there has been some extra bruising, but, as I said, that's not uncommon. Stealing? I can't do anything about that. Security would have to look into it."

Marvin pulled away and laughed sarcastically. "Not likely. That new security guy is darn near as old as we are."

"You almost sound like you think there's some kind of conspiracy. That's pushing it a bit far, don't you think?"

"That's what I've been trying to say. That's exactly what it is, a conspiracy. We think there is an organized plan, hatched at the top for whatever reason, to make things miserable for the old people."

She raised her eyebrows. "That's really far-fetched, Marvin. Look. I'll keep an eye out for unusual injuries. If I see anything, I'll report it to the doctor. But I'm not stirring up any hornets' nests around here. I need this job. My daughter split up with her husband, and she and her kids moved in with me, and she doesn't have a job, and her husband is a deadbeat. So I can't and I won't do anything to upset the applecart."

"Well, you'll forgive me for saying it, but that will put you square in the middle of it." Right away, he was sorry he said that. He looked at the floor. "Not that you are, of course. You'll have to excuse me. I have a way of running my mouth before my brain gets in gear."

"That's okay. You're forgiven." She was smiling at him.

"But you need to know that that's how it'll look when it hits the fan, like you were in on it. And it will hit the fan."

"How do you figure that?"

"Because I'm a natural born whistleblower is how. Particularly when helpless people are being hurt, old people, people who never did anything to anybody." Marvin rubbed under his eyes to soak up the unwanted tear. He didn't like showing this much emotion.

"What whistle would you blow? What proof do you have?"

"None yet. But I intend to get to the bottom of it. And find the proof. And when I do, I'll be talking to state officials, the county health board, the district attorney, the cops, the news-papers, the families, the President, the Pope, and anybody else who'll listen." He was getting worked up again. "Of course, I wouldn't want management to know my plans. That's why I asked if I could trust you."

"Settle down, Marvin. You look like you're about to explode. If you want evidence to back up your theory, as off-the-wall as it sounds, this company has taken over nursing homes all around the state, and they claim to have turned each one into a profit-able enterprise. See what's happening at the other homes. I doubt that you'll find anything."

"I already did some of that. That's what the research was about. But it's not the profitable ones I'm suspicious of. It's the ones where there's been abuse and then they quietly close their doors. That doesn't make any sense."

"I don't know about that. I'm sorry I can't be of more help.

But be careful. If someone is beating up old people and killing cats like you say, which I doubt very much, there's no telling what they'll do to anyone who gets in their way."

"They don't scare me. They can't be any worse than the last war I fought."

"You never talk about that, Marvin. But I read your files. You were a hero with a bunch of medals."

"Let's keep that between us." Marvin wondered why people fixated on such things. "And in the past. We have bigger fish to fry. Do you know where they keep memos and forms for the government and communications between them and other nursing homes and such? And their books?"

"Those things would be on the computer. They're completely automated. But the computer is locked up in the main office when nobody's there. Besides, you shouldn't be messing with that stuff. You could get into trouble. And it's just plain wrong."

"Well, I don't know enough about computers. I never had one 'til I got here and used the one in the dayroom. My company had one, but I mostly let the young people deal with it. I was starting to learn when I retired. So that's not an issue. Thanks, Nurse Norma."

"That's okay, Marvin. You be careful, you hear? And just so you know, between you and me, I'm looking for another job. So are the gals. We don't like working for these people. Now get out of here and let me get back to work."

CHAPTER 9

Marvin walked back to his room and thought about the newest problem. The information he needed was on the main computer. Nurse Norma had said so. Even if he could get at the computer, he couldn't get the data. He knew what to look for but not how to find it.

It didn't bother him that Nurse Norma said it would be wrong. Somebody on staff was doing something wrong, too, something a whole lot worse. If Marvin had to bend a few rules, or even break a law or two to address the problem, he would.

"What can they do to me?" he said to himself. "What could be worse than this?"

He asked himself who could help. Then it hit him. Freddie. He could ask his grandson how to retrieve such data from a computer. If anyone could do it, Freddie could. Freddie was his only hope. Marvin got on his cell phone and called Freddie.

After the usual amenities between grandfather and grandson, Marvin said, "Okay, Freddie, here's what I need. Now please don't discuss this with anyone, not even your parents. First thing, I need new hearing aids."

"Sure, Granddad. Did your ear trumpet finally break down?" Freddie referred to the family joke, Marvin's antiquated hearing aid.

"No, it's okay. I'm doing some snooping around here, and I want people to think I can't hear, so I need the invisible hearing aids. The kind you can't see, that fit down inside your ears. One of the guys here has them, and he says he got them on the Internet, one size fits all. Good ones that let me hear folks talking clear across the room. They'll think I left my hearing aid in my room. Don't have them shipped here. Get them and bring them to me."

"Should be no problem."

Marvin got up with his cane in one hand and the phone in the other and paced around the room.

"Now, for the next thing," he said. "Keep this quiet. Do you think you can hack into the computer here?"

"Hack?" Marvin could hear the smile in Freddie's voice.

"Yeah. You're one of those computer hackers, aren't you?"

"Yeah. It's what I do. I can't wait to hear this. What kind of computer do you need hacked and why?" He was laughing.

"The usual kind. Screen, keyboard, mouse." Marvin didn't know how else to describe it. "Like the one we have in the dayroom."

"Mac? PC? Linux? Windows?"

"You just hit my wall of confusion, son. The one I want hacked is locked up in the office at night. Maybe we can bust in there somehow so you can hack it."

"Bust in? I'm going to have to know a whole lot more about what you're doing before I go breaking into a locked office in the middle of the night. Is the computer on a network?"

"I don't know. What's a network look like?"

"Can you go on the Internet with the dayroom computer?"

"Oh, sure. And is it something. You should see some of the stuff they've got on that Internet. Do you know about satellite imagery? I know how to look down at this place. And my house. I can see Charlie Danvers working in his garden. He's always there just like in real life. Do you know about that?"

"Sure do. Does the computer have wi-fi?"

"What's that?"

"Is it hooked to the Internet with cables or is it wireless?"

"There's all kind of wires in back of that thing. I don't know what they do. I can wire a lamp or fix a toaster, but that's about as far as me and wires go."

"I can check it out when I get there. But you have to tell me. Why do you need me to do this?" Freddie's concern was evident in his voice.

"Hold on."

Marvin walked over and looked out his door to make sure no one in the hallway could hear him. He lowered his voice. "Some of the old people here are being abused, and somebody's stealing their stuff and killing their pets. So, for starters, I want to look at the nursing home's business records, and I don't want them to know what I'm doing."

"Are you being abused?"

"No, they won't mess with the high-functioning residents."

"I'm confused. What do business records have to do with the abuse of residents?"

"It's complicated, but I think management is in on it, and I want to find out why. There might be something in their records to explain it."

"What kind of records do you need?"

"Financial records, personnel records, government forms, memos, like that, off the computer."

"You know that's illegal."

"Only if you get caught."

"That's an interesting attitude, Granddad. I bet you were a heck of an accountant."

"You said it. Especially at tax time. But what they're doing isn't exactly on the up-and-up either. I plan to prove it." Marvin was getting tired. He walked over and sat in his chair.

"Granddad, how do you plan to do that?"

"Just getting some information together. I don't know how

I'll use it, but that's beside the point. I don't want to be helpless if anyone comes after me."

Freddie's voice quickened. "Comes after you? What do you mean, comes after you?"

"We figure if they bust us, they'll try to stop us."

"Good grief! Can't we move you someplace else?"

Marvin fidgeted in his chair and adjusted the volume on the cell phone. "No. There's two reasons. First of all, your father and the rest of them agreed to me coming here because it uses up less of their inheritance than the other places they looked at. If I demand to be moved, they'll have me declared incompetent, grab my assets, and put me in the VA home in Harrisburg."

"You think they'd do that?"

"I know they would."

"But you'd let them do that? That doesn't sound like you, Granddad."

"I've seen it happen to others. They rationalize that it's in the best interests of the old guy. Keep him from spending all his money on a floozie or giving it to some charity or something like that. And the courts pay more attention to the younger generation than they do to us old geezers. Err on the side of caution, they say. The old boy probably has dementia but is having a rare lucid day in court. We're having the same problem here getting people to believe us about the abuse. One's credibility diminishes with age, and it has nothing to do with one's ability."

"I just can't see my Dad doing that to his own father."

Knowing that Freddie and his father were close, Marvin was reluctant to say what had to be said. "You don't know him like I do. I had to argue long and hard to keep your Granny Jessie at home with me and out of a place like this. Then he blamed me when she passed."

"These are things grandkids never hear about, I guess."

"It's best that way. Keeps you from having to take sides. I'm telling you now because I need your help."

"You said, 'two reasons.' What's the other reason you don't want to leave?"

"If I leave here, there's nobody left to look after the old people who can't look after themselves. I ain't much, but I'm all they've got."

"What about your friends?"

"They can't do it on their own."

"Okay, but I'm not sure about all this. What else do you need besides hearing aids?"

"That ought to do it for now. When can you hack the computer?"

"I'll look at it when I bring you the hearing aids. We might be able to get at those files without breaking down any doors. You do understand that I don't exactly approve of what you're doing."

"You will when I show you what's happening here."

"I can hardly wait."

"Okay, son. I really appreciate it. Is there any chance you could take me to my house, too? There's stuff there I want to get."

CHAPTER 10

That evening after supper, the three old collaborators assembled in Carrie's room. They set up the card table and sat around it as if they were going to play cards.

"Close the door," Marvin said.

"We better not," Carrie said. "They might get suspicious and look in on us."

"What? Are you worried about appearances, old gal?" Mike asked with a grin. "In the room alone with two men and the door closed?"

"No, I'm not worried about that. Neither of you geezers is equal to the task."

They all laughed. Mike closed the door.

"My grandson is coming by soon," Marvin said. "He's going to show me how to hack the computer."

Carrie wrote in her notepad and then said, "Hack the computer. What does that mean?"

"We should be able to get inside the main computer somehow and find all their records."

"What for? What can we do with them?"

"It depends on what I find. I hope there might be internal memos that help explain what's going on."

"What else do we need?" she asked.

"We'll need weapons," he added.

"Weapons? Whatever for?"

Mike said, "I can answer that. If these guys get onto who's

ratting them out, they'll come after us. We need to defend ourselves."

"Come after us?" she said. "They better not come after me. What kind of weapons do we need?"

Marvin said, "Ordinary items that don't arouse suspicion when they see them in our rooms but that we can use if we need to. I've got golf clubs and other stuff at my house in town."

"How about getting the bad guys in a bathtub and throwing in a hair dryer," Carrie said. "I saw that on a television show."

"How are you going to get anyone in a bathtub?" Mike said.

"I'll just use my charm," she said in her best Mae West voice, batting her eyelids and smiling.

"Forget it. Won't work."

"I do have a hat pin that would bring down an elephant," Carrie said.

"Good," said Marvin. "Keep it handy. What do you have, Mike?"

"You're not going to believe it."

"What?" the other two said in unison.

"I have a cattle prod."

"A cattle prod?" Carrie said. "Whatever are you doing with a cattle prod?"

"I used to work at a slaughterhouse. When I left, I kept my cattle prod as a souvenir. I think it needs batteries."

"Get batteries," Marvin said.

"Wait, guys. Slow down so I can get it all," Carrie said. "Hat pin, golf clubs, cattle prod. What do you do with a cattle prod?"

"Prod cattle."

"At the slaughterhouse, but what does a private citizen do with one?"

"Prod cattle."

"You have cattle?"

"No, but if I ever get any, I'm ready. I have an archery set, too. At home."

Carrie put her head in her hands and shook it.

"Archery set?" Marvin said. "That could be useful. Do you know how to use it?"

"Yeah. I took the blue ribbon for archery at the company picnic."

"When was that?"

"Nineteen forty-seven."

Marvin smiled. "Well, get somebody to send it here."

"The blue ribbon?"

"No, Mike, the archery set. Hide it in your closet."

"Could we use flashbulbs?" Carrie asked.

"You have flashbulbs?" Marvin asked. "I thought they went out with strobe lights."

"My husband was a professional photographer. He left behind a lot of old equipment."

"How old are the flashbulbs?" Mike asked.

"Probably thirty-five, forty years old. I have a big box full of them. Hundreds."

"Carrie," Mike said, "get someone to send you the flashbulbs and flash attachments and batteries if you have them."

"Flashbulbs, attachments, batteries," Carrie said and kept writing.

Marvin said, "You have an idea for the flashbulbs, Mike?"

"It's crazy but it might work. Can we get any wiring, electrical tape, stuff like that?"

"If I can get to my house. I have all that stuff in the garage. Make a list of what you want, and I'll try to get it. Let's just get anything we can think of that would make a good weapon or booby trap and that we can hide in our closets. Something tells me we're going to see action."

They took a break, and Carrie poured coffee for everyone. Then she started in.

"I kept an eye on some of the staff today, but they didn't do anything out of the ordinary."

"Do you think they knew you were watching?"

"Nah. None of the new staff really knows any of us. I just wheeled myself around and babbled like the Alzheimer patients. They didn't know the difference."

"Did you mess your pants?" Mike asked.

"No! Why ever would you ask that?"

"Just checking," Mike said. "If they think you're one of the drooling babblers, you'll be next on their list."

"How do I keep them from knowing I'm watching?" Carrie asked. "Besides messing my pants, that is."

"Here's what I do. Unlike old Marvin here, my hearing is really good. So are my eyes. So, when I'm watching these guys, I just keep my distance from the guy I'm watching. I see what rooms they go into and then I go in after they're gone to see if there are signs of abuse. Fresh bruises, somebody crying, and like that. I also watch to see if they bring out anything they didn't take in. It's hit or miss, but eventually something will turn up."

"Good work, people," Marvin said. "Somebody needs to watch Leroy. We can take turns so he doesn't get suspicious. You take him tomorrow, Mike. I've got research to do over the next few days. I want to see if there are any new state or federal guidelines, memos, whatever, that might be making them tighten their belts. And what they might gain by abusing residents. That's the part I don't understand. I can see cutting back on soap and food, but hitting us? What's that all about?"

"How do you know what to look for in the computer, Marvin?" Mike asked.

"I was an accountant. I had clients who operated with government funds. I knew what forms they had to fill out, what records they had to keep. I know what to look for. If I can find where they keep it."

"I used to work for an accountant," Mike said.

"We're lucky to have you, Marvin," Carrie said.

"Yeah, but I don't have a cattle prod."

CHAPTER 11

During the week that followed, Marvin, Mike, and Carrie worked shifts watching Leroy. Wherever he'd go, one or two of them would be there, hanging around, acting innocent and unconcerned. If he noticed them, he didn't say anything. Marvin wanted Leroy to get used to them being around. He might avoid abusing anyone with witnesses there, or maybe he would tip his hand.

Marvin spent his evenings correlating the newspaper articles he'd collected. If an article suggested something that might contribute to the chain of evidence he was building, he'd go to the dayroom and look up what he could find about it, make notes about where he'd found it, and print it on the nursing station printer the next day when Nurse Norma was on duty.

Gradually he built a case of purely circumstantial evidence, most of it against the investment corporation that held the lease on the nursing home. His case wasn't strong enough to prove anything yet, but he hoped the accumulated body of evidence would catch a prosecutor's interest.

Each evening at supper, the trio of sleuths was careful not to discuss anything about the investigation lest someone overhear something and get the gossip mill started. Then, after supper, they'd meet in one of their rooms with the door closed to compare notes. Progress was slow, but at least they were preventing Leroy from dishing out any serious abuse.

Marvin hoped things would pick up when Freddie showed him how to hack the computer.

That Saturday, Freddie came to visit after breakfast. Knowing Freddie was coming and hoping that they'd be going into town, Marvin had dressed as if it were Sunday.

Freddie was a tall, strapping fellow in his late twenties who took after Marvin not only in appearance but in character, too. He was the only one of Marvin's family who visited him with any regularity, at least once a month, although his job often took him away. Freddie was single and independent.

They chatted a while in Marvin's room, and Marvin got caught up on what Freddie was doing and all the latest family gossip.

"When are you getting married? I need great-grandkids."

"No time soon. How about you? Got any girlfriends here at the home?"

"Nah. When you've had the best . . ."

After they exhausted the small talk, Freddie said, "Okay, Granddad, what are we doing first?"

"Let's make a few house calls. I want you to see it firsthand."

Marvin took Freddie on his tour of the old people. In each room he pointed out new bruises and ones that were still healing.

"A lot of them don't respond now. That's only since they've been getting hit. They don't trust anybody, anymore, and they're afraid. You can see it in their eyes."

Freddie was visibly moved by the condition of the old people. At one stop, where an old lady had a black eye, a swollen lip, and bruises on both arms, Freddie's eyes filled with tears and he put his hand over his mouth.

Marvin explained. "Take my word for it, before all this, these old people were always happy to see me. And they did not have these injuries."

Freddie shook his head in disbelief. "Don't the nurses see this?"

"Probably not. They think it's normal. It's not their fault. They have a lot of patients to look after, and a bruise here and there isn't unusual. But I see an escalating pattern."

When they came out into the hallway after visiting the last resident, Marvin asked, "So do you still think I shouldn't be looking into it?"

Freddie's face hardened, and he looked straight ahead down the hall. "Let's go find that computer," he said.

Marvin led him to the dayroom. Freddie checked the back of the computer for connections. He turned it on and sat there a while, rummaging around in the computer's files and on the network.

"Man," he said. "This is really stupid."

"What's that?" Marvin asked.

"Nothing's password-protected or firewalled. All the company's files are on the network out there in the open available to anyone who logs on. It's wi-fi, so someone could sit out in the parking lot with a laptop and take anything they wanted. I wonder what idiot set this up. This is too easy."

"A minimum wage idiot would be my guess. These people don't spend any more money than they have to. How do I get to the documents?"

"You could do it here, but you might get caught. Do you have a laptop?"

"No."

"Okay, I'll leave you mine. Let's go back to your room."

Freddie turned off the computer, and they walked back to Marvin's room. Freddie sat with his laptop on the desk and typed on the keyboard. Marvin didn't know what Freddie was doing, so he just waited.

When he was finished, Freddie said, "Come over here, Grand-dad, and see this."

Freddie showed Marvin how to log onto a special account, one that opened a desktop with several icons that Marvin had never seen.

"Where'd all that come from? We don't have that in the day-room PC."

"I just put them there," Freddie said. "This one is your email. Each of these other icons gets you into an area on the main server where they store the documents. Click on the icon and there you are."

Freddie clicked an icon labeled, "Tax Records." A window opened with spreadsheet icons, each with a document name. He clicked one of the icons and a spreadsheet program opened with the document in place.

"Wow!" Marvin said. He leaned closer and examined the rows and columns of numbers. "That's tax data for last year. Before the turnover."

"Everything you want is here somewhere," Freddie said. "Here are copies of emails in and out, this one is for official government guidelines, here's interoffice memos, letters to family, personnel files, patient records, everything."

"I can see I'll be busy for a while. I hope I don't get caught doing it."

"You have to keep it to yourself. Patients' families could sue you for invasion of privacy, and the company could have you prosecuted. Anybody walks in, click this icon here, and turn the computer off."

"What does the icon do?"

"It removes all traces of your having logged onto the server. Use it every time you log off."

"That's clever. I hope I can remember all this."

"If it gets too complicated, call, and I'll come show you."

"Thanks, Freddie, this is great. When do I get my hearing aids?"

"Oh, I almost forgot. I had them sent overnight. Here they are." He took a small package from his jacket pocket and gave it to Marvin.

The hearing aids were in separate cellophane baggies. A third baggie had spare batteries. Marvin removed the aids and read the instructions. He took out his old hearing aid and put the new ones into his ears.

"Say something, Freddie," he said.

Freddie went to the other side of the room and said in a quiet voice, "What's happening, Granddad?"

Marvin grinned. Then he went to the door, opened it, and stuck his head out to listen to the sounds in the hallway. He came back in the room.

"Man!" he said. "These are great! I should have tried something like this years ago. I might start watching TV again. It's going to be hard to go back to my old one. I'll wear these if the family ever visits. They'll think I can't hear them talking about me."

"You'll probably change your will several times, Granddad. Let's go visit your house."

Freddie walked Marvin out to his car and helped him in the passenger's side. "I wish I could drive," Marvin said.

"Maybe someday. Let's go."

Freddie drove out the gate and down the driveway. He drove into town and to the street where Marvin's house was.

He helped Marvin out of the car and up the front steps to the door. He unlocked and opened the door and led Marvin into the living room.

The house was cold. The thermostat was set just high enough so the pipes wouldn't freeze but not warm enough to live in. Marvin pulled his jacket around him and looked around. It looked as if no one had touched anything since the day they carried Marvin out on a stretcher.

"Looks like nobody's been here," Marvin said.

"Nobody has. Dad said they didn't want to disturb your things until they knew for sure you wouldn't be coming back."

"That doesn't sound like him. I expected him and your mom and aunts and uncles to raid the place. I guess they didn't want any of it, and it isn't worth selling. But perhaps it's for the best. I'm hoping to get well enough to live here and have home care come in. Some day."

"Some day. Okay, Granddad, what do we need to get?"

"My golf clubs."

"You have golf clubs? I didn't know you played golf."

"I don't. Your dad got them for me. He thought we could hit the links every Sunday. A father-son bonding. That lasted about two weeks. But I kept the clubs. They're in the hall closet."

"Okay. I'll get them. What else?"

Marvin referred to the list Mike had given him. "Wiring and fixtures. It's all on this list. And wood slats. There's pieces of latticework out there. Bring in about ten of the strips. And wood glue and clamps. I've got to sit down." He sat in the living room recliner chair, pushed himself back, and said, "Ahh."

"What are you going to build with all that stuff?"

"Protection. There's some bad monkey business going on up there. As I get closer to it, I might need to protect myself."

"Do you still own that shotgun?"

"Yeah, it's in the closet upstairs. But don't get it. If they found it, they'd take it away from me. And if they didn't find it, I might shoot one of them. Or miss and shoot one of my friends. Or myself. Then I'd be the one in trouble. No, I'm better off without a gun. I haven't fired one since, well, since a long time ago. If I need it, I'll let you know."

"Anything else?"

"You remember that hickory cane I had with the deer's antler handle?"

"Yeah. Great-grandpa's cane."

"I don't remember where it is, but I'd like to have it. This aluminum cane doesn't have enough heft to bean anybody with."

"Granddad, you're starting to worry me."

"Don't worry. It probably won't come to anything. Do you remember where it is?"

"It's right here beside the piano where it always was. And here's your camcorder. You might want that. You can make a documentary of your escapades with your friends. Call it 'Marvin's Marauders.' "

Marvin chuckled at the thought. "Yeah, bring it along. There's a blank DVD in it. I never used it for anything."

"Is this all you're going to have to protect yourselves with?"

"No, the others are bringing things. We're prepared. Carrie has a hat pin and flashbulbs, and Mike has a cattle prod and an archery set."

"I don't believe what I'm hearing. Cattle prod? Archery set? Nobody would believe it. Oh, well."

Freddie went out to the garage and found the things Marvin had asked for.

"Is the Buick still there?" Marvin asked when Freddie came back in the house. He often worried that someone would steal the neglected and unprotected car.

"Still there. But it ought to be started every now and then and maybe run around the block. The battery might need a charge. I'll see about doing that."

"I'd appreciate it."

Freddie took everything to his car and then came back to get Marvin.

"Do you miss this place, Granddad?"

"Sometimes. But without Granny Jessie here, it isn't the

same. Just another dusty old house with a bunch of dusty old things. Let's go."

He started toward the door then stopped.

"One more thing, Freddie. Go up to my bedroom and look under the bed. You should find a strongbox. Bring it down."

Freddie went upstairs, and Marvin went into the kitchen and retrieved a key from the cookie jar in the pantry. Freddie came back with the strongbox. Marvin opened it. Among documents, coins, and an old pocket watch was a bundle of cash held together with a rubber band.

"How much did the hearing aids cost?"

"Four hundred each. I put them on my credit card."

Marvin peeled off eight hundred dollars and gave it to Freddie.

"I don't have much cash up there at the home," he said, and counted off two hundred dollars and put it in his wallet. Then he returned the other cash to the strongbox and put the key back in the cookie jar.

"The key is in here," he said, "along with keys to the Buick." He put the garage key back in the cookie jar. "If anything happens to me, make sure you get here ahead of the others. My will is in the strongbox. Get the cash for yourself, and don't tell anyone. There's about ten grand there. The will covers the rest of it. Here. Take the strongbox back upstairs."

Freddie returned the strongbox to the upstairs bedroom. Then he came downstairs and helped Marvin outside and into the car. He took Marvin to a local diner for lunch.

Marvin knew most of the people at the diner, staff and customers. They'd wave from across the room or say hello when Marvin spoke to them, but they avoided being near him or having a conversation, like they didn't know what to say, as if his circumstances were contagious.

"You'd think I had AIDS or something," Marvin said. "No

matter, pass the ketchup, please; this is the best meal I've had in six months."

A fellow about Marvin's age came in the front entrance. It was Charlie Danvers, Marvin's next-door neighbor from when he'd lived in town. He came over to the table.

"I was hoping you'd be here, Marvin. Mrs. Savitsky said she saw you at your house. I've been wanting to see you, see how you're doing."

Marvin was ready for that one. "Well, I live just up the hill, Charlie. You can come see me whenever you want."

Charlie made a face. "I don't know, Marvin. That place gives me the creeps."

"You think it gave you the creeps before? You ought to hang around there now."

"Rather not. My kids keep making noises like they want to send me up there for good."

That sounded familiar. "Are you getting to be a handful, Charlie?"

"I don't think so. I can still drive. But they keep asking me about my stock portfolio and my coin collection and where I keep my will."

"I'd worry about that. Maybe you'd be safer with me up at the nursing home." They both laughed. "Do you still have a key to my house?"

"Yep."

"If I was to need anything from there, would you get it and bring it up?"

"Sure. They won't make me stay, will they?"

Both men laughed again.

CHAPTER 12

When Freddie dropped him off, Marvin went into the dining hall and up to the counter between the kitchen and the seating area. He stood there a while. The kitchen workers went about their work and ignored him.

Finally, he said, "Hey you!"

A worker stopped and came over. "What?"

Marvin leaned forward against the counter. "Can I have a banana, please?"

"No." The worker turned to walk away.

"Why not? You have bananas, don't you?"

The worker stopped and turned around again.

Marvin said, "Under previous management, we could have fruit when we wanted it. So why can't I have a banana?"

"We have been instructed not to hand out extra food."

"It's just a banana, dadgumit! I don't see what's extra about that."

"Man, I'm sorry but we have our instructions. Look at this."

He handed Marvin a memo from Director Bates. Marvin read it aloud. "Residents are not to be provided with snacks or any other food except for the regularly scheduled meals. There are no exceptions to this directive."

Marvin stood looking at the memo in disbelief.

"Can I keep this?"

"Why not? We have another copy."

Marvin folded the memo and put it in his pocket.

The worker said, "Here, pop, hide these in your pocket." He gave Marvin a small bunch of bananas. "Don't tell anyone where you got them."

"Thanks, son. I appreciate it."

Marvin spent the rest of the afternoon at the laptop studying documents on the home's main computer. Every time he found an interesting one, something he could use, he'd store it on his hard drive and email a copy to Freddie just for backup. He concentrated on the home's financial records and found nothing out of the ordinary. Typical evasive bookkeeping practices by a business to impress stockholders and minimize its tax liability. These records could get them in trouble, but they didn't indicate anything relative to the abuse.

He was so engrossed in his studies that he almost forgot to go to supper and would have forgotten if Mike hadn't come to get him.

"We missed you at lunch, Marvin."

"Yeah, Freddie took me out. That was a treat. Real food. Let's go eat whatever culinary delight the kitchen staff has prepared for us tonight."

They walked to the dining hall. Carrie was waiting for them at their usual table.

"Are we meeting tonight?" she asked.

"Yep," Marvin said. "I've got things to report."

"Me, too," Mike said.

"Me, too," Carrie said.

It had been a productive day. Things were looking up.

The waitress brought the usual Saturday fare.

"Mac and cheese, again," Carrie said. "Undercooked and cold."

"Look at my coffee cup." Mike's cup had scraps of dried food stuck to the lip. "Hey waitress, my cup is dirty. Bring me another one."

The server looked over, gave a heavy sigh, and took the cup back to the kitchen. It took her ten minutes to return.

"What took so long?" Mike asked.

She glared at him. "You think you're the only old codger around here that needs attention, pops? I got other things to do besides waiting on you hand and foot."

Mike frowned and spat out the words. "Listen, young lady. We might be old and useless, but we deserve clean dinnerware at the very least. Particularly given what it costs to live in this rat trap."

About then, a tall fellow came walking over. "What's the problem here?" he said.

Leroy Parker was a rangy guy in his late thirties. He ran his hand through his red hair, dirty and uncombed, and glared at them. He moved the toothpick from one side of his mouth to the other with his tongue and folded his arms across his chest, calling attention to his bulging biceps, tattoos, and dirty fingernails. His clothes smelled of grease and oil, and his breath sounded like fingernails on sandpaper and reeked of a mixture of whiskey and tobacco. His scuffed, dirty cowboy boots left tracks on the tile floor.

"Dirty dishes is the problem," Mike said. "But, you aren't the dishwasher, so what business is it of yours?"

"You want me to make it my business, old man?"

Mike started to push himself up from his chair. He had a belligerent look on his face. "Easy, Mike," Marvin said. He pressed Mike's shoulder to sit him back down. "It's okay, sir," he said to Leroy, "we're fine now."

He made a point of fiddling with his old hearing aid so Leroy would know he depended on it.

When Leroy and the server left, Marvin said, "Let's take things as they come and don't make waves. It'll get better soon enough if we do our job right."

"Well, okay," Mike said, "but that clown doesn't know who he's messing with."

Just then a ruckus broke out across the room, and they all turned to see. Leroy was facing a tall, stocky man who was wearing a utility uniform. The man had his face pushed close to Leroy's and was speaking angrily to him. Marvin couldn't make out what they were saying.

"What's that all about?" Marvin asked the others.

Elsie Collins at the next table leaned over and said, "That fellow is Nurse Helen's husband. We met him last year at the family picnic. He delivers fuel oil. Nice fellow. I don't know why he's so mad at Leroy."

Marvin said, "Looks like we're not the only ones with complaints about Leroy. Maybe I can find out what this is about."

Carrie asked Elsie, "Do you know his name?"

"No," Elsie said.

"Okay, I'll just write 'Helen's husband' on my new list."

"New list?" Mike asked. "What's on it?"

"I'm keeping a list of people who might be able to help us with Leroy."

"Good," said Mike. "How many names do you have?"

"Just this one."

Carrie pushed her food around on her plate and made a face. "This stuff is dog food. Except what self-respecting dog would eat it? But did you ever notice that Sunday dinner is much better than the rest of the week? When the families come to visit? Dinner is better on Sunday."

"Yeah," Mike growled. "I really look forward to Sundays."

Marvin said, "I read somewhere that household pets, dogs and cats, have only three needs: Food, love, and safety. I guess we don't rate the same as household pets."

CHAPTER 13

That evening at their meeting, Marvin gave his report first.

"I've been looking at the books. They have definitely cut expenses over last year. And they have two sets of books. I'm guessing one is for them and the other is the cooked-books version to report to the state and the IRS. I have a good idea of their financial situation now. There's things going on here the IRS would like to know about."

"That's really something, Marvin," Carrie said. "How did you get them to let you look at the books?"

"I didn't. I never asked. I guess I'm now an official computer hacker. Like Freddie. This kind of snooping is illegal, so if I get caught, the story is I figured it out on my own. You two don't know squat. I need another day or two to go through their emails, corporate documents, and memos, to see what else is going on."

"That's great," Mike said.

"What do you guys have to report," Marvin asked. "Carrie?"

"Well, I'm getting the flashbulbs and stuff soon. I don't know how we can use them, but they'll be here."

"We'll figure something out," Mike said. "I have an idea."

"I followed Leroy around yesterday," Carrie said. "He's definitely stealing things. After the mail came in, several old people got packages from home. He went in the rooms of the ones that got stuff and that can't tell and came out with items that he didn't go in with. Just like you said he would."

"Did he hit any of the old people?" Marvin asked.

"Not that I could tell," Carrie said. "He mostly went in while they were out of the room."

Mike shook his head. "Some of them don't come out of their rooms."

"I guess he just waltzes in and takes what he wants. They can't tell anybody. I made a list of the folks whose rooms he went in."

"I'll type them in later to add to my documents. Thanks."

"You might not have seen it, Carrie, but Leroy is hitting people," Mike said.

"You've seen it?" Marvin asked.

"Almost. He went into Mr. Whitley's room today. I could hear Leroy talking but I couldn't hear what he was saying. Then I heard a slap and a yell. Leroy came out and walked away. I don't think he took notice of me. Just another old duffer wandering the halls. I went in Whitley's room. He had a big red hand-shaped mark on his face."

"Son of a—" Marvin caught himself. He never swore in front of a lady. "Sorry, Carrie."

"It's okay. I was thinking lots worse than that."

"I asked Whitley if Leroy hit him. He nodded that he did. He wrote a note saying Leroy wanted to see what he got in the mail. Whitley didn't get anything, so Leroy hit him."

They all sat for a while not saying anything. What Mike had seen verified everyone's worst fears.

"If only we had evidence," Marvin said, "besides just our word. Nobody will listen to us. Just the ramblings of old people. Mike, do you think you can operate a camcorder?"

"Sure. I used to work at a TV station."

"I swear," Carrie said. "If we were making a bomb, you'd say you used to work for a dynamite company."

"I did. Back in fifty-two. They fired me, though."

"Why?" asked Carrie, "Or do I want to know?"

"For smoking in the storage room."

"I was right. I didn't want to know."

Once again, Mike's quirks provided comic relief to the tension. When Marvin stopped laughing, he said, "Okay, Mike. I've got a camcorder. It's not one of the new ones, but it's about what they'd expect us to have."

"What do you use it for?" Carrie asked.

"Nothing. My kids brought it. I don't know why. I think they got a new one and didn't want this one any more. Mike, stop by later and get it. See if you can follow Leroy some more and catch him on video going into a room. Then after he leaves, go in and record what you see. Maybe then we'll have evidence. The camcorder has a date-time stamp that it puts on the movie frames. Keep that turned on so nobody can question the integrity of the recording, when each scene was made, and so on."

"Will do. He doesn't notice me much. He knows I can talk, so I'm not on his hit list."

"You will be if he catches you recording him. So be careful."

"Don't worry. I used to work for a private investigator. We caught cheating husbands on film that way. They never knew we did it until their old ladies showed it in court."

"Is there anyone you didn't used to work for?" Carrie asked.

"I never worked for a plastic surgeon. But I always wanted to."

"Whatever for?"

"Breast implants. I'd like to see how they do that."

"My god," Carrie said, looking at the ceiling and shaking her head. "Meeting adjourned, I hope."

"Yeah," Marvin said. "We'll get back together when we know a little more."

Mike said, "Carrie, bring me the flashbulbs and everything

87

that goes with them. Marvin and I are going to build something."

"What?" Marvin asked.

"A booby trap."

That night Marvin slept fitfully. His dreams were troubled by images of staff hitting him and his friends, them needing their clothes changed, needing baths, not getting the attention they needed, being left to die.

CHAPTER 14

Marvin spent the next morning at the laptop in his room. He read corporate documents, internal memos, and email from the files of the server. Document by document he found a pattern of carefully planned tactics designed to decrease the quality of life at the nursing home.

Trying to learn why, Marvin found zoning applications and business plans, and it all came clear. His years of experience managing the financial programs of large and small businesses led him to an astounding conclusion.

"They're waiting for us to die so they can build an amusement park," he said out loud to the empty room.

Next he browsed the personnel files. More revelations. Director Bates and their main suspect, Leroy, had been previously assigned to other nursing homes owned by the same company. Apparently they were a team that moved around the state with the express purpose of closing nursing homes.

He emailed copies of everything to Freddie.

Nurse Helen came in the room with his morning meds. "Good morning, Mr. Bradley. Ready for your pills?"

Helen Crenshaw was about thirty, a pretty woman with short hair. Marvin liked her. She was always cheerful and brought a beam of light into any room she entered. Helen was from the old regime. She had been there at least as long as he had.

Marvin turned the laptop off just as Freddie had shown him.

"Always ready for your visits, Nurse Helen. How's everything today?"

"Just fine. Here, take these. I'll get you a glass of water."

"Nurse Helen, do you know why your husband was here the other day arguing with the maintenance man?"

Nurse Helen seemed surprised by his question. "No, I didn't know about that," she said. "I'll ask him when I get home. Maybe it was about the furnace. Sam delivers the fuel oil."

She got his water, watched while he swallowed his pills, said a cheery good day to him, and went out to continue her morning rounds.

Just then Carrie stuck her head in. "Busy?" she asked.

"Come on in. Look at what I found."

"I have the flashbulb stuff in my room. My daughter brought them. You know how our kids are. Ann just had to know why I needed them. I didn't want to tell her what we're doing, so I told her someone here collects old photographic equipment. That satisfied her."

"Thanks for getting them. I don't know what Mike has in mind, but it's bound to be something clever. Come on in and put them over there. I want you to see this."

She wheeled in, put the box on the floor next to his bed, and pulled up to his desk. He scooted over to make room for her so she could see the laptop screen.

"Want a soda?" he asked.

"Diet?"

"Nope."

"No, thank you."

"Look at this document, Carrie," he said and gestured toward a document that was open in a window on the laptop's screen.

"I don't understand. What does it mean?"

"The company that's running Orchard Hills Nursing Home is a real estate investment and development company."

Carrie looked from the computer screen to Marvin and back again. "Is that significant?" she asked.

"It is when you see what they've done with other nursing homes." Marvin opened another folder on his laptop and opened several documents for Carrie to see.

"Do I need to write all this down?" Carrie asked. She reached for her notepad.

"No, it's all in the computer."

She put the notepad back in her purse. "What did they do with the other nursing homes?"

"They closed most of them. Here's a file of zoning change applications and building permits. They're tearing down nursing homes and building commercial properties, shopping centers, apartments, industrial parks."

"Isn't that illegal?"

"No, not on the face of it. But a lot of residents have the guarantee that they can stay here until they die. To tear a place down, they have to deal with that."

The sound of a vacuum cleaner from out in the corridor interrupted their conversation. Marvin looked at his watch.

"Eleven o'clock," he said. "Right on time. You want to break for lunch?"

"Soon. So when they close down the homes, what do they do with the residents?"

"I think that's where Leroy comes in."

Carrie put her hand on her chest. "Oh, dear. Well, it must be working. We have a lot of empty rooms here."

"And have you noticed? No new admissions since the new regime took over. I think Mr. Whitley was the last one."

"What would they do with this property?" Carrie asked. "This isn't exactly a major metropolitan area."

"I learned the answer to that one here," Marvin said and opened another document. "They plan to build an amusement park here. A really big one."

"Can they do that? They don't own the property."

"They have an option to buy it after Mrs. Simpson passes away." Marvin brought the lease document up on the screen and pointed to the option clause.

"They sure do. Maybe we should start worrying about her."

Marvin turned in his chair. He formed a picture in his mind of someone hitting a frail ninety-seven-year-old woman. He shuddered. "At least we ought to warn her." He turned back to the computer. "And here's a scary clause. Even after she dies and they exercise the option, they have to keep the nursing home running as long as there are any residents left."

"Oh, my stars. They want us all to die." Carrie looked as if she was going to cry.

"And they might be scheming a way to hurry it up, which we are going to nip in the bud." He reached over and patted Carrie's arm.

"Now, look at this." Marvin clicked on Oliver Bates's personnel file. "Bates is married to Mrs. Simpson's daughter. If anything happens to Mrs. Simpson, Bates and his wife inherit the property. Or at least half. She has another daughter."

"And sell to the development company?"

"Now for the admissions files." He closed the documents on the screen and opened another file that listed the residents and their histories.

She took the mouse from under Marvin's hand and used it to scroll Mike's file up on the monitor's screen.

"Oh, my stars!" she said. "Do you know why Mike came here?"

"He said it was a spinal injury."

"More than that. It was a gunshot wound. Do you believe that? He's here on a full government disability." She scrolled further down. "But there's nothing about the government in his employment records. Just all those goofy jobs he talks about."

Marvin was not comfortable with what they were doing. "Probably just a filing error. Let's move on. We shouldn't be prying into Mike's background like this."

She handed the mouse back to him. "Do me a favor. Don't read mine either. There's probably things in there I'd rather keep to myself."

"Same here." Marvin's wartime experiences were like that, so far in the past, so hard to forget. He pushed those memories down as he always did and concentrated on the task at hand. "Now, what else do you want to see?"

"Are there records about the staff in there?" Carrie asked. "What's Leroy's background?"

Marvin opened the personnel files of the employees and downloaded Leroy's file.

"He was a correctional officer for a while. Then there's a gap in his employment history. Say, wait a minute."

Marvin took the stack of printed newspaper articles from his desk drawer. He leafed through them until he found what he was looking for.

"This is starting to add up," he said. "It doesn't make sense, but things are starting to fall into place."

"What?"

"This is a report of someone abusing an elderly prisoner at the prison, a con named, let's see, Willie Hunt. The guy is older than us. I didn't pay it any heed before because it doesn't involve nursing homes. But I printed it just in case. And guess who was a correctional officer until just after this article was published." Marvin clicked on Leroy's personnel records.

"Leroy?"

"Leroy."

"I'll be darned. Did you check on Bates? What's his background?" Carrie strained to get a better look at the documents on the laptop's screen.

"He was a high school teacher. Phys ed. How could a slob like that teach phys ed? And he married Freda Simpson last year, not long before Mrs. Simpson signed that lease."

"The plot thickens."

"It sure does," he said. "We have what could be called coincidences, but we don't have enough to blow the lid off. But we have to do something to protect Mrs. Simpson."

"I agree. Got to go now. I'll see you at lunch." She wheeled herself out of the room and down the hall toward her own room.

Marvin opened the admissions files and found the records for Portia Simpson, the upstairs resident who was also owner of the nursing home property. From there he found her daughter Freda Bates, who was married to Director Bates, and Penny Montana, her other daughter. He didn't want to alert Bates's wife, so he picked up his cell phone and punched in the number for Penny Montana. He got a recording saying to leave a message.

"Ms. Montana, this is Marvin Bradley. I'm a resident at the nursing home where your mother lives. I have reason to believe your mother is in danger. Please call me as soon as you can." He left his number and hung up the phone.

He picked up the newspaper article about abuse in the prison. He read it again and did some searches with the laptop. Certain he was on to something, he got his phone book out and looked up the home phone number of Hardin Lindemuth. He dialed the number.

Hardin had been an administrative assistant at the prison when Marvin met him. Now he was the warden.

"Hardin, this is Marvin Bradley."

"Marvin. How are you? To what do I owe the pleasure?"

"What can you tell me about a former correctional officer there named Leroy Parker?"

"I can't tell you anything about him. I'm under an injunction to never discuss him or even admit that I know him. Otherwise the union will have my head on a platter."

"Okay, I understand. In that case, I want to visit one of your inmates. Willie Hunt. Can you grease the way?"

"Not a problem, Marvin. Why do you need to see him? Is this about Parker?"

"I'm doing research on elderly abuse, and it led to Hunt. I just want to ask him a few questions."

"I can arrange it, but he probably won't tell you anything. The inmates frown on any of their own becoming a snitch even when they snitch on a guard."

That didn't make sense to Marvin. "Why's that?"

"They don't like their own cooperating with the system. But you can try. When would you like to see him?"

"Tomorrow if that can be arranged. About noon, I guess. I have to get myself up there somehow."

"Can't help you there, but I can put in the paperwork to get you through the visitor process. I'm in meetings all day tomorrow, so I won't get to see you. Maybe I'll come up there one day."

"That would be nice, Hardin. I don't get many visitors."

"Will do. When you get here, go to the visitor center. I'll have someone there who will bring you in without you having to go through all the red tape that it usually involves. Do you need a private room?"

"That would be best if you can arrange it."

"Okay, I'll set you up like you were his lawyer. Or financial advisor. That would be better given your background."

"If I need to convince Mr. Hunt to talk to me, is there anything I can promise him?"

"Well, he's a lifer. And pretty old. Older than you, I'd guess. Murdered his wife back in the forties. He works in the library.

Too old for anything strenuous, so you can't offer him an easier job. Tell him you can arrange an extra dessert for him once a week. There's not much else he needs or wants. I'll go ahead and set that up. Just let me know if he doesn't cooperate."

"Thanks, Hardin. I really appreciate your help. And I hope to see you soon."

CHAPTER 15

The next morning, on Monday at breakfast, Marvin told his friends that he'd be gone for most of the day.

"Where are you going?" Mike asked.

"Mike, maybe Marvin doesn't want to tell us," Carrie said.

"I'll tell you about it later," Marvin told them. He didn't want them to try to stop him.

He met the shuttle bus at the curb for its nine o'clock run to take residents to the mall. Marvin boarded and said to the driver, "Could you drop me off in town? I need to see my doctor."

"Sure, Mr. Bradley."

Mike was on the bus, which surprised Marvin.

"I didn't know you were going shopping," Marvin said. "How did you get here ahead of me?"

"I hurried. Didn't want to miss the bus. When you said you were gone for the day, I figured I'd come out for a field trip. Sit in the mall and ogle the teenage girls. Carrie's watching Leroy today. It's her turn. Where are you headed?"

Marvin leaned over and whispered, "To prison."

"What? What do you mean—"

"Shh. The driver thinks I'm going to the doctor. I'll explain later."

The bus stopped on Main Street about two blocks from the turnoff to Marvin's house. "Is this close enough, Mr. Bradley?"

The driver opened the door, and Marvin stepped down the

first step. "I'll be here about the time you're scheduled to take us home. I'll go shopping until then."

"Are you sure you'll be okay by yourself out here?"

"Everybody in town knows me. If there's any problem, they'll call up to the home. And I have my cell phone."

Marvin got off the bus and watched it drive away toward the mall. He walked slowly to his house so he wouldn't get winded. He sat on the front steps to rest and catch his breath. Then he went around to the garage.

He took the key ring from his pocket and unlocked the garage door. With a great deal of effort, he got the door open. The Buick sat inside just as he'd last seen it. Out of breath, he opened the driver's side front door and sat on the seat for a while with his feet hanging down to the dirt floor. When he felt rested enough, he swung around, put the key in the ignition, and turned it. Nothing. It didn't crank over.

"Dadgumit," he said out loud. "Dead battery." Apparently Freddie hadn't gotten there yet to charge it.

The battery charger sat over against the wall where it had always been. He pulled the hood latch, got out, went around front, and raised the hood. A mouse went scurrying away from on top of the air cleaner where she'd built her nest.

He wheeled the charger over, plugged it into a wall socket, and connected the cables to the battery. Then he got in the car and turned the key. The engine labored to turn over with a grind and then went quiet. He switched off the key and waited. After about a minute, he tried again. This time the engine didn't respond.

This was a problem. He needed his car to start so he could keep his appointment. He couldn't call a cab. The only cab company was two towns away.

Maybe his neighbor Charlie Danvers was home and could give him a jump start. But his car was parked nose in. Jumper cables wouldn't reach from another car in the driveway to the Buick's battery. Maybe Charlie could drive him up there.

He walked toward the garage door to go to Charlie's house. He saw the problem and stopped. The charger was set to charge a battery, not start a car.

He switched it to the Engine Start setting, got back in the car, and turned the key. The engine fired up with that satisfying grumble that the old V-eight had always produced.

He got out, went around, turned off the charger, disconnected it from the battery, and wheeled it back to its place against the wall. He closed the hood and got in the car. Getting the car started had taken a lot out of him, and he needed a moment to rest. He looked at his watch. "If I hurry up, I'll be late."

After a few minutes to get a second wind, he put the car in reverse. "Well, here goes nothing," he said aloud. He backed out of the garage and continued into the street. He looked around. Everything looked the way he remembered it. He drove to the intersection, stopped, waited for traffic to clear, and pulled out onto Main Street.

"So far, so good. Who says I can't drive?"

The drive went without incident but not without apprehension and anxiety. Traffic was light, and he drove slowly to give his reflexes time to react to whatever might come his way, but he worried that he might miss something. It felt good to be behind the wheel after so long, but he wondered what would happen if anyone found out. He could hear his son, now. "Dad, what are we going to do with you, driving in your condition?" That made him laugh.

Cars in the oncoming lane seemed to go by too fast and too close. He flinched at every one that sped by. He didn't remember it being that way, but he held on to the wheel firmly and drove with deliberation toward his destination. His confidence grew with each minute spent behind the wheel. By the time he got to the turnoff to the prison, he felt like he was in charge again, in control, master of his own destiny.

He drove up the incline to the prison entrance. He parked in the visitor's parking lot, turned off the engine, got out, went to the visitor center, and told the receptionist who he was.

"We've been expecting you, Mr. Bradley. Come this way."

They took him to an interview room with a long table and several chairs.

"Take a seat, sir. The prisoner will be right out."

After a moment, a door at the far end of the room opened, and an elderly man in prison clothes came into the room. He was short and looked ancient. He wore a green pullover shirt, green slacks, and sneakers. His look was one of defiance, distrust, and attitude, and Marvin instantly feared the man, an automatic reaction. Marvin was sure that Willie Hunt could sense his discomfort, and he tried to relax. Hunt looked around the room, pushed his cigarette into a standing sand-filled ashtray at the door, walked over to Marvin, and sat across the table from him. He didn't say anything but just looked at Marvin, a sneer on his face that seemed to be permanent.

"Mr. Hunt, my name is Marvin Bradley. I am not associated with the prison or any law enforcement organization. In fact, I am not associated with anything. I retired over twenty years ago."

Hunt spoke. "I can tell that. You look older than dirt." He took a cigarette from a crumpled pack and lit it with a match. "Mind if I smoke? Too bad if you do."

"No, that's okay. I smoke a pipe, myself." Marvin struggled to find a common bond, a way to crack Willie Hunt's shell. It didn't seem to be working.

"What do you want, Mr. Bradley?"

"I read a newspaper article from several years ago that

reported a number of incidents of inmate abuse here by the guards."

"Oh, that."

"The article mentioned your name as one of the ones abused. The paper singled you out apparently because of your age."

"Yeah, human interest. Old convict gets the crap beat out of him by the guards."

"It said you were beaten rather badly. That you spent time in the hospital."

"I ain't supposed to talk about it."

"This talk is private, Mr. Hunt. It's between you and me."

"These walls have ears. And eyes. What's in it for me?"

"The warden said if you could help me, he'll see to it that you got an extra dessert once a week."

"No kidding. Well, ask away."

"Who beat you up?"

"One of the guards. He was known for beating up the old cons whenever he could. They fired him when it hit the news-papers. But I won't tell you who he is. He's still out there somewhere. Those guys can have a long reach. Other guards might be his pals. Plus we have a code about snitching. Break the code, somebody breaks your face. I guess I'll have to pass on the extra desserts. Too bad."

"The guy I'm dealing with is beating up old people in the nursing home where I'm confined." Marvin hoped the "con-fined" would give them something in common and garner him a measure of trust.

"You live in a nursing home? Confined? How'd you get here? Somebody bring you?"

"No. I busted out and stole a car." Maybe that would impress the old convict.

"Good for you. I can work with that. Go on." Hunt snuffed out his cigarette and put the butt in his shirt pocket.

"The guy I know was a guard here," Marvin said. "He left just about the time the story about you came out. The details of his hasty departure are not in the records, and he isn't mentioned in the newspapers with regard to the abuse."

"Yeah, the other guards protected him. And they have a union. We all have to look out for our own. They ain't no exception."

"After that he worked at nursing homes around the state. Since coming to where I live, he's been hitting the old people. He killed a blind resident's seeing-eye dog and another old guy's cat."

"Man, that's cold. Sounds like our boy. But I ain't saying his name."

"Let's try it this way. I'll say a name. If it isn't him, you get up and walk out of here. If it is him, you stay and have another cigarette. Either way, you didn't rat anybody out, I know what I need to know, and you get your extra desserts."

Hunt didn't speak. He just sat there and stared at Marvin.

Marvin said, "The guy I know is named Leroy Parker."

Willie Hunt looked around, then took another cigarette from his pack and lit it. He drew the smoke into his lungs, blew it out into the room, and continued to look directly at Marvin's face. When he finished the cigarette, he got up and went across the room and out the door.

CHAPTER 16

Marvin stood looking at the Buick in the prison parking lot, hoping it would start. He was reluctant to climb in and learn otherwise, but when he opened the door, the dome light shone bright. He got in, put the key in the ignition, turned it, and listened with satisfaction to the engine turn over and start. The drive from home to here had been enough to charge the battery. At least enough for one start.

He drove out of the parking lot and into town. He was tired from the interview and the walk afterwards, and his vision was slightly out of focus from the exhaustion. He drove north through the town at about twenty miles an hour. When he got out of town, he continued to drive at the same speed on a two-lane winding road. A line of cars formed behind him, impatient commuters eager to get home after their day's work.

He tried to ignore the other cars and crawled along at his most comfortable speed. At a long, straight stretch of road, the cars behind him swerved into the oncoming lane and shot past him, going as fast as they could. The blur as they sped by made him uncomfortable and nervous. Several of them blew their horns to assert their disapproval of his driving.

The cars raced past him, and he instinctively shifted his shoulders to his right as if to keep from making contact. He inched his car closer to the dirt shoulder. Then, worried that he'd go off the road, he inched back toward the center line. With this back and forth, left to right, he tried to switch his focus from the rear and side mirrors to the road ahead, his lane, and the oncoming one, so he could keep track of everything and react to whatever might happen, but his eyes would not converge fast enough on the rapidly changing scenes.

With reluctance, he conceded that maybe this motor trip outing had been a bad idea. At least in rush hour.

He was almost in town when, to his relief, the last batch of cars passed him. Just when he had it made, blue lights flashed in his rearview mirror. A city police car was pulling him over.

He pulled over and kept his engine running. A cop got out of the police car and walked up alongside of Marvin's car. Marvin rolled down the window. He was sure the cop would arrest him. His license had expired. Even if he got off, there would be the humiliation of having it known around the nursing home. This was indeed a piece of bad luck.

"Was I speeding, officer?"

The cop laughed. "Not hardly, sir. Your driver's license and registration, please."

Marvin got the registration out of the glove compartment. He said, "I don't have my driver's license. I forget where I left it."

"What is your name?"

"Marvin Bradley."

"Where do you live, Mr. Bradley?"

"Orchard Hills Nursing Home. Why did you stop me? Did I break any laws?"

"Your tags expired two months ago, Mr. Bradley. Turn off your engine, please."

"I'm afraid if I do it won't start."

"Doesn't matter, you won't need it. Without a license and valid tags, you aren't driving it anywhere. Get out of the car, please."

Marvin got out with his cane. The cop led him by the arm

back to the patrol car, opened the rear door, and helped him get in.

"What about my car?"

"We'll send a tow truck to get it. We could impound it but I'd rather not. Paperwork. Where would you like it taken?"

"To my house here in town. You can leave it in front. My grandson will take care of it."

"What's the address?"

Marvin told him his home address and the cop wrote it down.

"How will you pay for the towing, Mr. Bradley? And the fine?"

"Do you take plastic?"

"Sure. We can take care of that down at the police station."

"Am I going to jail?"

"No, sir. You can wait at the station until we can get you home. If no one can come get you, I'll take you there myself when I have time. Why did your grandson let you drive in the first place?"

"He doesn't know. He lives in Philadelphia."

Marvin looked around outside the patrol car hoping nobody he knew had seen him. This was humiliating. He'd never even had a traffic ticket, much less a ride in a cop car.

The cop drove him to the police station and took him inside. He paid his fine with his credit card and arranged to pay for the tow truck, too.

"Can you just take me to Main Street near my house? I'm supposed to meet the bus there."

"Rather not do that. It's getting colder. You shouldn't be outside. Can they pick you up here?"

"I guess so." Then he said, "This is the part I'm dreading."

He called Mike's cell phone.

"Mike, see if the driver can stop at the police station. I've been picked up."

"For what?"

"D.W.E."

"What's that?"

"Driving while elderly."

They both laughed. The desk sergeant, who could hear Marvin talking, laughed, too.

"Actually, I was driving on expired tags without a license."

"Driving? You were driving?"

"To the prison. And it was worth it. I learned a lot about Leroy."

Marvin sat in the police station until the bus pulled in. He thanked the cop and the desk sergeant and went out to board the bus. The driver shook his head in disbelief. Mike grinned. The others just looked at him. He got on the bus and said, "Not a word, don't say a word," and rode home in silence.

They got there just before suppertime. Marvin and Mike went straight to the dining hall and joined Carrie.

Mike said to Carrie, "Guess what our boy did today."

"What?"

"He got his car out and drove to the prison."

"What? Whatever for?"

Marvin said, "I did some research on Leroy. He's definitely our guy. He was fired from the prison for beating up elderly inmates."

"Can we use that to get him fired here?" Carrie asked.

"I doubt it," Marvin said. "There's no way they don't already know about it. Which kind of implicates management in the abuse."

"That's not proof," Mike said. "That's speculation. We need more than that."

"We'll get it. Now that we know where to concentrate our investigation. If only we don't get caught."

CHAPTER 17

The next morning Marvin was well-rested. He went to breakfast and was almost cheerful. He told Mike and Carrie about his trip the day before and his encounter with the cops.

"What was it like talking to a convicted murderer?" Carrie asked.

"Just like talking to anyone else. He was cautious at first, but I managed to win him over. And I learned that Leroy was the abuser there. I'm going to do some snooping today. What are you two doing?"

"Just following the usual suspects," Carrie said.

"I have to go to the clinic," Mike said. "The ultrasound lady is here. I'm due to have my corroded artery scanned."

"That's carotid artery," Carrie said. "What's wrong with it?"

"It's corroded."

After breakfast Marvin returned to his room, put in his new hearing aids, and went out to go snooping. He headed toward the reception area to see if he could overhear anything useful. He sat in an easy chair placed there for visitors and pretended to read a magazine. Every now and then the telephone would ring. Loretta sat at a big desk near the entrance and answered the phone, "Orchard Hills Nursing Home." A couple of times she said, "I'm sorry, but Orchard Hills is not accepting applications for new admissions at this time."

Loretta Swann was a lady in her forties who had come in with the new regime. Just as he had suspected, she was turning away customers. There were plenty of empty rooms; the home was at about seventy percent capacity according to Marvin's estimate. The accountant in him told him that you don't turn a losing enterprise into a profitable one by turning away business. But based on what he'd discovered so far, he began to understand the losing strategy. He'd need more evidence to back up his theory, though.

After a while, Leroy came strolling down the hall from the residential section. He sat on the edge of Loretta's desk and started talking to her.

"Hi, sweet thing," Leroy said. "How's by you? I brought you a present."

Leroy gave her a box of chocolates. Marvin recognized it. It had been delivered to Mr. Whitley with a sympathy card from his daughter for the loss of his cat. Even though Leroy and Loretta spoke quietly, Marvin could hear every word they said, thanks to his new hearing aids.

"Thank you, Leroy. How's the project going? I heard about the cat."

"Shh," Leroy hushed her up. "Don't you see that old geezer sitting over there?"

"Don't worry about him. That's old Marvin. He can't hear squat without his ratty old hearing aid. And with it, he can't hear much. Looks like he left it in his room again. You can speak up. He's deaf as a post."

Leroy walked over and stood in front of Marvin. "What's up, grandpa?" he said.

Marvin cupped his hand behind his ear and said, "Eh?"

Leroy laughed, walked back to Loretta's desk, and sat on its edge.

"Deaf as a post," he said. "Soon to be dead as a doornail, I expect."

The threat registered with Marvin, and it angered and scared him, but he didn't let them see his reaction.

"So, what have you been up to?" she asked Leroy.

"I managed to intercept medications a couple of times. Might hurry things along if they don't get their pills."

"How do you get their pills? The nurses hand out all the medications."

"I sweet-talk them. Offer to help. Take a cup of pills in for an old poop and flush them down the toilet."

"You be careful how you sweet-talk the nurses, Leroy. That's not allowed."

"Don't worry. It's all part of the game. You're still number one."

"I better be. And there better not be any number twos."

"Besides the meds, I'm still knocking the old geezers around when I can."

"I don't like that part. Stealing candy and flushing meds is one thing, Leroy, but hurting old people doesn't seem right."

"Yeah? Well how else do you hurry along their demise?"

The more they said, the angrier Marvin got.

"I suppose. I just wish there was another way. Some of these people are nice. The other day three of them shared their pizza with me." She didn't tell Leroy that Marvin was one of the three.

"Pizza? Where did they get pizza?"

"I don't know, dear, but they gave me some. Why do we have to hurt them?"

"Bates's idea. Didn't he tell you? No, I guess he wouldn't. I break a bone or some skin. Infection sets in. Out of their misery soon enough."

Marvin perked up at that. Bates was part of it. He was in charge of it. Just as Marvin had suspected.

"They don't have much longer anyway," Leroy said. "We just help Mother Nature along. I'm keeping it to slaps and punches now to get them used to being pushed around and to get the nurses used to seeing the minor injuries."

That comment registered with Marvin, too. It told him that the nurses weren't part of the conspiracy. He was glad to hear that.

Leroy continued. "I'll get rougher later. Break some hips, ribs, or whatever. Then, when the numbers get down far enough, we'll do the consolidation thing with the high-functioning ones. Bates calls it 'natural attrition used to our advantage.' Don't that sound high spoken? We've done it before at other homes. We just help nudge along the natural part. Step in when Mother Nature is taking too long."

It took all of Marvin's control to keep from reacting to that. He gripped his hickory cane, pushed his anger down, and kept his eyes on the magazine and his ears on the conversation. Apparently the "consolidation thing" was how they reduced the resident populations. Whatever that meant, it probably tagged his own fate, the plans they had for him. Marvin was one of the high-functioning ones.

Leroy went on. "I ain't supposed to be telling you any of this, Loretta, but being as how we're involved and all, I figure you should know. The bonus Bates promised me might just pay for a cruise to the islands."

"That would be nice, Leroy." She removed one of Whitley's chocolates from the box, slipped it into her mouth, and winked coyly at Leroy. "I just wish there was a better way."

Marvin wondered about the character of someone who would condone this kind of vile abuse just to get a box of chocolates or a cruise with a guy. Loretta wasn't as nice as Carrie had said.

Director Bates came out of the director's office, and Leroy's and Loretta's body language changed to suggest a less intimate relationship.

Oliver Bates was a disagreeable man of about fifty, pudgy

with a ruddy complexion that changed constantly from red to scarlet and back again, suggesting a cardiovascular system about to erupt. He wore a rumpled brown double-breasted suit that looked like a Goodwill reject. His shoes needed a shine, his tie was stained with the droppings of numerous meals, and he did not button his jacket because it wouldn't close across his abundant belly.

"What are you doing here, Parker?" he asked.

"Just visiting with Loretta. I brought her a box of candy. From my latest raid."

"Dad blast it, Parker," Bates said in a harsh whisper. "Keep your voice down." He gestured toward Marvin.

"Deaf," Leroy said.

"So you think. And why are you discussing this stuff with Loretta? It's supposed to be between us and only us."

Marvin was glad to hear that. Now they didn't have to worry about other, unknown conspirators. Just Bates and Leroy.

"It's okay, Oliver," Loretta said. "Leroy and I are friends."

"So I see," Bates answered. "But how many times have I told you? When others are around, call me Mr. Bates."

"I'm sorry," Loretta said. "I forgot."

"Get back to work, Parker," Bates said and went back into his office.

Just then the telephone rang again. As Loretta reached to answer it, Leroy waved at her and left. Marvin sat there seething. When he'd regained control, he got up and walked away.

On his way back he passed the nursing station. He stopped. This could be a chance to address the medication part of the problem. He went back to the station where Nurse Norma was making entries in a log.

"Nurse Norma, you didn't seem to believe me when I told you about the abuse. Well, see if this changes your mind. I just overheard Leroy say he kept residents from getting their meds."

"What? How?" She put the log down and came over to the counter.

"He offers to help the nurses, and then he takes the pills and flushes them down the toilet. I think you should instruct your nurses not to accept anyone's help."

"I'll do more than that. I'll report him to Director Bates. Get him fired."

"Not a good idea. That would probably get you fired. Bates is in on it."

"What? How do you know?"

"I heard them talking about it."

"Oh, my goodness. Why are they doing it?"

"It's that conspiracy you don't believe in. We've just about got this thing wrapped up, so trust us for a few days. Please don't say anything to Leroy or Bates. We don't have all the evidence we need yet. Just tell your nurses to hand out the meds themselves."

"Okay, Marvin. Keep me posted."

Marvin spent the rest of the day at his computer, correlating files and facts and summarizing everything in a report for the authorities. He was so deep into the project that he skipped lunch and had a candy bar and a soda for supper. When Mike poked his head in after supper to see where he'd been, Marvin said, "Here. Busy. No meeting tonight. I'll see you tomorrow," and got back to work.

CHAPTER 18

At breakfast on Wednesday, Marvin told Mike and Carrie, "Come to my room at lunchtime. I got solid information."

"Can't you tell us now?" Carrie asked.

"No. I want this to be as private as possible. I think the case is cracked, but I need more time to finish organizing my records."

"I'll bring lunch," Mike said.

Later Marvin paced in his room and waited for the meeting to begin. He had organized everything on the computer and polished up his report, and now he was excited that he had broken the case and learned who the bad guys were. He looked forward to the next stage when they'd reveal the conspirators and put a stop to the abuse. He understood their motives now, but he'd need more evidence to make a strong case, something that the authorities would believe. He moved around the room, not even noticing that he was doing it without his cane.

Soon, Mike came in with a pizza and six-pack. Carrie wheeled in right behind him, rolled up to the table, and busied herself opening beer bottles and passing out pizza slices.

Marvin sat in his chair, and Mike sat on the bed and leaned back on his elbows.

Marvin started the meeting. "I've got good news and bad news. What do you want first?"

"The good news," Carrie said.

Marvin explained to Mike what he and Carrie had discussed

a few days back about the lease and management's plans to close the nursing home. Then he said, "I think we know from that why they're doing it. That's the good news."

"What's the bad news?" Mike asked.

"They're planning to kill us off one at a time."

"Kill us?" Mike said.

"I heard Leroy say so. He and Bates and Loretta were talking about it."

"I knew it," Mike said. "Killing cats and dogs, knocking us around, taking our stuff. Why are they doing it?"

"So they can close nursing homes and develop the properties."

Mike sat up off his elbows and leaned forward. "This is all about real estate? They're beating up old people so they can bulldoze the building and build something else?"

"An amusement park."

"Holy crap!" Mike said.

"That's my theory, anyway," Marvin said. "We have to move fast. We need hard evidence. Mike, you got to get that camcorder going. Leroy is our only suspect at this time."

"I'm on it," Mike said.

"I don't think anyone else on the staff is part of it. Bates as much as said so. Just him and Leroy. Except maybe Loretta, and that's just because she and Leroy are having a fling. So don't say anything to her."

Carrie gave them each another slice. "What could she see in that ugly man? I can't figure it. Can't we just turn them in?" she asked.

Marvin twisted in his chair and shook his head. "Nobody'd believe us. Heck, I know it to be a fact, and I can hardly believe it myself. We have to have ironclad proof. The other good news is that the medical staff isn't part of it."

"I'm glad to hear that," Mike said. "The last thing we need is for the people who handle our meds to be in a conspiracy to bump us off. But how do you know they aren't in on it?"

"I heard Leroy say he was getting the nurses used to seeing the occasional bruise. But the other bad news is that the nurses are all looking for jobs. Nurse Norma told me. Who knows who they'll get to replace them? We need to move fast. Mike, do you have the cattle prod and archery set?"

"Not yet. My son is sending them. I ought to have them in a day or two."

"How will you get them past the receptionist?"

"I already got permission from Director Ollie to set up hay bales with targets in the recreation yard when it warms up. He wants to see the set when it comes in to make sure it will be safe."

"He probably hopes you'll shoot somebody by accident," Carrie said.

"I will if Leroy is out there. My son is going to hide the cattle prod in the quiver when he ships the archery set."

"A cattle prod," Carrie said. "What next?"

Everyone was animated now, excited, with a mission and a purpose. Mike and Carrie congratulated Marvin on his snooping expedition. Then they left to go to their own rooms and prepare themselves for whatever would come next.

Right after they left, Marvin's cell phone rang.

"Mr. Bradley, this is Penny Montana. You left me a message about my mother being in danger. What's going on?"

"We're seeing a pattern of patient abuse around here, and I was worried that your mother might be one of the targets."

"Abuse? Didn't you report it to management?"

"No, ma'am. We aren't sure who we can trust."

"But the director is married to my sister. My mother is his mother-in-law."

"Yes, ma'am, I know. As I said, we don't know who we can trust."

"Have you called the police?"

"No, ma'am. I'm afraid if I do, they'll brush it off as an old man with an overactive imagination and then whoever is doing it will know we're on to them."

"Thank you, Mr. Bradley. I'm really finding this difficult to believe. But I never liked that worm my sister married. I'll see what I can do without revealing your part in it."

"Just make sure your mother is protected. We've just about got this cleared up. If you'd like, I'll look in on your mother from time to time."

"That would be helpful. You have my number. Call if there's anything I should know. Thank you very much."

CHAPTER 19

It was mid-morning on Thursday. Marvin went to the dayroom to set up for Bonnie Meade's weekly piano recital. He always helped her by moving the card tables out of the way and setting up the chairs. She was sitting at the piano when he got there.

He had almost forgotten to come. The investigation and its recent developments had distracted him. He thought about how to deal with the problem and whether he was putting himself and his friends in danger. So much to think about, so much that could go wrong, all of it his responsibility. He was worried.

While he got the folding chairs out of the storage room one by one, she practiced today's program of selections by Debussy. That was one advantage of his volunteer work. He got a private concert.

She deftly ran down the three Nocturnes, never missing a note. Her technique wasn't what it used to be. Arthritis had slowed her down a bit, but her touch was delicate, and her musical selections were always well organized and planned. Marvin had known her for years and had attended many of her student recitals when they both lived in town.

The room's acoustics added a natural reverberation to the sounds of the piano. Even with his old hearing aid, the piano had sounded wonderful. Now, with the new ones, the sound was marvelous.

When everything was ready, Marvin waited for Bonnie to end the piece she was practicing and then said, "That was beautiful,

Mrs. Meade. That piano has such a beautiful tone."

"Particularly in this room. Such grand acoustics. As if it belongs here."

"It does as long as you are here to play it. We're lucky that you brought it with you. And that you play it for us every week."

"Well, it will still be here after I'm gone. I left it to the nursing home in my will."

"That is very generous, Mrs. Meade."

"I only hope my friends can make good use of it."

"I'm sure they will." He looked at his watch and said, "I'm going to lunch, now. Care to join me?"

He always asked, and she always answered, "No thank you, Mr. Bradley. I have a few more numbers to practice."

CHAPTER 20

At lunch Marvin said, "Coming to the concert with us, Mike?"

"Don't we have more important things to worry about?" Mike asked.

"We don't want to tip our hand by breaking routine. Carrie and I go every Thursday."

"Criminentlies, Marvin! There's somebody out there who wants to kill us."

"Staying away from the concert won't change that. And we'll be in a crowd. Safe enough. I wish you'd come."

"Well, what about the old people who can't go? Who's going to protect them?"

That made sense to Marvin. "Good point, Mike. Tell you what. If Leroy isn't at the concert, we can come back and hang around the old people's rooms."

"Well, I'm not going anyway."

"It's Debussy, Mike," Carrie said. "She'll probably play Clair De Lune."

"Why would I want to go hear some old biddy pounding out 'Clear the Room' on a rickety old pie-anna?" Mike said. "I got better ways to spend my time. I've about got Leroy's schedule figured out. He's a creature of habit. I can be most places ahead of him with my trusty camcorder at the ready."

He got up from the table and left for parts unknown.

"Should we let Mike go out alone knowing what we know now?" Carrie asked.

119

"He should be okay. I don't think any of us is on the hit list yet, anyway. It's still just the old people."

They walked from the dining hall on their way to the concert. When they were near the dayroom Leroy came rushing out and brushed by them without a word.

"I wonder what he's been up to," Carrie said.

When they got to the dayroom they got a shock. Bonnie Meade was lying on the floor beside the piano bench. They rushed to her side.

"She's got a bruise on her face," Marvin said. "Her jaw looks broken. Quick, Carrie, you're faster in the chair. Go get Nurse Norma."

Carrie sped off toward the nursing station.

"Mrs. Meade," Marvin said, "Are you awake?"

Bonnie Meade moaned.

"Oh, God," Marvin said to no one in particular. "It's already started."

In less than a minute, Nurse Norma rushed up with a cell phone held to her ear. "Get back, Marvin, so I can tend to her. The doctor will be right here."

She began poking and prodding Bonnie, feeling for broken bones. Just then the doctor got there. He went down on both knees next to Bonnie and listened to her heartbeat and breathing with his stethoscope. Then he said to Nurse Norma, "Call nine-one-one. We need to get her to the hospital."

People were beginning to arrive for the concert. Carrie positioned herself at the door to head them off. She told them, "The concert for today has been cancelled. Mrs. Meade is not well."

Marvin said, "Doc, take notice. She's on her left side. That's how we found her. The bruise is on the right side of her face. I think somebody knocked her off the piano bench."

"I noticed, Mr. Bradley," the doctor said. "Now go on about

your business. People here fall down all the time. Her face might have hit the bench on her way down."

"Not the way I see it."

Just then Mike came rushing up. Word had already spread around the home. He was carrying the camcorder.

"Get a shot of that, Mike," Marvin said. "Make sure you get her jaw and the bruise and where she's positioned relative to the piano bench."

Mike pointed the camcorder at Mrs. Meade and began recording.

"What are you two doing?" asked the doctor. "Go on along now."

"Just making a record," said Mike. "You'll thank me later."

"Or not," Marvin said. The doctor was ignoring the obvious when every indication was that this woman had been assaulted. Now Marvin wondered whether the doctor was part of the conspiracy. "Doc, this is not something you should sweep under the carpet. You haven't heard the last of it. Get on board with what's going on around here and do something about it, or else."

"Or else what, Mr. Bradley?"

"Or else start planning on what you'll do for a living after they yank your license," Marvin said over his shoulder.

"What?" the doctor said.

Marvin didn't respond but walked away, hot under the collar. Marvin, Mike, and Carrie went to Marvin's room where he took the DVD from the camcorder, uploaded the video of Mrs. Meade on the floor into his laptop, and emailed it to Freddie.

"This is sooner than I expected," he said. "Now it's worse than just bruises. And Mrs. Meade wasn't one of the old people. Leroy has taken it to the next level. We've got to step up our investigation."

"Can we prove Leroy did it?" Mike asked.

"Not directly. But Carrie and I saw him heading out of the dayroom right before we found her. There's no doubt about who did it, at least in our minds. But would anyone believe us?"

"Woo," Carrie said. "This has knocked the wind out of my sails. That poor woman. I feel so bad for her."

"Yes," Marvin said. "I'm out of steam myself."

"We need to rest," Mike said. "This has been a busy day. We can't be effective when we're bone tired. Let's take a break."

CHAPTER 21

Marvin was in his room trying to rest. He had changed out of his concert clothes and into his usual daily attire, slippers, pajamas, and robe. The morning's activities had worn him down. He lay on his bed but he couldn't sleep. Then Mike was at the door.

"Marvin, come on out. They're moving Mrs. Meade's piano out."

"What? Who is?"

"Piano movers. They're taking it."

"Let's go see."

Marvin pulled himself off the bed. They hurried as fast as they could down the hall toward the dayroom. Two workmen were there with the grand piano on its side strapped to a skid board, its legs and pedals folded under. They hoisted it onto a dolly. Mike had the camcorder going, making a video for the files.

"Where are you going with that?" Marvin asked the movers.

"To the piano shop in town."

"Is something wrong with it?"

"No. They're going to sell it, I think. On consignment. Do you want to see the work order?"

Marvin took the work order and looked it over. "Can we make a copy of this?"

"You can have that one," the mover said.

"Boy, that didn't take long," Mike said. "Let's go see if

anyone knows how Mrs. Meade is doing."

They walked to the nursing station. Nurse Norma was sitting there filling out forms.

"Nurse Norma, how's Mrs. Meade?" Marvin asked.

"She died in the ambulance, I'm sad to say. They're saying it was from the accident, the injury from when she fell."

"Accident, my Aunt Fanny's hat!" Mike said. He choked back a sob and turned away, pulling his handkerchief out.

Marvin was stunned. He sat on a bench against the far wall, put his face in his hands, and waited for a brief spell before speaking. Then, his composure back, he sat up straight and said, "Such a dear lady, she was. All she ever did was give of herself and her talent to others. To die like that. At the hands of a worthless, no-good . . ."

He got up and walked back over to the counter. "Nurse Norma, would you scan this document in for me? I want it for my files. You can email it to me."

Nurse Norma took the piano mover's work order over to her computer. A while later she brought it back. "It's in your email, Marvin." She paused for a moment and said, "You two guys better watch yourselves. I don't like what's going on around here. Keep your eyes open and quit meddling. I don't want to see you guys get hurt, too. I wish I knew what to do. You don't just accuse people without evidence. You could lose everything."

They walked away from the nursing station. When they were out of earshot, Mike said, "Mrs. Meade isn't even in the ground yet, the body's still warm, and already they're selling her piano."

"And look at this work order," Marvin said. "Look at the date the order was cut." He handed it to Mike.

"Yesterday," Mike said. "They arrange to move and sell the piano the day before she has her so-called accident. This means only one thing."

"What?" Marvin asked.

"He meant to kill her. He hit her hard enough to put her down. He did it on purpose. She just took a couple hours longer than he intended. And look at the name on the work order authorizing the move."

Marvin took the document back. "Bates."

CHAPTER 22

Marvin returned to his room and got dressed. Then he went to the reception area. Loretta was busy filing. He interrupted her work.

"Loretta, you know who Mrs. Simpson is?"

"You mean the old gal who owns this place? Sure."

"Is her room still upstairs?"

"Room? She has a suite. The only residence quarters on the second floor."

"Is she allowed to have visitors?"

"Sure. I wish she'd get some."

"Doesn't she have daughters?"

"They never come."

"Not even Director Bates's wife?"

"You know about that? He didn't want it spread around. Worries about nepotism. But, no, Mrs. Bates doesn't come around here. I don't think Mr. Bates has ever visited her, either."

"Thanks. I think I'll add her to my morning rounds."

"That would be nice, Marvin. I never met her, but I bet she'd appreciate it. Now, excuse me, I'm behind in my filing. I'm always behind in my filing."

"Don't you keep all that in the computer?"

"These are old resident and staff records from before. I have to update them because of all the turnover."

"I see. Thank you."

Marvin went down the corridor to where the staircase was.

He'd often wondered what was on the second floor, and now he'd see for himself. He had always conducted business with Abel Simpson in his first-floor study. Marvin could still negotiate a flight of stairs, so he didn't need to use the chair lift. He climbed to the second floor landing and looked around. A desk and chair sat where you had to go past it to get to the other rooms. He walked around looking at the closed doors, wondering which one was Mrs. Simpson's.

Just then a door opened and a woman in a nurse's uniform came out. She carried herself in a sturdy, in-charge way. Her uniform was different from the ones worn by the nursing staff downstairs.

"Can I help you?" she asked in a cautious voice.

"I just came to visit Mrs. Simpson."

"Sure. Go right in. Leave the door open."

Marvin went through the door. Mrs. Simpson sat in a wheelchair looking out a large bay window onto a balcony. She was frail in stature and appearance.

"Mrs. Simpson, I'm Marvin Bradley. Do you remember me? I was your husband's accountant."

"Of course I remember you, Marvin. What brings you here?"

"I'm a resident. Have been for a year. Penny asked me to look in on you from time to time."

"How nice, young man, come in and sit down."

Marvin hadn't been called "young man" in years. But he was younger than Mrs. Simpson by about ten years. He sat with her and exchanged small talk. She asked all about him.

"And how is that pretty wife? Jessica, as I recall."

"She passed away several years ago."

"How sad. I'm so sorry for you. Are you happy here?"

"Yes, ma'am. It's very nice." He did not wish to alarm the old lady with what had been going on.

"Well, if you have any problems, you just let me know. I'm

still in charge around here."

Marvin smiled and thought, *If only you knew.*

After a while when they ran out of small talk, he said good-bye, promised to come back, and went out into the lobby area. The nurse sat at the desk. He walked up and said, "Hello, I'm Marvin Bradley. I haven't seen you here before."

"I'm Rhonda," she said. "I'm new."

"You mean with the new management?"

"No, sir, I'm a private nurse. Retired Marine. There are three of us hired to take care of Mrs. Simpson. And watch over her. Her daughter hired us."

"Okay, Rhonda, I have one piece of advice for you and the other two nurses. Don't let anyone in the room with Mrs. Simpson alone. Particularly the maintenance man."

"We already got those orders from Mrs. Montana. But thanks for the heads up on the maintenance man."

"One more thing. I know you can't keep the director out of her room, but don't let him in there alone."

"Really? Want to say why?"

"Just a hunch. Better safe than sorry."

Rhonda looked puzzled. "That sounds mysterious. But it sounds like you have your reasons. I'm not paid to put my nose in where it isn't needed, so I'll just take it for what it's worth. I'll let the other girls know. And the cook and housekeeper. They're private staff, too."

"And ask them to please keep it to themselves. Too much gossip can keep us from getting to the bottom of all this."

"Bottom of all what?"

"Of all the reasons Mrs. Montana hired you to guard her mother."

"Got it. Thanks."

CHAPTER 23

Marvin went down the stairs and stood at the bottom of the staircase. He looked at his watch. It would be suppertime soon. He looked around the hallways. He wasn't familiar with this part of the facility. A door was on the side of the staircase, closed.

"Wonder where this goes," he said to himself. The position of the door on the side of the staircase suggested either a cellar or a storage room under the stairs.

He opened the door, which squeaked as it rotated on its rusty hinges. It opened onto a landing above a dark descending flight of rough wooden stairs. A string hung from a bare light bulb above the landing. He pulled it, and the forty-watt bulb cast a weak light onto and down the stairway into the cellar.

The furnace would be down there and he'd be able to solve another problem if only for a while. He started down. The old wooden stairs creaked under his feet, and he ducked to keep from bumping his head on the underside of the staircase above. He was barely able to make out the details of the room below. It looked like a typical cellar, although bigger than most. He steadied himself with his cane and went down the stairs. He looked from side to side with each step. He could make out the furnace over to the left and rows of shelves containing dusty Mason jars of canned vegetables, jellies, and fruit at the bottom of the stairs.

Food. The gang would sure like to know about this.

When he got to the bottom, he brushed away spider webs and wandered around the room on the cold concrete floor. He looked for another light switch, and he had to bend over for his head to clear the floor joists above him. He found a candle and a box of matches on a shelf. He lit the candle, held it in front of him, and continued his exploration.

If I can get to the furnace, I'll turn it up.

The home would be warm at least until someone discovered what he'd done.

The door squeaked at the top of the stairs and thumped loudly as it closed. He blew out his candle and looked up. Leroy stood on the landing looking down, his rugged face bathed in the light of the overhead bulb, a grin on his face.

"I been following you, Bradley. How come you went up to Mrs. Simpson's suite?"

Marvin looked around him. There was nothing he could use as a weapon except his cane. This could be it.

"I went up for a visit. Anything wrong with that?"

Leroy came down a step. "No, nothing wrong. What did you talk about?"

"The weather. What else do you say to a ninety-seven-year-old lady?"

"Uh-huh. The weather. So what are you doing down here? Residents ain't allowed down here."

"I was looking for the furnace. Thought maybe I could get things to warm up around here."

"Is that so? You shouldn't touch the furnace, pops. The furnace is my job."

"Then maybe you ought to start doing your job. People are getting cold."

"Do tell. Well, Mr. Bradley, I figure an old guy wandering around this big old house could get lost and might stumble in here and fall down the stairs. You know, an old guy that has your kind of disabilities."

The threat was not lost on Marvin. He looked around for some way, any way, out of this dangerous situation.

"Nobody comes down here except me when I adjust the furnace, old man, so that old guy might not be found for days until he starts to stink." He started slowly down the stairs. "I think maybe that could happen. That's what I think."

Marvin looked around for a place to hide, a place to get behind so he could ambush Leroy with his cane. He stumbled in the dark back toward the furnace. With only the dim light from the stair landing to show him the way, he moved away with caution.

"Where are you?" Leroy said.

The flashlight came on and swept the cellar. Marvin's heart started thumping. Then a cell phone ring tone startled him as it reverberated through the dark room. It wasn't his; he hadn't brought his cell phone along. The flashlight beam stopped moving and then went out. Leroy answered the phone.

"What?" A few seconds passed. "Where?" More time. "Okay, I'll get right over there." He snapped the lid closed on his phone. "I'm going out, Bradley. But I'm coming right back. You better not be here." He went up the stairs and out, closing the door behind him.

Marvin moved carefully toward the stairs. He didn't want to be around when Leroy returned. Then the door opened again.

Bad luck. He's back already.

"Marvin? Are you okay? I can't come down there." Mike was at the top of the stairway.

"I'm okay. I'll be right up." Marvin went up the stairs as fast as he could and out into the hallway. He and Mike headed back to their rooms.

"Leroy had some kind of emergency call," Marvin said. "Otherwise I was a goner."

"Yeah, that was me."

"You?"

"Yeah. I was following Leroy like I've been doing. He was following you. Who were you following? I wonder if anyone was following me."

"I think it was just the three of us, Mike."

"Yeah. When he followed you into the cellar way, I right away called Loretta on my cell phone and said there was a flood in the kitchen and that the pipes were gushing and that Leroy better get in there pronto. I guess she called Leroy, which was what I was hoping."

"That was quick thinking, Mike. You sure saved my bacon."

"The bacon around here isn't worth saving. What were you doing down there?"

"Looking for the furnace. But Leroy told me in no uncertain terms that that was his job, that he was the only one allowed to touch it, and that nobody else ever went in the cellar."

"Really? That's good to know."

"You know, there's lots of canned food down there, probably from when Mrs. Simpson lived here in the mansion before it was a nursing home. Food. Good food. Veggies, fruit, preserves. Maybe we can get some of it later. We can cook it in our rooms. Better than pizza."

"Nothing's better than pizza. Except for strawberry preserves. Was there any strawberry preserves?"

"Probably. I didn't have time to read the labels. I'm tired. It's time for my nap."

CHAPTER 24

The next afternoon, Mike came to Marvin's room and woke him up. "Can you give me a hand, Marvin? My package is here. The weapons of staff reduction." He laughed at his own joke.

Marvin yawned and sat up. "Don't talk like that. This is just to defend ourselves if we have to, and we hope we don't."

They walked together toward the front desk and discussed Marvin's encounter with Leroy in the basement. "Man. That was close," Mike said. "You better start carrying a nine-iron with you."

They went to the reception area where a UPS delivery man waited with a large package. "Mr. Charles? Sign here, please."

Loretta said, "Don't forget you have to get Mr. Bates to approve you having that."

"Right. We'll take it to my room and unpack it. Then we'll bring it back. Is he in his office?"

"He's always in his office."

They took the package to Mike's room. Marvin had to carry it tucked under the arm opposite his cane. Mike couldn't manage it and his walker at the same time. Once in the room with the door closed, Mike opened the package and put the contents on his bed.

"One bow, one quiver, five arrows, and, aha, one cattle prod."

He took the cattle prod from the quiver and tested it. The end glowed and it made a buzzing sound. He put it in his closet and leaned it against the wall behind where his suits and shirts hung. Then he said, "Let's take the archery set for Ollie to look at."

Mike put the bow over his shoulder and Marvin wore the quiver. They went back to the reception area.

"We're ready to see Ollie, er, Director Bates," Mike said.

"Go on in. He's expecting you."

They went into the office. Bates got up from his desk and came around to where they stood. "Let's see what we have here," he said and took the bow from Mike. He pulled back on it and said, "Mr. Charles, tell me again why you want this here."

"For the recreation area when it warms up. I used to be a tournament archer. I thought maybe we could set up targets out by the garden, and I could teach the other residents to shoot."

"Not with this bow, you won't," Bates said, pulling on the bow. "It's for hunting. Too powerful for target practice. The old folks won't be able to pull it. I doubt that you could now, either."

"Well, I can get another bow. But in the meantime, is it okay if I keep these things in my room?"

"I don't see what harm it can do. You couldn't pull it if your life depended on it. That's a Bear Kodiak fifty pound bow. Go on, keep it, but plan on getting a smaller one. Once you get targets set up and classes going, I'd like to use this one. I was pretty good with a bow myself years back. I'll see about having hay bales brought in."

They left the office to take the archery set to Mike's room. Loretta said, "Be careful with that thing, you two. Don't shoot yourselves."

On the way back to their rooms, they talked about their meeting with Bates.

"Can you picture him doing anything athletic?" Mike asked. "He looks like a basketball with feet."

"Probably his younger days when he taught school."

Mr. Peters was coming toward them feeling his way along

with his white cane.

"Hello, Mr. Charles, Mr. Bradley. How are you today?"

"Look at this, Mr. Peters," Mike said.

"At what?"

"I have a bow and arrows."

"Oh, let me see it." He felt along the bow. "This is a nice one. I used to go bow hunting back in the day."

"Before you went blind?" Mike asked.

Marvin started laughing. "No, Mike. After he couldn't see."

"Mr. Whitley used to go with me. He never could shoot a deer, though."

"So you two knew one another before you came here?" Marvin asked.

"For years. We're best friends. He just couldn't bring himself to shoot anything, though. Such a nice man. What a shame about his cat."

They took the archery set to Mike's room. He stored it in the closet. Then he used Velcro that his son had included and fastened the cattle prod to a vertical bar on his walker.

"Look at this," he said. "You can hardly tell it's there. I wonder if there's laws against carrying a concealed cattle prod."

"I doubt it. I'm going back to my room now. Don't forget, we're meeting in about an hour."

CHAPTER 25

Carrie and Mike came to Marvin's room for their meeting. Marvin was sitting at his desk with the laptop. Mike fell back on the recliner, and Carrie wheeled up to the desk.

"I sent the piano mover's work order to Freddie," Marvin said. "Do either of you have anything to report?"

"Well, there's one piece of good news," Carrie said. "Mr. Whitley's daughter surprised him with a visit this morning and a kitten. Gray and white. Same markings as Toby. Mr. Whitley named her Tabitha. It's a friendly little kitty. It likes everybody."

"That is a nice piece of news," Marvin said. "Mr. Whitley might perk up. Nothing like a kitten bouncing around to keep a guy company. Now if only we can keep Leroy away from it."

"My archery set and cattle prod came in," Mike told Carrie. "Ollie doesn't think us old folks are strong enough to pull the bow, though."

"Are you?" Carrie asked.

"If not, I can smack somebody upside the head with it."

"Anything else to report?" Marvin asked.

"Just you wait. I got that rat Leroy on video tape a little while ago."

"Actually, it's a DVD, not tape," Marvin said.

"I know. But Leroy doesn't. He saw me walking around with it. He asked if I had any tape in it. I said, what tape, I didn't know I needed tape, which is true, but he doesn't know that. He just laughed and walked away. Figured I was a doddering old man playing TV cameraman. I am a doddering old man, but I'm not playing. Dumb jerk."

"What did you get?"

"Well, just play it back and you'll see."

Marvin took the DVD from the camcorder and put it in his laptop so they could watch the video on the monitor. Then he started it up.

The video showed what Mike had seen through the view-finder when he walked out of his room, turned left, and proceeded down the hall.

"Don't you ever put the camera down?" Carrie asked.

"Got to get it all. I can't risk missing anything. You know if that guy Zapruder wouldn't have stopped filming, we'd have seen those other assassins behind the picket fence on the grassy knoll. I don't plan to make the same mistake he made."

"Zapruder? What does he have to do with this?" Carrie asked.

Mike pressed the Pause button. "Look, there were other shooters there in Dallas. And I know who was behind it."

"You do?"

"It was that guy Pascrow."

"Who?"

"Pascrow. Fidel Pascrow. Cuban dictator."

Carrie laughed and they turned their attention to the moni-tor again.

"How do you see where you're going?"

"Through the viewfinder. How else?"

The camera proceeded down the corridor. A voice called out from the laptop's small speaker.

"Mr. Charles," the recorded voice said, "whatever are you doing?"

The voice was that of Mrs. Ghent, an invalid who seldom left her room.

"Making a documentary, Mrs. Ghent," Mike's voice said

from the audio track. "About my life here at the nursing home."

"Well, isn't that grand. Do you want to interview me? Will it be on America's Funniest Home Videos?"

Mike's voice said in a low whisper, "It will if I interview you." Then he said out loud, "Maybe later, Mrs. Ghent. Just now I have to finish this scene," and he moved past her door down the hall.

"Now, Mike," Carrie said. "Your documentary wouldn't be complete without Mrs. Ghent telling about her great-grandchildren."

"My life would be complete if I never had to hear it again," Mike said.

The video proceeded down the hallway. A loud clank sounded out, and the camera jerked all over the place.

"What was that?" Marvin asked.

"I ran into the fire extinguisher hanging on the wall. Don't have much peripheral vision with this camera stuck in my face."

They watched Mike steady the camera and turn left at the next cross corridor. Then they heard his voice again, in that low tone.

"This is where Leroy usually comes this time of day. He's been working on the furnace controls. Probably to get it colder in here. And this is the wing where nobody lives. Ouch!"

The camera jerked again in the video, and a garbage can went bumping and rolling away from the camera down the hall.

Mike's recorded voice again, "What lazy lout left that out in the hallway?"

Marvin had to stifle a laugh. Carrie didn't stifle hers. Mike ignored them both.

The camera moved a little further and took another turn, and Mike's voice whispered, "Oops."

The camera picked up the silhouettes of two people, a tall man and a short woman embracing in the dark hallway about thirty feet away.

"That's Leroy and Nurse Helen," Mike said to the other two. "I caught them in the act."

"Nurse Helen?" Carrie asked.

"One and the same."

"Maybe that explains why her husband was arguing with Leroy," Marvin said.

"Now, watch this," Mike said.

The lovers were groping at one another within view of the camera. Then came the sound of a woman's gasp from closer to Mike than the couple were. The camera spun around to show Loretta's unmistakable backside. She stomped away from the scene and down the hall. The camera picked up her footsteps and her voice, "Well, I never."

"Yeah," said Marvin. "She says she never. But she did. I heard her and Leroy talking about it. He'll be in hot water now."

The camera turned back toward the couple. In the heat of the moment, they had failed to notice either Mike or Loretta. Then they slipped into a room, and the camera went dark.

"Why did you stop recording?" Carrie asked.

"What, you want to see what they did next? There's laws against that."

"They did that right there in plain view of the hallway?"

"No, ma'am, Miss Carrie. They closed the door. That's when I left."

"Did you get anything else?" Marvin asked.

"Isn't that enough?"

"I suppose. It might give us leverage if we need it."

"What leverage?" Mike said. "Who could we tell? Loretta already knows."

"I don't know. Maybe we can use it to get Nurse Helen to spy for us."

"That's blackmail," Mike said.

"What's wrong with that?" Marvin asked.

"Nothing. I think it's a good idea. I was just telling you what it is."

Marvin uploaded the video into his laptop and emailed it to Freddie. Then he erased the DVD, put it into the camcorder, and gave it back to Mike.

"Okay gang," Marvin said. "Sit back and listen up. Here's what I've learned. Carrie was with me when I uncovered some of it and we talked about it day before yesterday. I've since gotten it all together and written it up in a document. You can read it here if you want, but I'd rather not have copies floating around. I sent one to my grandson for the archives. Anyone want a soda?"

"Do you have diet?" Carrie asked.

"Sorry. How about you, Mike?"

"I'd rather a beer."

"I'm all out."

Marvin got himself a soda from the refrigerator and continued.

"First off, consider the home's income. Most residents pay as they go. So much a month."

Carrie said, "I had long-term disability coverage from my job, and it pays for me."

"Some residents, such as Mrs. Meade, paid a lump sum when they were admitted. Those residents are at risk. So are Medicare and Medicaid patients. It appears that management wishes they would all die."

"Me, too?" Carrie asked.

"Probably. I found directives to the kitchen and maintenance staffs to cut back on operating expenses. That's why the food has gotten as bad as it is. And why the rooms are cold and a lot of stuff doesn't get fixed. But here's the big surprise. Mrs. Simpson leased the home to a real estate development and investment corporation. They are acquiring nursing homes up and down the east coast. According to their business plan, they'll shut down the homes, level the buildings, and redevelop the land."

"What do they do about the residents?" Carrie asked.

"They stop accepting new admissions and wait until the resident population is down to half capacity in two homes. Then they consolidate them."

"Oh, my stars," Carrie said.

"Their business plan has this all laid out in a schedule. The problem is that we aren't dying off fast enough to meet their schedule."

Mike and Carrie looked at one another.

Marvin continued. "Investors are putting pressure on, so they have to speed up attrition."

"So, they're targeting the ones that can't fight back," Mike said.

"They are."

"What can we do about it?" Carrie said.

"About all we can do is make it difficult for Leroy to carry out his plans," Marvin said. "If we can slow him down, that gives us time to collect more hard evidence."

CHAPTER 26

The next morning after breakfast, Marvin and Mike met in Marvin's room to begin building their project. Marvin closed the door and gathered together his tools, wiring components, and Carrie's flashbulb paraphernalia. He arranged them on his dinette table and desk.

"Okay, now what?" he asked Mike.

Mike looked the things over and drew simple circuit and assembly diagrams on a sheet of stationery.

When his design was complete, he said, "Okay, let's start building."

"What's it going to be?" Marvin asked.

"One big bright flashbulb. It'll put Leroy out of commission for a few days."

"Who's going to set it off?"

"If we do it right, Leroy is."

They fabricated components from the materials from Marvin's garage to build the device.

Marvin stripped wires and attached them with wire nuts, and he built a wooden frame five feet wide and two feet high of slats glued together. Mike soldered wires to sockets and insulated everything with electrical tape.

When they were done, they had a jerry-rigged array of fifty-five flashbulb sockets wired together and mounted on the frame. A standard wall switch would turn the array on and off, and the contraption would be powered by household current. Marvin inserted fifty-five flashbulbs into the sockets, after which the rig was ready to be put into action. But where?

"I'm not going to ask how you know how to do all this," Marvin said, "but I sure am having fun."

"Ask me when Carrie's around," Mike said with a grin and a wink.

"How are we going to use this thing?" Marvin asked. "Where will we install it?"

"I've given that a lot of thought. It needs to be located where it will affect only Leroy. No one else should get in its line of fire. And it needs to be in a place where we can lure him. And I think I know where that can be."

Then he went to the door and looked up and down the hallway. No one was in sight.

"Come on, Marvin."

They took the contraption down the hall to just outside Mr. Peters's room.

"What do you think? In here?"

"No better place," Marvin said.

The door was closed. Marvin knocked and called out, "Mr. Peters, can I come in?"

"Sure, Mr. Bradley, come on in."

Peters was lying on his bed listening to the radio. The lights were off.

"Have a seat," he said.

"No thanks, sir, we just want to leave something here. It won't be in your way. Do you mind?"

"Not at all."

Marvin stood the rack of lights in Bruno's bed, now unused with no dog to sleep in it. He leaned the rack against the wall so that the flashbulb array was aimed at the door. Mike ran the electrical wire around the baseboard and up the doorframe. Then, using a hand stapler, he attached the wire to the doorframe where the switch could be reached from outside the door.

He made sure the main light switch in the room and the switch on the array were both off. Then he plugged the array into the wall outlet corresponding to the main light switch.

As configured, if either switch was turned on without the other, nothing would happen. But when one was on, the other would trigger the array. They were proud of their work.

"Mr. Peters, do you ever turn any lights on in here?"

"No. Why would I?"

Mike said, "When the nurse comes to give you your meds, she might turn it on."

"She doesn't. I go to the nursing station for my pills. The only one who comes in here is the housemaid. She just left, so I won't see her for a while."

"I'm guessing it'll be out of here by then," Marvin said.

"What's this all about?" Peters asked.

"Best you don't know until after," Marvin said.

"Whatever you folks say. Close the door behind you, please. I like to keep my door closed."

Marvin closed the door and said, "That's good. No one will be able to see what's in there."

Nurse Helen was in the hallway making her rounds. She wore dark glasses.

"Mr. Bradley, I have your meds for today. Come on in your room."

Mike returned to his room, and Marvin followed her into his own room. His tools were still all over the place.

"What have you been building here, Mr. Bradley?"

"Just a hobby. Electronics."

"I don't understand that stuff," she said. She had to lift her dark glasses to read the labels on the meds. She had a prominent bruise under her right eye.

"Nurse Helen, who gave you that shiner?"

"No one," she said, lowering the dark glasses over her eyes. "It's nothing. I tripped at home and bumped the dining room table."

"Nurse Helen, did Leroy Parker hit you?"

She drew back and looked at him with surprise. "Leroy wouldn't hit me. He wouldn't hit anyone. Why would you think it was him?"

"How do you know he wouldn't do that? Have you known him long?"

"No. Only since he hired on. But he didn't do this. I fell at home."

She gave him his pills and a glass of water and left.

Marvin considered what had just transpired. Nurse Helen was from the old regime and was one of the more popular day nurses among the residents. Marvin couldn't imagine what she saw in Leroy, the abuser of old people. And now she herself showed signs of abuse and seemed to be in denial about it.

He went looking for Mike and Carrie to discuss it with them. He found Carrie in the dayroom reading a book. She had a shawl over her shoulders.

"I wish they'd light a fire in the fireplace like they used to," she said. "This place is getting so bleak."

"Firewood costs money," Marvin said. "Where's Mike?"

"I haven't seen him for a while," she answered. "He headed out with the camcorder a while back. Said he was going to go stalking Leroy. We'll probably see him at lunch."

"Somebody gave Nurse Helen a black eye."

"I saw that. I wonder if Leroy did it."

"She said it wasn't Leroy. That she fell at home."

"You asked her about Leroy?"

"Yeah. I wanted to warn her somehow without spilling the beans. But she doesn't think he can do anything like that."

"Women," Carrie said. "Maybe her husband did it. Leroy

145

better be careful. He'll have them coming at him from all sides."

"Worse things could happen. Let's find Mike."

"Okie-dokie." She put down her book and wheeled out of the dayroom following Marvin. They went from hallway to hallway until they were in the corridor where their rooms were. They went to the far end of that corridor where it took a ninety degree turn.

When they reached the turn, Mike was hurrying along toward them with his walker. The camcorder swung from its strap around his neck.

"Follow me. He's headed into the old people's wing."

He turned into another corridor, and Marvin and Carrie fell in behind him.

"He turned left next corridor," Mike said.

"Does he know you're following?" Carrie asked.

"I don't think so. Come on, but stay back a ways."

They went to the turnoff and looked around the corner. "He's going into Mr. Partlow's room," Mike said. "Stay here."

Mike crept slowly toward the room. He stopped at the open door, aimed the camcorder inside, and began recording.

A loud slapping sound was followed by a groan and the thump of something hitting the floor. Then Leroy's voice. "You! What are you doing there?"

Mike dropped the camcorder so it swung from its strap and began clumping as fast as he could with his walker toward Marvin and Carrie.

"Leroy saw me! I'm busted! Let's get out of here."

Mike headed down the hallway turning first right, then left, with Carrie right behind him and Marvin with his cane trying to keep up.

"Where's Leroy?" Marvin asked, panting. "He should have gotten here by now."

"Taking his time, I guess. He knows we don't move fast and

don't have many places to go. And he can't run in those cowboy boots."

"What happened in Mr. Partlow's room?" Marvin asked, panting. He was running out of breath.

"He hit Mr. Partlow," Mike said without stopping. "I got it on DVD. I got the actual hit. He saw me. Just me, though. I don't think he saw you. You two better get out of sight before he sees you with me. Hurry."

"Oh, no," Carrie said. "We're in this together. We aren't going to leave you out here unprotected."

They kept moving, constantly looking over their shoulders to see if Leroy was in sight. When they reached the reception area, all three were breathing hard and slowing down. They stopped, and Marvin leaned on the counter to catch his breath. Loretta looked up at them. "What's the big rush, you three?" she asked.

"Hide and seek," Mike said.

She looked at them, shrugged, and went back to her work.

"In here," Mike said, opening the door to the men's room.

"Me, too?" Carrie asked. "In the men's room?"

"Just get in here," Mike said. "Hurry."

They went into the men's room. The door began to shut slowly. It had a slow pneumatic door to accommodate folks with walkers and wheelchairs.

Mike said, "Stay over there against the wall by the door. And watch where you step when we leave. I saw Rockford do this on a TV show."

He removed the hand soap dispenser and poured the liquid soap on the floor just inside the door. Then he stood on the other side of the door and turned the light off. The door was still closing.

Leroy's voice came from outside the door. "Where did he go?"

"Where did who go?" Loretta said.

"Old guy with a TV camera and a walker."

"I'm sure I don't know. What did he do?"

Leroy must have noticed the door still closing. "Who went in here?" he asked.

"Mr. Parker, I'm sure I have better things to do than watch where the old people go. So do you. Now why don't you get your worthless butt out of here and back to work?"

Mike whispered to the others, "What goes around comes around."

"What's wrong with you?" Leroy said.

Loretta didn't answer.

Leroy yanked the bathroom door open and rushed into the dark room. When his boots hit the soaped floor, his legs went out from under him, and he fell on his hindquarters, his head hitting the tiled floor. Stunned, he tried to get up, but his knees slid away under him in the soapy film and he went down again. He yelled and rolled over. The door was closing slowly again, and they could see him in the light from the hallway trying to get up. Marvin raised his hickory cane and swung full strength at Leroy's head, striking him just above his right ear. Down he went. He yelled and tried to get up again. Carrie wheeled over toward Leroy. The glint of her hat pin shone in the light from the hallway. She rolled alongside Leroy and struck him in his right buttock with the hat pin. Leroy screamed. Then Mike moved toward Leroy's left side. After a loud buzzing noise Leroy shrieked.

"Let's get out of here," said Mike. "Don't step in the soap."

They rushed out.

"Say, Marvin," Mike said, "you can move pretty fast when you have to."

"Adrenalin," Marvin said.

"You two are in the clear," Mike said. "He's after me. I'll meet you back at my room."

Marvin didn't want Mike out there unprotected. "Wait in my room, Mike. He won't look for you there."

"I've got something else up my sleeve."

That worried Marvin. "If you say so. But be careful. We'll hang out around Loretta's desk and see what happens."

"Okay." And Mike took off.

Marvin and Carrie went to the reception area's lounge and sat on a couch. Marvin picked up a magazine, and Carrie took a needlepoint project out of her purse. Loretta looked up at them and said, "What was all that noise in there?"

"Leroy fell down," Marvin said.

She smiled at that. Leroy came limping out of the restroom. "Which way did he go?"

"Who?" said Loretta.

"That old buzzard with the camcorder." Leroy was rubbing his rear end and grimacing.

"I didn't see anyone like that? Besides, it's not my week to watch him."

Leroy turned to Marvin and Carrie. "How long have you two been here?"

"We just got here. Why?" Marvin said.

"Where did the guy go who came out ahead of me?"

"What guy?" said Marvin.

"What guy?" said Carrie.

They both had innocent looks on their faces. Leroy shook his head. "Senile old geezers." He walked away.

Marvin and Carrie covered their mouths to keep from laughing. Then they got up and followed Leroy, keeping their distance, acting unconcerned. The door to Mike's room was partially open. Leroy pushed it all the way open and peered in. A large scrub bucket of nuts, bolts, and rocks fell from the top of the door in a loud crash. Leroy hit the floor again. Nuts and bolts bounced everywhere, and the bucket rolled around on the

floor. Leroy was stunned. Mike came out, stepping over Leroy
with his walker. He unholstered the cattle prod and gave Leroy
another hit with it. Leroy groaned and rolled over. Mike came
toward them and said, "Let's go before he comes to."

They headed down the hallway. Mike looked back at Leroy.
He had his back to them and was pulling himself up. "This
way," Mike said, and led them down the corridor toward the
wing with the staircase.

"Why are we going here? This is Leroy's territory."

"I'll wait here where he can see me when he gets up. You two
go down to the stairway and get out of sight. Don't go in the
cellar, whatever you do. I'll come on after he spots me. Get him
to follow."

"What's going to happen?" Carrie said.

"Go! Go!" Mike said.

Marvin and Carrie went to the stairway and waited. Soon
Mike showed up, puffing and panting. He opened the door to
the stairway.

"You said not to go down there," Marvin said.

"We won't, but Leroy will." He reached in and turned on the
light in the landing and said, "Let's go. Hurry." He left the door
ajar, and they went down another corridor.

"Hide in here," Mike said, "He'll think we're in the cellar."

"Are you going to lock him in there?" Carrie asked.

"Nope. Shh."

Leroy said, "You think you can hide down there, Charles?
That was a big mistake." Then a couple of seconds later there
came a loud, "Ahhhhhhh!" along with the bumpity-bump of
Leroy falling down the stairs followed by the crash of wood
splintering and glass shattering when he hit and toppled the
shelf full of canned food at the bottom of the stairs.

"How did that happen?" Marvin asked.

"Trip wire," Mike said. "I hope he didn't knock over the

strawberry preserves. I was hoping to get a jar. He'll be down there a while. Wait a minute."

He went to the cellar door and reached in. He came out with a length of cord. "This is the trip wire. I need to get rid of the evidence in case we killed him."

Mike led them toward Mr. Peters's room. He opened the door, reached in, made sure the main switch was off, and turned on the array switch to enable the flashbulb array.

"Who's that?" Peters called out.

"Just us looking in on you, Mr. Peters."

"What's all the racket out there?"

"I'll explain later." Then to Carrie and Marvin, "Come on around that corner." He left Mr. Peters's door ajar. "We want Leroy to think we went in there."

Marvin laughed, "I'm beginning to understand."

"Don't look at Mr. Peters's door," Mike said, "and whatever you do, don't let Leroy see us."

They waited about three minutes. Mike peeked around the corner.

"There he is," Mike whispered. "The fall didn't kill him, but he sure looks terrible. What a mess! He's covered with vegetables. Good. He missed the strawberry preserves. Now wait. He's about to go in."

Marvin stood behind Mike and looked, too. Then Carrie wedged herself and her wheelchair alongside them. Three heads lined up vertically, Carrie, Mike, Marvin, bottom to top, watching to see what would happen.

Leroy was at Mr. Peters's door, which was normally closed but was standing ajar, leaving the impression that someone had recently used it, just what Mike said they wanted Leroy to think.

"Think you can hide in here in the dark?" shouted Leroy.

Mike whispered, "Look away. Quick!" The three heads bobbed back behind the corner.

Just then there was a loud pop! and the hallway around them lit up in the most brilliant flash of light any of them had ever seen. Leroy screamed. Mike raised his fist in a victorious gesture, pumped it down like a golfer who'd just made a long putt, and said in a loud whisper, "Yes!"

They looked around the corner as Leroy came out, bumping into things, rubbing his eyes with his fists. He stumbled down the hall going away from them and toward the nursing station.

"I saw the light, I saw the light . . ." Carrie sang in a whisper.

"I'm going to get him again with the cattle prod," Mike whispered and started for Leroy.

"No, Mike." Marvin had him by the arm and pulled him back. "Let's quit while we're ahead. Let's go."

The three co-conspirators crept back toward their rooms.

When they got to Mr. Peters's room, Marvin said, "Wait for me out here." He went into Mr. Peters's room and retrieved the light array. "So long Mr. Peters," he said. "Thanks for the use of your room."

"What happened in here? I heard a heck of a popping sound."

"We set a trap for a rat. Couldn't have done it anywhere else. We got Leroy."

"Gee, I'm all broke up about that. Him being such an upstanding fellow and all."

"Don't tell anyone who did it."

"Not a chance," Peters answered, a big grin on his face.

Marvin brought the light array out into the hallway.

"Where are you going to hide it?" Mike asked.

"In Mrs. Ghent's room. He'll never look there."

"Good thinking."

"Mike, how did you get that bucket of hardware up on your door?"

"I stood on a chair and balanced the bucket on top of the door so it leaned back against the wall."

"Don't you know you can hurt yourself with that kind of stunt?" Marvin said.

"Not as bad as Leroy got hurt. Did you see him hit the floor? I'd pay money to see that again."

"Well that about uses up all our weapons," Carrie said.

"Not quite," Mike said. "I still have my archery set, and Marvin has his golf clubs."

"After I stow the flashbulb array, let's go upload that video," Marvin said. "With that, we'll have Leroy in our pocket."

"What more do we need?" Carrie asked.

"A direct tie to Bates and maybe even upper management. Then we'll have them all."

They stopped at Mrs. Ghent's room. Marvin stuck his head in the door. "Mrs. Ghent, can I hide something in here for a few hours?"

"Sure, Mr. Bradley, if you can find room."

He went in and put the array behind Mrs. Ghent's desk and came back out into the hallway. "That's done. I'm going to check on Mr. Partlow."

"Marvin," Carrie said, "you're all red in the face. Shouldn't you rest first?"

"Later. He could be hurt bad. We should split up for a while, anyway. Meet me in my room in about an hour."

Marvin walked slowly through the corridors to Mr. Partlow's room. He maintained a constant watch for Leroy, although he was sure Leroy was out of commission for a while.

He found Mr. Partlow laying on the floor. He was conscious and breathing but just barely. He had a huge bruise on his cheek.

"Are you okay?"

Partlow didn't make a sign one way or the other. Marvin wasn't strong enough to help Mr. Partlow up to his bed. He picked up the room intercom and pressed the Nurse button.

Nurse Norma answered.

"Nurse Norma, I'm in Mr. Partlow's room. He's on the floor and hurt. Could you send someone?"

"We're kind of busy here, Marvin. One of the staff had an accident."

Marvin almost smiled at that. Then he got back to the issue at hand. "I think Mr. Partlow is hurt bad, too."

"Okay. I'll send someone. Please wait with him."

In less than a minute a nurse and an orderly were there.

"What happened here?" the nurse asked. She and the orderly lifted Mr. Partlow to his bed.

"He was hit."

"Did you see it?"

Marvin stopped. He'd better wait to reveal what he knew. "No," he said. That was the truth. He hadn't actually seen it. "How is he?"

"He'll be okay," the nurse said. "Nothing broken. I'll have the doctor look in on him later."

Marvin left Mr. Partlow's room and returned to his own. Mike and Carrie were already there. Marvin plopped down on his recliner, exhausted.

"How's Mr. Partlow?" Carrie asked.

"They say he'll be okay. I hope so."

Mike picked up the room intercom and punched a button. Loretta's voice answered, "Administration."

"This is Mr. Charles. There's a bucket of nuts and bolts all over the floor in front of my room. Send someone to clean it up, please."

Loretta let out a whoop that they could have heard without the intercom. "I'll get someone down there right away."

CHAPTER 27

They gathered together at lunch, wondering whether their activities of the morning would return to haunt them. Surely Leroy would try to get even. Marvin started the conversation. He spoke in whispers so that no one could overhear what he said.

"Somebody is bound to look into what happened this morning. I don't think we've heard the last of it."

Carrie said, "Do you think we'll get in trouble?"

"I don't think so. Leroy isn't going to rat us out. He probably knows we have the video. But sooner or later everyone will know that he got hurt."

They ate their lunch quietly.

When they were finished eating and the dishes cleared away, Mike said, "Leroy won't be in any condition to do anything for a while. He won't be able to see. I'd give a month's pay to have been there when the nurses had to clean the vegetables off of him. I bet that was a sight to see."

"How much is a month's pay?" Carrie asked.

"Don't remember," Mike said.

Carrie looked around the room. "Do you think Leroy told the nurses what happened?"

"Not a chance," Mike said. "Mr. Macho Man would never admit that three old fogies got the best of him."

"What do we do next?" Carrie asked.

"Wait for when he shows himself," Marvin said. "Then figure

it from there."

That afternoon they stayed in their rooms and rested. Marvin was tired but exhilarated. He reorganized his documents yet another time and began to assemble a package that he could give to the authorities. He figured he'd start with the district attorney.

That evening at supper, Marvin, Mike, and Carrie sat together as usual. They resumed their discussion from lunch about the day's activities and laughed at the notion of big bad Leroy Parker being disabled by three disabled old codgers.

Marvin was proud of his friends and their bravery. He was particularly impressed by Mike's ingenuity in rigging the booby traps and foiling Leroy at every turn.

Although no one had mentioned the incident earlier at lunch, the room was buzzing now with stories of what had happened, except that no one seemed to know who was responsible.

"Let's keep it that way," Marvin said.

Elsie Collins leaned over and said, "Did you hear? Leroy Parker had an accident. Nurse Norma told us about it. He was all battered and bruised and beaten. Cuts on his head and shoulders, covered with string beans, carrots, and peas and nearly blind. What do you suppose happened?"

"No telling," Marvin said. Then he turned back to his dining companions and said in a low tone, "I wonder if those flashbulbs did any long-term damage to his eyes."

"I hope not," Carrie said.

"I hope so," Mike said. "Oops. There he is."

They looked to the door as Leroy came into the dining hall, wearing dark glasses and with band-aids and bruises all over his head and arms. Nurse Helen, also in dark glasses, led him by the arm. Everyone in the room watched him come in. He pulled away from Nurse Helen and hobbled over to the table where

Marvin, Mike, and Carrie were seated.

He stood for a time, trying to stare them down. Except he couldn't stare; he squinted at them instead. Marvin and Mike stared back. Carrie took some needlepoint out of her tote bag and concentrated on her sewing.

"I know the three of you are behind this," Leroy said in a harsh whisper. "Don't think it's over. When I get my vision back, I'll be coming for you. Especially you, Charles." He pushed his face right into Mike's face.

Mike had his hand on the cattle prod, still fastened to his walker. He stared back at Leroy with defiance on his face. "Try it, you sheepherder," Mike said, his voice trembling. "Just try it. Today was nothing. Just try it."

"Easy, Mike," Marvin said. "There's time for that later."

People at adjacent tables got quiet and turned to see what was happening.

Leroy turned and tried to focus on the rest of the room. "What are you looking at?" he said to the other residents. "Mind your own business."

"Mr. Parker," Marvin said, loud enough to be heard by everyone in the room. "You don't scare us any more. Anyone who beats up helpless old people and kills cats is a yellow, spineless coward. We know you were responsible for what happened to Mrs. Meade and Mr. Partlow, and we know the rest, too. You are the lowest of the low, and today you found out what happens when you take on real men. And a real woman. Come after us again, and you'll get more of the same and worse. As it is, you aren't going to be around much longer. I'm going to see to that."

Leroy squinted and looked around the room. All the residents were listening and watching to see what would happen next. He leaned over toward Marvin and said in a harsh whisper, "I figured you were the ringleader, Bradley. You're on my list, too.

You'll be first. I'm coming to get you." He turned and groped his way back to Helen's side.

"Gee whiz," Mike said. "I guess we made it worse."

"How much worse could it be?" Marvin said.

"Sheepherder?" Carrie asked Mike.

"Yeah. That's what movie cowboys called the bad guys before they could cuss."

"At least you didn't cuss," Carrie said. "What do we do now?"

"Nobody goes out alone," Marvin said. "Don't let Leroy catch you without any witnesses around. Keep your weapons handy."

Carrie flashed her hat pin. Mike patted his cattle prod.

Marvin went on. "When we have our case built up and documented, Leroy won't be a problem any more. And I'm almost there. Another few days of cyber-snooping." Marvin was proud that he could even come up with that term. "I'll have iron-clad evidence that implicates not only Leroy, but Bates and the executives of the corporation, tied up in a neat package. They'll all go up the river. In the meantime, we have to watch out for one another."

"What about when we're sleeping?" Carrie asked. "We can't lock our doors. They don't have locks."

"I don't know," Marvin said. "Maybe we'll have to sleep together in one room. But keep your intercoms nearby when you're alone in your rooms. Beep for a nurse or security at the first sign of trouble. And yell your brains out."

After supper, Marvin returned to his room and called Freddie on his cell phone.

"What's going on, Granddad?"

"Have you looked at the stuff I sent you?"

"It paints a grim picture. That tall guy hitting the old man was over the top. I really want to get you out of there."

"You can't just yet. Leroy Parker, the guy doing the beatings, is after me and my friends. If I left, they'd be here alone and without protection. I'm pretty sure Leroy has already killed at least one old person. I'm going to ask Charlie Danvers to bring my shotgun."

"You're scaring me, Granddad, but I can't be there until Sunday. Is that soon enough?"

"I think so. The guy can't see too well just now." Marvin told Freddie what they had done with their weapons and booby traps.

Freddie was laughing. "Man. I wouldn't want you three after me. I'll see you soon, Granddad."

He said goodbye to Freddie and speed-dialed Charlie's phone.

"Charlie, this is Marvin. I need a favor."

"Name it."

"Go in my house and get my shotgun. It's in the upstairs closet. There's a box of shells on the closet shelf. Bring them, too. You'll have to sneak it in past the receptionist. I don't want anyone to know I have it. I need it soon. Tomorrow at the latest. Can you do it?"

"Sure. What's this all about?"

"Long story. I'll explain tomorrow. You're not going to believe it."

That night, Marvin's dreams were of combat scenes like the nightmares he used to have when he came home from the war in 1945. Except that every enemy soldier had Leroy's face, and every one of his fallen comrades was either Mike or Carrie.

CHAPTER 28

The next day, Saturday, Charlie Danvers came into Marvin's room. He had the shotgun wrapped in a vinyl tablecloth. He left it wrapped up and put it on Marvin's bed.

"How did you get the shotgun past the desk?" Marvin asked.

"I told her it was a telescope for you to go stargazing. It's short enough that it doesn't look like a gun."

"Good story. Did she believe you?"

"She didn't say anything. I guess so."

"I knew I could count on you. Did you bring the shells?"

"Yeah. I checked to see if they were still okay. They look like they've been reloaded."

"Did it myself. Remember? I used your equipment. It's rock salt."

"What good will that do?"

"Intimidation. It'll keep me from killing somebody."

"If you say so. So tell me what's going on around here."

"A maintenance man is abusing the old people. Nobody believes us, so we're trying to catch him in the act. We think he's responsible for at least one death. Mrs. Meade. You remember her."

"She was murdered? Man! Molly used to take piano lessons from her. I heard she died, but I didn't know she was murdered. That's a shock."

"They ruled it an accident, but we know better."

"That's awful."

"He killed pets, too. A cat and a seeing-eye dog. We got him on video hitting people and stealing. We need a little more evidence. He's on to us. So if he comes after me, he'll meet a load of rock salt."

Charlie looked at his friend with concern and pointed at the shotgun. "Rock salt won't stop anyone, Marvin. As long as you don't get up close and personal."

"He won't know that."

"You always did have big, well, you know," Charlie said. "Like in forty-four. Remember?"

"Don't start up with that again," Marvin said.

Charlie ignored him and kept talking. "That machine gun nest had us pinned down in the street from inside that house. Man, I'll never forget you crawling across the street and lobbing that grenade in the window, machine gun tracers flying all around you, noise, smoke, dust. Saved us all. Then you went in and got three more of them. We saw you run in, heard all the gunfire, and then out you came, waving us to come ahead. Man, those were the times. That one earned you the Croix de Guerre. Do you still have it?"

"I don't know. Maybe one of my kids has it."

"Didn't you get a Silver Star, too? What was that for?"

"I forget."

"Come on, Marvin, how could anyone forget something like that?"

"It wasn't easy."

"You keep saying that. Why don't you come with me to the next VFW meeting? I'll pick you up."

"No, why would I go there? I'm not a member."

"Why, indeed. You were the most decorated soldier from here and half the guys don't even know it. It'd be an honor to have you come as a guest speaker. You could talk about that day. And a lot more."

"We've been having this conversation for how many years, Charlie? I don't have anything important to say to those guys. It was a terrible time. All any of us ever wanted was to come home. Well, we came home. And right away they up and join some club and act like they want to go back. Like those were the good old days. I'm sorry, that's not me. I respect all you guys and what you did, the sacrifices you made, the terrible memories you brought home with you."

His own memories brought to the surface feelings he had always tried to suppress. Deep regret and sorrow for what he'd done in those awful times. He wiped his eyes with his handkerchief.

"I respect you all because I had to do that, too. I've been trying to forget it ever since. What could I possibly say to those guys that they'd want to hear?"

"You could say the things you just said to me here and now, Marvin. It's not all chest-thumping and flag waving. A lot of our guys use these clubs as a way to cope with what we saw, what we did. Imagine having to deal with that alone."

"I don't have to imagine it. It's what I've been doing since forty-five."

"Maybe that's your problem. Maybe it would be easier if you got support from guys who went through the same thing."

"Don't you see, Charlie? We killed people. We shot them, we stuck them with bayonets, we blew them to kingdom come with grenades, we burned them out with flamethrowers. And they looked just like us, scared kids, sent out there into that horror to do the unthinkable and have it done to them all in the name of some higher cause that they didn't understand. Just like us. Why in God's name would anyone want to do anything except forget?"

Charlie waited to let the moment simmer down. "You know,

we're dying off, Marvin, us World War II veterans. Not many of us left."

"Nope. Not many. But we're the lucky ones. It's the ones who didn't come home that I think about. Why do we always wind up talking about this?"

"Maybe it's what we have in common."

"No, we have more than that, you and me. We went to grade school and high school together. We played baseball and football. We double-dated at the prom. We live side by side in identical houses. We both lost our wives. We both have kids who wish we weren't an inconvenience. We both like beer and pizza."

"And you saved my life and a bunch of others in forty-four in a town in France. I can't forget that."

"And you saved mine last year in a kitchen when I stroked out. And I can't tell you how grateful I am. That makes us even. Let's forget the war."

"Forget? Can't you see the hypocrisy? What's happening now? From what you say, you're back in there fighting the good fight again. Somebody's hurting people. Somebody has to stop them. And it might even involve somebody getting killed. Yeah, it might come to that. And you just armed yourself to that purpose. You haven't changed all that much."

"Charlie, you're hopeless. I can't get through to you."

"You old duffer, if I outlive you, which I fully intend to do, I will personally come to your funeral, open the coffin, and pin those medals on your chest. And the members of VFW Post 1420 will fly the flag at half-mast, the honor guard will give you a twenty-one-gun salute, old Tally Withers will play taps and fluff the high note like he always does, and we'll all line up and salute your sorry butt. And when the speeches are over, the band has played, and the mayor has given his usual long-winded eulogy, the town will finally know, as they should have known all along, that they've had a hero in their midst for all these years and didn't know it because he was too modest and too dad-burned stubborn to let on."

"Thanks, Charlie. That really means a lot coming from you. You were the bravest of the brave. Nobody knows that better than I do. But it's not how I want to be known today, and it's not how I want to be remembered after."

CHAPTER 29

On Sunday, Marvin was waiting in the lobby. Freddie came through the front entrance and waved while he signed in. Then he came over. "Good morning, Granddad. How's it going?"

"Let's walk."

Marvin got up and walked with Freddie down the hall toward his room.

"Nothing's happened so far, Freddie, but that guy Leroy keeps glaring at me in the dining hall."

"Did you get the blunderbuss?"

"Yeah. Charlie brought it yesterday. If Leroy comes after me again, he's going to have a heck of a surprise."

"Again?"

"Yeah, he had me cornered in the cellar, but Mike bailed me out." Marvin told Freddie what had happened in the cellar.

"That's really scary, Granddad. Do you think he really meant to harm you?"

"No doubt about it."

They went into Marvin's room. Freddie sat at the desk, Marvin in his easy chair.

"Why don't you alert security about this guy?" Freddie asked. "Or call the police?"

"Well, in the first place, security here is a joke. The guard spends his shift sleeping in one of the vacant rooms. And then no one pays any attention to us; it's the rantings of old people. They laugh it off and call it dementia."

"Even when they know your mind is okay?"

"Well, think about this. Suppose I had told you what's going on around here and hadn't sent you all those documents and videos. Would you have believed me?"

"I see your point. Aren't the documents and videos enough evidence?"

"Enough to get Leroy, sure, but except for that one video it's all circumstantial. Besides, I'm after bigger fish."

"But in the meantime you're in danger, Granddad. I can't get that through to you."

"I know it, son. That's what the shotgun is for. I've been in danger before and fought worse men than Leroy. Lots worse. I'm not scared of him."

"That's what bothers me, Granddad. You're eighty-seven years old. You ought to be scared."

"Of what? You just said it, I'm eighty-seven. I can't hear without a hearing aid, I can't walk without a cane. Soon I'll need an oxygen bottle to breathe. I need people to bathe me and give me my meds, and I wear a diaper. I can't even go out for a haircut. And that's what I have to look forward to for the rest of my life. What do I have to lose? Don't worry about me. At least I'm enjoying some adventure."

"You can't bathe yourself?"

"No, or so they tell me. I fell in the bathtub last month. Now I get a nurse in here every day to help me with my shower. Actually, it's not all that bad, depending on which one they send in." Marvin chuckled at the surprised expression on Freddie's face.

"When did you start wearing diapers?"

"After the stroke. For the occasional accident."

"Oh. Sorry." Freddie seemed embarrassed. He changed the subject. "So, do you have shells for the shotgun, or do you just plan to scare him with it?"

"Here they are. Rock salt." Marvin pulled the box of shotgun shells out of his desk drawer.

"Rock salt? What's that for?"

Marvin took a shell out of the box and handed it to Freddie. "Non-lethal except at really close range, but painful. We were having burglaries several years back. I didn't want to kill anybody, just scare them, so I reloaded these shells with rock salt and kept the shotgun loaded and handy."

"If it's non-lethal, how would it deter a break-in?"

Marvin laughed. "They didn't know that. Even if they did, anyone who's ever taken a load of rock salt in the butt won't chance it again."

"Is that from experience?"

"From when I was a boy. We used to steal watermelons out of the farmers' fields. I beat many a load of rock salt down the road."

Freddie looked at his grandfather with what appeared to be new respect. "I learn more and more about you every day."

"Stick around. There's lots more to know. Just everybody knowing I had the shotgun kept the burglars away. I never had to use it, and I hope I don't have to use it now."

"I wish you'd let me call the police, Granddad. They'll believe me when I show them the evidence you sent."

Marvin shook his head. "A lot of that evidence is illegal. It might get Homeland Security after me. Stealing computer files is a felony. And it wouldn't solve the problem. The cops might take Leroy away, but a lawyer would get him out or management would just replace him, maybe with somebody worse than him. I want to get him and the top dogs, too. And I don't want them to know I've hacked their computer yet. We bust Leroy and the walls go up. I'm waiting for that one document that seals their fate."

"What would it take?"

167

"A memo from the top telling Bates to go the extra mile. Or, a confession from Bates. I figure if I can implicate Bates, he'll roll over on the others."

CHAPTER 30

That evening and for the next several evenings, Marvin leaned his golf clubs against the closed door. If anyone opened the door, the clubs would fall to the floor, and the noise they made would wake him up. He put the camcorder on his desk positioned to cover the room. He put pillows under his blanket on the bed and slept in his chair, his hearing aids in, and the shotgun under his quilt. His dreams continued.

Always the same dream. Mike, Carrie, and Marvin in midnight, moonless combat with an unseen, unknown enemy. They're hunkered down in a trench, huddled together, gunfire, grenades, and bombs going off all around them, machine gun tracers etching the air overhead, enemy fighter planes strafing their position from above, the unmistakable smell of burning gunpowder and smoke all around them. He pulls himself up to the rim of the trench and looks toward the enemy's position. In the light cast by a single flare from somewhere behind him, he sees a company of enemy soldiers coming across the ridge, bayonets fixed, swastikas emblazoned on their helmets, fierce and murderous grins on their faces, every face the spitting image of Leroy. The old, familiar fear in the pit of his stomach, the knowledge that the situation is hopeless and death is near. Then, just before the army reaches them, he wakes up in a cold sweat, tangled in his blanket, thankful that the dream has ended, thankful that it had been only a dream.

He could not return to sleep after the dream, tossing and

turning until morning when he'd ask Mike and Carrie whether they had been disturbed. So far, nothing. He worried that they could see in his tired face the toll this ordeal was taking. But he did not tell them about the dreams.

A week later at about midnight, Marvin sat in his chair in the dark with the shotgun under his quilt and on his lap. He was fighting off sleep and trying to postpone the nightmares. He was about to doze off when a noise came from near his closed door. The shadows of two feet showed in the light under the door from the hallway. He came wide awake.

He reached over and pressed the record button on the camcorder. Then he readied the shotgun under the quilt and pushed the safety with his thumb to the off position. When the door opened, the golf clubs hit the floor, making a loud clattering sound. The figure behind the door was only a silhouette. It stopped short, looking around, trying to determine what the noise was and where it came from.

Marvin was frightened. He knew his intruder. Tall and lean, the smell of grease, whiskey, and tobacco, and the raspy breath, Leroy was there as expected, come to make good on his promise. Marvin's heart pounded so hard he could hear it. He braced himself, waiting for whatever would happen next. Leroy reached for the light switch and then hesitated. Marvin laughed silently. Leroy was obviously worried about another flashbulb booby trap.

No such luck, Leroy, this is a lot worse.

Leroy lit a match and looked around. The flicker of the flame cast dancing lights and shadows upwards onto his scruffy face, giving him a demonic appearance. Marvin tightened his grip on the shotgun as Leroy slowly opened the door all the way and stepped in, a pillow clenched in his hands. He intended to suffocate Marvin in bed, of that Marvin was sure. He would press the pillow tightly into Marvin's face until Marvin stopped breathing, stopped struggling. The perfect crime. No autopsy, no coroner's inquest, no police investigation, just another old man dying in his sleep at a nursing home. Happens all the time. Marvin could hear and feel his heart pounding.

Leroy crept across the room toward the bed. He held the pillow out in front of him. When he reached the bed, he pushed it into the place where Marvin's head should have been. Marvin reached over and turned on the lamp on his desk. Leroy pulled back and froze in place.

"What do you think you're doing in here, Parker?"

Leroy's eyes darted around the room, looking to make sure they were alone before speaking. His voice was like ice. "Just what I said I'd do, Bradley, what I should've done in the cellar. So, now, I'm getting even for what you and the others did. It's payback time, old man, and you're first. Say your prayers and get ready to meet your maker."

Thank God for camcorders, Marvin thought.

Leroy turned and began moving toward him. Marvin pulled the quilt back exposing the shotgun. He had it aimed at Leroy's groin.

Leroy stopped, no doubt surprised by the sight of the shotgun, something he could not have expected and was not prepared for. His jaw dropped and the toothpick fell off his lip and hit the floor.

He backed away toward the door and said, "What do you think you're going to do with that? I think you're bluffing." He hesitated then took a step toward Marvin.

Marvin raised the shotgun and aimed it at Leroy's face. "I think I'm going to blow your ugly head off if you don't stop where you are. That's what I think."

Leroy stopped. Then he said, "You can get in a lot of trouble having that shotgun in here."

"Not as much trouble as you're in right now, Parker. Don't come any closer, or you're dead meat."

Leroy didn't move. He showed less bravado than before. The shotgun had him scared, that was clear.

His words were rushed and a slight stammer crept into them. "You'll get the death penalty, old man. Think about that. You brought a shotgun in here planning to shoot somebody. That's premeditation. A date with the executioner. You're not going to shoot anybody."

"You stupid jerk. You know how long it takes to litigate a death penalty? They'll have to dig me up to execute me."

With the video, whatever he did here would be self-defense. But he'd have to coax Leroy to come a lot closer for the rock salt to do any serious damage. Instead, he'd encourage him to leave.

"Now you turn around and get out of here before I leave a hole where your ugly head used to be."

Marvin couldn't believe he was saying all this. What movie did it come from?

"I'll go, old man, but I'll be back."

Marvin decided to try a bluff. "Really?" he said. "Well here's something you better keep in mind, you spineless rat. Most of the other residents know what's been going on around here. But nobody would listen to us. So, my friends got guns the same as me, but they don't have my patience; they'll shoot first and forget to ask questions later. The next time you enter a resident's room with a pillow in your hands is likely to be your last. And my friends and I have a pact. If any of us gets hurt or dies, the others come after you. You do anything like that, and you better not go to sleep in this place. Like the man said, we know what you did, and we know where you live."

Marvin waited for his bluff to sink in.

Then he continued. "Now. If you're still here by the time I

count to ten, I'm going to paint the hallway with your worthless insides." He pointed the shotgun at Leroy's midsection and began counting, "One, two, three—"

Leroy turned and ran out the door. Marvin was able to breathe at last. He reset the safety on the shotgun and put it on the floor leaning against his chair. He pressed the stop button on the camcorder. He got up from the chair, closed the door, and put the golf clubs back in place. He picked up Leroy's toothpick and threw it in the trashcan. Then he sat at his desk, inserted the camcorder's DVD into the laptop, uploaded the video he had just made, and emailed it to Freddie. The adventure had exhausted him, so he went to bed and slept soundly with no nightmares to disturb him for the first time in many nights.

CHAPTER 31

The next morning, Marvin went to breakfast at the usual time. Mike and Carrie were already there.

Marvin sat, waited to catch his breath, and then spoke quietly. "Leroy came into my room last night. He came to kill me. I scared him off with the shotgun."

"That rat," Mike said. "Well he said you'd be first. I'm the one he ought to be after."

"He knows I'm the instigator of all the things that happened to him, and he knows we're on to him. He said he was there to get even and that you two were next."

"Oh my stars," Carrie said. "What do you suppose he'll do?"

"He's sitting over there staring at us," Mike said. "Let's go ask him what he plans to do."

Marvin chuckled. "He was really surprised when he saw the shotgun."

"He probably went to his room and changed his drawers," Mike said. "Nothing like staring down the barrels of a twelve-gauge to fill a guy's Jockey shorts."

"I told him we all have guns, hoping to keep him from busting in on one of you. I guess it worked. You're both here. But I got the whole thing on video and emailed it to my grandson. I don't think Leroy will be around much longer."

They stopped talking as their breakfast was served.

"Is this the blue plate special?" Mike asked the server. "Oh, my mistake, it's not the plate. It's the eggs that are blue."

She ignored him and walked away. They concentrated on the food and didn't talk. Then Carrie said. "Speaking of your grandson, look who's here," she said.

Freddie had come into the dining hall and was standing there inside the door. He looked around the room and spotted the three of them. He waved and then kept looking. The room was full with residents and staff having breakfast.

"What's he up to?" Mike asked.

"Darned if I know. I asked him to stay out of this, but I guess I can't blame him. I sent him the video."

Freddie looked toward Leroy sitting at a table with Bates. He walked over and stood in front of Leroy.

"Are you Leroy Parker?" Freddie spoke loud enough that everyone in the room got quiet and turned their attention to the table where Leroy sat.

Leroy looked from side to side. He sized up Freddie. Freddie wasn't as tall, but he was younger and with more bulk. "Who wants to know?" Leroy asked.

Freddie leaned over and put his face within inches of Leroy's. He raised his voice. "Get this straight, Parker. If you threaten my grandfather again, if you harm him, if you harm any of his friends, I will come here and kill you."

The room became abuzz as people commented to one another about what was going on.

"What? Are you threatening me?" Leroy asked. He slid his chair back away from Freddie.

"What part of it isn't clear?" Freddie said. He moved toward the retreating Leroy. "Do I need to speak slower, use smaller words? You are a disgusting piece of trash that beats up sick and helpless old people. You don't deserve to breathe the same air they do. And if I hear that you do anything more like the things I know you already did, and if the authorities don't take care of you, I will."

Leroy was sliding his chair away and looking around the room frantically as Freddie moved closer.

"Sir," said Bates, "who are you and what is this about?"

"I'm Fred Bradley, grandson of Marvin Bradley, a resident here. Who are you?"

"I am Oliver Bates, the Director of Orchard Hills Nursing Home, and if you don't leave immediately, I'll call security."

"Yeah, Bates, you do that. And I'll call the cops. And you and Mr. Parker here and anyone else involved in what's going on around here will be eating prison food for the rest of your miserable lives. Which, I'm sorry to say, will be an improvement over the swill you're feeding the residents here."

"What grounds do you have to suggest that there has been any kind of conspiracy here, Mr. Bradley? Those are slanderous statements, and I'll have no more of it." He took out his cell phone and started to call someone.

"I have more than grounds, Bates. I've got it all. The next time you see me, it will be in court when I testify against you and this piece of . . . And then I'll watch them lead both of your sorry butts away to prison."

At that, Leroy jumped out of his chair. "Hold on, here. Nobody said nothing to nobody about no jail time."

Mike leaned over to Marvin and Carrie. "How many negatives was that?" he whispered.

Carrie said, "I lost count."

"I hope they lock him up in the prison," Marvin said, remembering the abused Willie Hunt. "He'd learn about payback there. Oh, how I hope."

Leroy backed away from the table toward the door, turned to leave, and shouted over his shoulder, "You better fix this, Bates, or the next time you see me, I'll be what they call 'state's evidence.' I'm not taking the rap for you," and he stomped out.

"Good," Marvin said. "Everybody heard that."

Carrie took out a list and scribbled a note on it. "Everybody heard . . ." she said to herself.

After Leroy left the room, a uniformed security guard came in. He was in his late sixties and looked unsure of what he was doing there. Bates signaled him to come over. Freddie walked away and toward the table where Marvin, Carrie, and Mike sat. The entire room was quiet, everyone watching to see what would happen next.

"Granddad, I want to take you out of here. Now. Let's go get your things."

"No, son, I can't leave my friends at the mercy of these people."

"Then I'm staying with you."

The security guard shuffled over. "Sir, you have to leave now," he said. "Mr. Bates said so."

"Are you in on it too?" Freddie asked.

"Huh? In on what?" the guard asked.

"I need to stay with my grandfather and his friends. Someone here is trying to kill them. If anything happens to them, you'll be sharing a jail cell with Parker and Bates."

The guard looked confused. "I don't know anything about that, sir. You have to leave now or I'll call the police."

"That might be a good idea," Freddie said. "Why don't you ask Bates if he wants the cops coming in here?"

"Go ahead and go, Freddie," Marvin said. "All these witnesses here heard everything. I don't think Bates or Leroy will try anything."

Freddie looked around the room as if trying to assess the situation. He seemed reluctant to leave. The security guard stood firm between Freddie and the other side of the room where Bates seemed to be trying to take it all in.

"Okay, Granddad. I'm going to put together a file to present to the authorities using the stuff you sent. You did a good job with that, but it's out of your hands now. You and your friends did the community a service. I'll take it from here."

"What should we do?" Marvin asked, unwilling to stand by idly waiting for something to happen.

"Stay close to your friends and out in the open where lots of people can see you if possible. Keep your cell phone handy and call me right away if anything happens. I should be back tomorrow afternoon at the latest." He looked at the guard. "With real cops. You are going to be looking for another job, pops. You better hope it isn't making license plates." He turned and walked out of the dining hall, the security guard following close behind.

"Man," Mike said. "Your grandson is something else."

"Runs in the family, I bet," Carrie said.

"He said it's out of our hands," Mike said. "He'll take it from here. But I bet he doesn't have a cattle prod."

"Let's go play cards," Marvin said. "I can't wait to see what we'll get for lunch after this."

"Maybe we should hire professional tasters," Mike said, "like the kings and pharaohs had. In case they try to poison us."

"You have such an imagination," Carrie said.

CHAPTER 32

In the early morning of the following day, Marvin awoke to a ruckus in the hallway outside his door. He got out of bed, opened the door, and peeked out. Two uniformed policemen and a man in a suit were in the hallway talking to Director Bates, the security guard, and Loretta, who was pointing at Mike's door. Marvin didn't know what was going on, but a lot of strangers were milling around, so he got dressed and put his new hearing aids in.

Loretta said to the cops, "It's in there somewhere. I saw it when he brought it in."

Bates added, "He said it was for target shooting, but it's designed for hunting deer and elk."

Marvin wondered what that was all about. Why were they interested in Mike's archery set? He closed the door quietly. They hadn't seen him. After he shaved, dressed, combed his hair, and brushed and inserted his teeth, he opened the door. The people were gone. He walked to the dining hall. The cops and the civilian were there talking to residents. Mike was sitting alone at their table. He was already eating breakfast. Marvin sat across from him and said, "What's going on?"

"I don't know," Mike said. "But it's something important. Ollie is here with the security guard and those cops. We'll find out soon enough."

Just then Carrie came in, joined them, and said, "I guess we don't have to worry about Leroy any more."

"Why not?" Marvin asked.

"Didn't they tell you? I thought everyone knew. Loretta told me when I went to get my newspaper."

"Told you what?" Mike asked.

"Leroy is dead."

"Dead? How?" Marvin asked.

"I'm not sure. Loretta didn't say. Only that she found him in the empty wing early this morning. She was all broke up about it, so I didn't push for details. I figured we'd learn soon enough."

"Well, I guess Leroy has gone to a better place," Mike said.

"Mike," Carrie said, "if Leroy is anywhere, he's in Hell."

"That's what I said. A better place." He pushed his powdered eggs around on his plate. "At least the food has to be better."

Elsie Collins was sitting alone at the next table. Marvin leaned over and asked her, "Elsie, did you hear what happened, how he died?"

"Sure did," said Elsie Collins. "They already talked to most of us. He was murdered."

"Murdered?" Mike asked. "How?"

"They found him face-down with an arrow in his back, of all things."

"An arrow?" Mike said. "Holy crap! I'll be right back." He got up and rushed out of the dining hall.

"He can sure move with that walker when he wants to," Marvin said.

"Where's he going?" Carrie asked.

"My guess is he's going to see if his archery set has been disturbed."

The food server came over with their breakfast.

"Where's the other one?" she asked.

"He'll be right back," Carrie said. "He went to the bathroom."

"Well, he better not complain if the food is cold."

"What difference would it make?" Carrie said.

The server glared at her, put their dishes down, and walked away. Marvin looked at the powdered eggs, greasy fried potatoes, and burned toast in front of him. "I think I'll learn to cook," he said.

"What did you eat when you lived alone?"

"TV dinners. Home delivery pizza. Sandwiches. Cereal."

"No wonder you had a stroke. I think I'd rather eat here. No, on second thought . . ."

Mike came back into the dining hall, not in as much of a hurry as when he had left. He plopped down in his chair, looked at the food, and made a face.

"It's gone," he said.

"What's gone," Marvin asked.

"The archery set. It's not in my room. Come to think of it, it wasn't there this morning, either. Not where I left it."

"Who could have taken it?" Carrie asked.

"Maybe Leroy stole it and committed suicide," Mike said.

They all laughed. Then Loretta's voice from the doorway interrupted their laughter. "That's him over there, officer. That's the one with the archery set." She was pointing at Mike.

The cops and other guy came over to their table. The other guy introduced himself.

"Good morning, folks. I'm Detective Barney Murray. Have you heard what's happened here?"

All three nodded that they had.

"Mr. Charles," Murray said to Mike, "I understand you own an archery set."

"Well, I used to. Somebody stole it this morning. Or last night, maybe."

"We have it, sir. We took it from your room. If I might ask, sir, how many arrows do you have?" Murray asked.

"I don't have any arrows. I used to have arrows. But you say you took them. How many arrows do you have?" Mike sneered at the detective.

"I see," Murray said. "Well, since you own the only archery set on the premises, and since one of its arrows is in the back of the deceased, and since you and the deceased are reported to have had recent difficulties, I'm afraid you'll have to come with us to answer some questions."

"Well, you can take me if you want. Not much I can do about that. But I am not answering any questions. Not until my lawyer tells me what questions to answer. I know my rights. Marvin, would you call Lawyer Epstein in town and ask him to meet me wherever they take me?"

"Sure, Mike," Marvin said. Then to Murray, "Where are you taking him?"

"The police station in town. Stand up, Mr. Charles, and put your hands behind your back. We have to put the cuffs on you."

"Then you'll have to carry me, too, sonny, because I can't move inch one without this walker. Which, you'll notice if you are even a tad smarter than you look, operates from in front of me, not in back." He didn't mention his wheelchair, which was back in his room.

"Okay, you can be cuffed in front. Sorry we have to do it, but it's standard procedure."

"Yeah, better cuff me. I'm quite the wise guy. I might just whip a crossbow out of my shoulder holster and shoot an apple off your ugly head. Let's see. Where did I put that apple?"

The two cops stood Mike up and cuffed his hands in front of him.

"Uh, take a look at this, detective," Mike said. "The cuffs are too close together. I can't reach the handles."

"Very well," Murray said with a sigh. Then to the uniforms, "Undo one cuff and snap it onto the handles."

"Aren't you going to tell me I have the right to remain silent?"

"You have the right to remain silent," Murray said with a

tired look on his face. "And we'd really prefer it if you would."

Mike took hold of the walker and looked at the cops, making a scoffing noise. "So long, folks," he said to Marvin and Carrie. "It's the third degree for me, the bright lights and rubber hoses. Except these guys are so dumb they'll probably just give me the second degree, a bug light, and a wet noodle. Well, don't just stand there, boys. Let's go. What are you waiting for?"

Marvin and Carrie watched Mike and the cops go across the dining hall toward the exit. Mike stayed in front and clumped along with his walker, and Detective Murray and the uniforms followed behind.

"Look at him," Carrie said. "Milking it for all it's worth. Going as slow as he can. That's our Mike."

Marvin called information on his cell phone to get the number for Lawyer Epstein. Then he called the lawyer and explained the situation.

When Marvin hung up, he said, "He thinks the notion of a guy in his eighties shooting someone with a fifty-pound hunter's bow and arrow while leaning on a walker would be enough to get Mike off the suspect list. He said not to worry. He'd have Mike back home in time for lunch."

"You should have told him to take his time," Carrie said. "The jail probably serves a better lunch than we get here."

"Couldn't be any worse. Do you think Mike did it?" Marvin asked.

"I don't think so. But Leroy did threaten us. If Mike did it, he was protecting us. Or else Leroy came after him."

"They said it happened in the empty wing. What would Mike be doing down there with his bow and arrow in the middle of the night?" Marvin was worried that maybe Mike really did it. "That lawyer thinks Mike couldn't pull the bow, but could he? He was able to set that trap with the bucket of bolts in his room. I couldn't do that. I guess we have to wait and see."

CHAPTER 33

After lunch Marvin and Carrie waited for Mike, or news of him, in the dayroom. At about two o'clock Mike came clumping in on his walker.

"Mike, how did it go?" Marvin asked before Mike even got to where they were sitting.

Mike came over and took a seat. "It was fun," he said. "Lawyer Epstein got there before I did. He told me to keep my mouth shut, which I did."

"That must have been very difficult," Carrie said.

"It wasn't easy," Mike said. "A life or death situation. I'd be looking at the electric chair."

"They don't use that here, any more," Marvin said.

"Epstein knows his stuff. He got them to show him my archery set. Then he asked me to pull the bow back. I tried as hard as I could, but it wouldn't pull back. I don't remember it being that tightly strung."

"When did you last try it?" Carrie asked.

"About thirty years ago. I entered an archery contest with it. It was easier to pull then."

"What happened next?" Marvin asked.

"I took second place."

"No, not then, Mike. What happened today, after you showed them you couldn't pull the bow?"

"Lawyer Epstein told them to imagine being in a courtroom testifying that an eighty-five-year-old man who can't walk used

184

a bow he couldn't pull standing behind a walker that he needed to grip with both hands and killing a man fifty years his junior from about fifty feet away."

"How do they know he was shot from that far away?" Marvin asked.

"Oh, they got it all figured out from the angle the arrow went in and the strength of the bow. They explained it to Epstein. The arrow was at a down angle, which means it needed to be released from at least fifty feet away, which is all the longer the hallway is. Man, those CSI guys are sharp."

"CSI?" Marvin said. "We don't have any CSI team."

"I guess not. But their dispatcher majored in math. He figured it out for them. Then Lawyer Epstein said to picture themselves explaining the same thing to a jury in a false arrest lawsuit."

"So they let you go?" Marvin asked.

"Not right away. They waited for the prints they'd lifted from the bow to be compared to mine. There was only one set of prints on the bow, and they weren't mine."

"Whose were they?" Carrie asked.

"They didn't say. Lawyer Epstein told me at lunch that it takes a while to have prints checked against all the law enforcement and military databases to see if those prints are on file anywhere."

"He bought your lunch?"

"No, I bought his. That was my retainer. If they charge me, he'll be my mouthpiece. He thought the whole thing was funny. Nice guy. Darn good lawyer, too. Just like Perry Mason."

"Okay, Mike," Marvin said, "we have to ask. Just between us." He looked around and lowered his voice. "Did you kill Leroy?"

"I wish I could say I did. But I didn't. Whoever did it must have got my bow from my room while I was sleeping. But I can't figure out why there was only that one set of fingerprints on it. I've handled it several times since it arrived here. My prints should have been on it, too. And my son's from when he packed it. And Director Ollie's, too. He handled it when I showed it to him. He knows a lot about them."

"That's probably because he used to be a phys ed teacher. Or maybe he hunted. Did you try to pull the bow when you first got it?" Marvin asked.

"You mean thirty years ago?"

"No, Mike, the other day when you got it here."

"Of course not. It might have gone off accidentally."

"Uh . . . Oh, never mind," Marvin said.

"Did they find the cattle prod in the quiver?" Carrie asked.

Mike started laughing. "No, that's the best part. It's still right here Velcro'd to my walker. It was there the whole time I was in custody. They frisked me, but they never even looked at my walker. When I went through the metal detector, they passed the walker, cattle prod and all, around it and handed it to me. When I told Lawyer Epstein about it at lunch, he about peed his pants laughing."

"Did you tell the cops about the abuse?" Marvin asked.

"None of the cops abused me. They were very nice."

"No, the abuse here at the nursing home."

"No. When we got there, Lawyer Epstein made them let him and me talk alone. I told him about it. He said I shouldn't mention it to the cops unless they asked about it. If we needed to go to trial, it would be part of our defense, and he didn't want to tip our hand right away. But the cops knew that Leroy had threatened us. Everyone in the dining room heard it, and someone must have told the cops this morning before we got there."

"Well," Carrie said, "I guess we don't have to worry about Leroy anymore. I guess our worries are over."

"Not necessarily," Marvin said. "We don't know who killed him or why. And Bates is still with us. Don't forget, he's the one who was giving Leroy his instructions. He'll probably just recruit another goon, and we'll have to go through this drill all over again."

"Do you have any flashbulbs left?" Carrie asked.

"I wonder where I can buy a bow that I can pull," Mike said. "And arrows. They kept my other ones for evidence."

Just then, Murray, the detective who had arrested Mike, came into the dining hall. He looked around the room until he spotted the three of them. He walked over and said, "Marvin Bradley?"

"That's me," Marvin answered.

"I wonder if you would come downtown so we could ask you some questions."

"Ask me here. I'm too feeble to travel," Marvin said.

"Not according to the uniforms. They say you were out for a joyride the other day."

"Some days are better than others. Today is a bad day."

"Shall I place you under arrest, sir?"

"For what?" Clearly the cop was bluffing, trying to intimidate him.

"I can always come up with something."

"Go ahead. But I'm not as easygoing as Mike here. If you do that, first, I will exercise my right to remain silent, and second, you will definitely be facing false arrest charges. Now, if you have any questions, ask away. I know enough law to know when to shut up and call a lawyer."

"Could we talk alone?" Murray asked.

"Nope. Anything I say to you will be with witnesses present until I know what you want."

"I really don't want anyone else in on the questioning, sir."

"Then, ask away and see how quiet it gets in here. I exercise

187

---

my right to remain silent."

"Very well. They can stay. Do you have in your possession a shotgun?"

Marvin wondered where Murray was going with this line of questioning. "Got one in my room."

"Is that permitted here?"

"Didn't bother to ask."

Murray slid his chair closer to Marvin's. "Did you threaten to shoot Leroy Parker with that shotgun?"

"I did."

"Why?"

"Because he came to my room to kill me."

Murray slid back and looked puzzled. "How do you know that?"

"Because he snuck into my room in the middle of the night while he thought I was sleeping. He was tiptoeing toward my bed with a pillow in his hands. I don't think he was looking for a pillow fight."

Carrie and Mike laughed. Mike looked around the room to see if anyone else had heard what Marvin had said.

"And you didn't call for help?"

"Wasn't time. And I didn't need help. Let that be a lesson to you, sonny. Never bring a pillow to a gun fight."

Mike laughed and looked around again.

Detective Murray smiled at that, too. "But you didn't report him the next day."

"Young fellow, what with all that's been going on around here, who was I going to report him to? Who could I trust?"

"How about the security force?"

Marvin laughed. "I take it you haven't met our stellar security force."

"What do you mean, all that's going on around here?"

Marvin raised his hands and made circles in the air. "Staff

trying to kill us, for one thing. What more do you need?"

"Why did Mr. Parker want to kill you?"

"You'd have to ask him. But then I guess you can't since he's on a slab in the morgue. Well, you could ask, but he wouldn't answer. Oh, well."

Murray referred to his notes. "According to what others have told us, you had a run-in with Mr. Parker in the dining hall the other day. Can you explain that?"

"We had a disagreement."

"About what?"

"He wanted to kill us, and we didn't want him to."

Murray wrote something down and said, "And the nursing staff tells us he had an episode with someone in which he was injured and nearly blinded. They thought you had something to do with that."

"Why would they think that? No matter, seems to me he had it coming." Marvin looked to Mike and Carrie for approval. They nodded at him.

"So it would appear that you have a strong motive for killing him yourself."

"So it would. And it would've been self-defense if I'd done it. But I didn't."

"Where were you last night?"

"In my room. With my shotgun. Waiting for Leroy. He never showed up."

"Can anyone vouch for that?"

Marvin leaned forward and stuck his nose close to Murray's face. "Yeah, sure, the can-can girls, the caterer, and the band. Get serious. I was in my room alone."

He leaned back.

"Did you know about Mr. Charles's archery set?"

"I did."

The detective put his notebook away. "Well sir, that adds up to means, motive, opportunity, and no alibi. Which makes you a prime suspect."

"Do you know how stupid that sounds? I already told you I have a shotgun. Why would I use a bow and arrow to kill anybody?"

"Hey, Marvin," Mike said, "why don't you confess? I understand that jailhouse food is a lot better than what we get here. Maybe we should all confess."

"Thanks, Mike. But Inspector Clouseau here doesn't have anything on me."

"We have enough to justify an arrest, sir. I'd rather not do that yet, but we definitely need you to come downtown so we can take your fingerprints."

Marvin picked up his cane and held it between himself and Murray. "Tell you what, son. I'll be here. I can't drive and I can barely walk. Why don't you wait until you get the results from your fingerprint search. I've never handled that bow, so I know they're not my prints. It can save you time. If you need my prints, bring the fingerprint kit here. But I'm not going anywhere. Call your chief. He'll vouch for me."

The detective took his cell phone over to the other side of the room and made a call. Then he returned to where they were sitting.

"I guess we can do that, sir. But only because the chief knows you from before you came here. I'll let the security guard know that you are effectively under house arrest."

"If you can find him and wake him up. But go ahead, there's nothing new about that. I've been under house arrest for a year."

The detective left the dining hall. Marvin figured he went to find the guard. Marvin's cell phone rang. Freddie was calling.

"Granddad, it was on the news. That guy Leroy was shot with a bow and arrow. Like the one your friend has."

"He sure was. We're all broke up about it."

"Did you or one of your friends do it?"

"As far as I'm concerned, whoever did it is a good friend."

"You know what I mean, Granddad. You or one of the two people you hang around with?"

"No, we didn't do it, but we're being questioned. They already took Mike in for questioning and released him. I guess I'm next on their list of usual suspects."

"I'm on my way, Granddad, after I get some sleep. Been up all night. I'm at a motel by the Interstate. I'll be there later this afternoon."

"How come you didn't go back to Philadelphia yesterday?"

"I wanted to stay nearby in case you needed me. I'll see you later. Be careful."

"Nothing to worry about, son. We're safe for now. Leroy's out of the picture, and there's enough cops here to make a Dirty Harry movie."

Marvin hung up his cell phone, and Detective Murray came back into the room. He was talking on his own cell phone, and he walked over to Marvin's table. When he hung up, he said to Marvin, "Mr. Bradley, what is your first name?"

"Marvin."

"Who is Frederick Marvin Bradley?"

"That's my grandson. He was named after me and my wife's father. We call him Freddie."

"Where is he now?"

Marvin took a moment, then said, "I just spoke to him on the phone. He heard about the murder on the news and is coming here to see if I need any help. He'll be here later today. Why do you ask?"

"Just routine. We need to talk to him. What time will he be here?"

"He didn't say a specific time."

191

"Do you know where he is now?"

"No, just that he'll be here."

When Detective Murray left, Marvin called Freddie back.

"Freddie, the cops want to talk to you."

"I bet they do. Do they know where I am?"

"No, just that you're coming here. Why do you think they want to talk to you?"

"Just guessing, Granddad, but I bet they found my finger-prints on that bow. I'll explain later. I have to get out of here."

CHAPTER 34

The next day after breakfast, Lawyer Epstein met with Marvin, Mike, and Carrie in the dayroom. They were on the sofa; he sat in a facing lounge chair. Marvin had met the lawyer years before when Morris Epstein came to town as a young lawyer fresh out of law school and having just passed the bar examination. He was in his thirties now, had substantial criminal law experience throughout the region, and was well-regarded in the professional community.

"Okay, here's how she sits. Mr. Bradley, your grandson is in the lockup in town charged with murdering Parker. I am representing him. The chief recommended me to him because he knows you and because I represented Mr. Charles here in his recent questioning on the same matter."

Epstein shifted his ample weight on the chair and fidgeted with some papers in his briefcase. His pasty complexion reddened from the effort. He took some papers out, selected a couple of pages, and read them to himself. The others waited without speaking, paying full attention. Then he took out three business cards and handed them out.

He returned the pages to his briefcase, closed it, and continued, his face now its original pale shade of pink. "A lot of people here heard Freddie threaten to kill Parker in the dining hall. The cops got his name from the sign-in register at the front desk, and they made a quick match of the fingerprints on the bow to his, which are on file with the FBI. The state police pulled him over on the Interstate and turned him over to the local police, who charged him with murder."

"How did his prints get on the bow?" Marvin asked.

"Yeah, how?" Mike said. "As far as I know, he never even saw it, much less handled it."

The lawyer leaned back in his chair and folded his well-manicured hands across his chest. "Freddie admitted that he spent all last night here."

"He was here when Leroy was killed?" Marvin asked.

"He said he came back because he was worried about what might happen to you three. He told me that he has a video of Parker attacking you in your room, Mr. Bradley."

"I made that video and emailed it to Freddie. I've been sending him lots of material about what's going on around here. Videos, memos, financial records, and like that."

"Where did you get all that?" Epstein asked.

"Downloaded it from their server. Don't tell them. According to Freddie, they don't have adequate security on their computer."

"Maybe because that computer security stuff costs money," Mike said.

The lawyer touched his fist to his chin and rubbed it from side to side. Then he asked, "Mr. Bradley, no offense, but how did you manage to survive an attack by a much younger man?"

"Didn't Freddie tell you? A double-barreled, twelve-gauge equalizer."

"Impressive. And you have other videos?"

"A few."

"If anything, we can use them and the documents you've collected to justify, or at least explain, the killing, so let's keep it under wraps. Get copies of your files to me right away. I must advise you that what you did is illegal and Freddie's complicity in the act makes it look worse. So we don't want the authorities knowing about it until it's to our advantage to do so."

Carrie fussed with her hair, then asked, "Doesn't all that stuff make a case for self-defense? Or at least for Freddie protecting us?"

Epstein shook his head. "Whoever shot Parker got him in the back between the shoulder blades. That kind of makes self-defense less than believable. As for protecting you, the murder didn't happen during any act of aggression on the residents as far as we can tell."

"Did Freddie say he did it?" Marvin asked.

"No. He denies it. He says he was here watching over your rooms and found the archery set on the floor in Mike's doorway. He said he just figured you dropped it there, Mike, so he picked it up and put it in your closet without waking you."

"See, Marvin? I told you that good deeds can get you in trouble."

"You did? When?"

"I don't know. Last year sometime. Anyway, whoever did it took the bow from my room, shot Leroy, wiped the bow down, and tossed it back into my doorway. Freddie saw it there, picked it up, and that was that."

"That's one theory, but the cops aren't buying it."

"Are they looking at anyone else for this murder?" Marvin asked. "Leroy had a lot of enemies."

"No. They questioned a lot of people. The fuel oil delivery man got into a tiff with Leroy."

"Yeah, we saw it."

"So did everybody else. The cops questioned him, but he has an explanation for the argument."

"His wife was fooling around with Leroy," Marvin said. "That's a pretty strong motive."

"I don't think they know about that. It's the first I heard of it. He said the argument was over the condition of the furnace here. He said he couldn't continue to deliver fuel oil until they fixed it."

"Doesn't matter," Mike said. "They never turn it on, anyway."

"It is kind of chilly in here. Anyway, they think they have an iron-clad case against Freddie. He had motive: Parker was threatening to kill his grandfather. He had means: he knew about the archery set and where Mike kept it. He had opportunity: he was on the premises when the murder took place. And they have evidence: his fingerprints are on the murder weapon, and a bunch of people heard him threaten to kill Parker. They can get an indictment with a lot less than that."

"Wait," Carrie said. "Let me get this all down. Motive, means, opportunity. Did I leave anything out?"

"Fingerprints and witnesses," Marvin said. "Were there any fingerprints on the arrow itself?"

"No, it was wiped clean."

"Then how do they explain that? A killer with enough savvy to wipe down the arrow shouldn't be stupid enough to leave his prints on the bow."

"They don't try to explain it. But I will if we go to court."

"Look, this should be a piece of cake," Mike said. "Freddie goes on trial for murder. But he has you defending him. During the trial, you get the real murderer to stand up in the courtroom and confess. That's how Perry Mason always did it."

Epstein laughed. "It doesn't work that way. I wish it did."

"Oh," Mike said. "I thought you were as good as Perry Mason. I guess I was mistaken. Sorry."

Chapter 35

Marvin and his little band of investigators sat in Marvin's room after Lawyer Epstein left.

"It looks like we're going to have to solve this mystery for the cops," he said. "They think they already have it wrapped up. They think Freddie did it. Lawyer Epstein clearly plans to argue that all the evidence is circumstantial and to use a defense based on reasonable doubt. Nobody is trying to find the real killer. So I guess it's up to us."

"Maybe Lawyer Epstein has the right idea. Maybe he can get Freddie acquitted," Carrie said.

"Maybe, maybe not," Marvin answered. "But there's three things wrong with that strategy. First, it might not work. Second, if it does, Freddie's name isn't cleared; people will just think he got off on technicalities, and his career is ruined. Third, we still have a killer in our midst."

"That's right," Carrie said. "Whoever did it is still walking around out there. I never thought of that. That's scary."

"And that person is the key to clearing Freddie's name. We have no choice," Marvin said. "We have to find the real killer."

"Yeah, then we make him confess in the courtroom, just like Perry Mason," Mike said.

"If we do this right, it doesn't go that far," Marvin said. "Freddie's name is cleared before any trial begins, and the real killer is behind bars. All's well that ends well."

"How do we start?" Carrie asked.

"I'm not sure. Any suggestions?" Marvin asked.

"Let's say we identify a suspect," Carrie said. "What do we do first?"

Mike said, "The cops face down a suspect. They accuse them outright and then force them to prove they didn't do it. That's what they did to me. Or tried. I didn't confess."

"We can't do that," Marvin said. "We don't have the clout a cop has. We can't threaten anyone with being locked up. And as soon as word got out we were snooping around, nobody would even talk to us. Maybe we can use psychology to get people talking about it and to make the guilty party reveal himself with too many evasive answers. I guess we'll have to play it by ear."

"Well, that's a good start for when we have a likely suspect. So how do we go about building a roster of likely suspects?" Mike asked.

"We need a list," Carrie said. She reached in her purse and pulled out her notepad and pencil.

"Well, for starters, who are the obvious ones?" Mike asked. "Besides us, I mean."

Carrie wrinkled her brow and gave it some thought. "Well, everyone heard Leroy tell Director Bates that he'd turn state's evidence to keep himself out of jail. That gives Bates a motive." She wrote Bates's name on her new list.

"And I got Loretta on video catching Leroy cheating on her with Nurse Helen," Mike said. "Add Loretta to the list. A woman scorned and all that."

"And Nurse Helen's husband," Marvin said. "We saw him arguing with Leroy. He probably learned about Leroy and Nurse Helen."

"Don't forget Freddie," Mike said. "He threatened to kill Leroy in front of everybody."

"Mike," Marvin said. "We're trying to clear Freddie, not implicate him."

"I'm just trying to be thorough."

"But think about it. When he found the archery set in your doorway, he put it in your closet, which implicated you. Do you think Freddie would have done that if he had just killed somebody with it?"

"I don't know. I guess not."

"Okay," Carrie said. "So far we have three people on our list. Not counting Freddie." She looked at Mike and shook her head.

"And you can bet that none of them did it," Mike said.

"How's that?" Marvin asked.

"Well, it's never any of the obvious ones," Mike answered. "Didn't you ever watch *Perry Mason*?"

"I don't think we can count on that," Marvin said.

"Well, you just mark my words. It won't turn out to be any of them."

"How about if we just list all the people who could possibly have done it?" Marvin said. "We start with them, investigate, and eliminate them one by one."

"Who would that include?" Carrie asked.

"Anyone who knew Leroy and could have been here that night," Marvin said.

"That's going to be a long list," Mike said. "All the staff and all the residents."

"No problem," Carrie said. "I already have that." She rummaged around in her purse and brought out several loose leaf sheets of notepad paper. "Here's your list."

"When did you do that?" Mike asked.

"Months ago. I always keep lists of the people in my world. It helps for things like Christmas card lists, party invitations, and so on. So I don't forget anybody."

"Is it up to date?" Marvin asked.

"Oh, yes. I scratch names off when somebody leaves and add to the list when somebody new comes on board. Look here."

She showed them the entry for Leroy Parker. "See? It's already crossed off." Sure enough, Leroy Parker's name was lined out on Carrie's list. "I did that as soon as I heard about the murder. And for Mrs. Meade, too, after she died. See?"

"Very efficient," Marvin said.

"You were going to send Leroy a Christmas card?" Mike asked.

"No, silly. But I like for my lists to be complete."

"Can we just work from your list and cross out names as we eliminate suspects?" Marvin asked.

"Oh, no. We'll have to make a copy. I don't want to give up my list."

"We can do it on the computer," Marvin said. "Can either of you type?"

"Ninety words a minute," Mike said.

"How did you learn to type that fast?" Carrie asked.

"I used to work for a company that made computers."

"I might have known," Carrie said.

"What did you do for them?" Marvin asked.

"Groundskeeper," Mike answered.

"So how did that—?" Carrie started to ask. "Oh, never mind."

Marvin went over to the computer and turned it on. "We'll make a database. I learned how to do that before I retired."

He opened the database program and made a new database with one column labeled "Suspect Name." Then he surrendered the computer to Mike, who typed the names from Carrie's list into the database. He hadn't lied. He could indeed type fast. He was done in no time.

"I'm impressed," Carrie said.

"Me, too," Marvin added.

"Okay," Mike said. "How do we eliminate names from this list? How do we identify the ones who aren't likely suspects?"

"Hold on," Carrie said. She searched her purse and came up

with the list she'd made when they talked to Lawyer Epstein. "To be a suspect, you have to have means, motive, and opportunity. That's what Lawyer Epstein said the police have on Freddie. He has all three. Then, to charge you with murder, there has to be evidence. Like Freddie's fingerprints on the bow and witnesses that heard him threaten to kill Leroy."

"That's everything. Are we sure Freddie didn't do it?" Mike asked.

"We're sure," Marvin said with a heavy sigh.

"How do we start?" Carrie asked.

Marvin took over the computer and added columns to the database labeled "means," "motive," and "opportunity." He explained, "We'll put a text entry in each column next to anyone who matches the category."

"Let's go down the list one by one and eliminate anyone who is physically incapable of shooting the bow and arrow," Mike said.

"You mean like you?" Carrie asked.

"I mean like Mr. Peters." Mike said.

"Yeah," said Marvin, moving the cursor down to the entry for Mr. Peters. "He can't even find his own room, much less locate the bow in Mike's room and aim it at anyone." Marvin put an X into Mr. Peters's "opportunity" column. Then he crossed out all the old people, the ones who couldn't have handled the bow.

"Now let's see if we can eliminate the ones with no motive," Marvin said.

"Everybody on the list had a motive. Nobody liked Leroy," Mike said.

"Not everybody," Marvin answered. "Most of the new regime staff had no ax to grind with him. That we know of."

"Nurse Helen was fooling around with him," Mike said. "I don't think she had a motive."

201

"No. She didn't even think he could hit anyone," Marvin said.

"Love is blind," Carrie said.

"Besides," Mike said, "she's a nurse. She's bound to the hypocritical oath."

"That's Hippocratic Oath," Carrie said. "And nurses don't take it. Only doctors."

"Whatever. How about the guys Leroy replaced when the new regime fired everybody?" he asked. "They're not even on our list."

"They'd be more likely to go after Bates for firing them," Marvin said. "But only the current staff would have known that you had that archery set. The old regime wouldn't."

"Do we know who did and who didn't?" Carrie asked. "Among the new regime?"

"No," Marvin said. "Loretta and Bates knew. But we don't know who else they told."

"Which means everyone not crossed off on the list might have had the means," Mike said.

"But how many of them could have known the bow and arrow were in your closet?" Marvin asked.

"It wasn't in my closet. I left it on the chair just inside my door."

"Was the door open?"

"Yes."

"That's significant, Mike," Marvin said. "Anybody could have seen it there. Who else can we eliminate?"

"Can we eliminate the ones who are just too nice?" Carrie said.

"How do we know that?" Marvin said. "Anyone can be pushed too far."

"Okay," Mike said. "Instead of crossing them off, maybe we

should just add a probability factor to your database of suspects."

"What's a probability factor?" Carrie asked.

"A numerical value that weighs which ones are more or less
likely to have done it," Mike said.

"How do you know about that?"

"I used to work for a statistician."

"What? Mowing his lawn?"

"No. I was his caddy."

"Instead of a factor, why don't we just move the likely ones
to the top of the list?" Carrie asked.

"Same thing," Mike said.

"We have to do something like that," Marvin said. "Otherwise
there won't be time to investigate everyone on this list. Now,
who can we move to the bottom?"

"The ones we think did it," Mike said. "Because none of
them did it. The *Perry Mason* syndrome."

"It's lunchtime," Marvin said. "Let's go avail ourselves of the
sumptuous banquet they've prepared. Then we can return and
work on the list some more."

They left Marvin's room and headed for the dining hall.
Three old troupers, a tall guy with a cane, a short guy with a
walker, and a heavyset lady in a wheelchair, making their way
down the corridor, with yet another single purpose, a crime to
solve.

CHAPTER 36

After lunch, when Marvin, Mike, and Carrie finished organizing the database, they had a list of suspects in three categories: "Possible," "unlikely," and "no way." That was Mike's idea. They went down the lists of residents and staff one by one and used the "means," "motive," and "opportunity" checkboxes to assign a category to each person.

"How about Nurse Helen's husband?" Carrie asked.

"Put him on the 'no way' list," Mike said. "He's such a likely suspect that there's no way he could have done it. It's never the one you think it is."

"Oh, Mike," Carrie said.

"Besides, didn't Lawyer Epstein say the cops already questioned him, and he has an alibi?"

"Right, he did say that," Marvin said. "I'll move him to 'unlikely.' "

"Why not 'no way'?"

"I can't forget Nurse Helen's black eye. I'd bet her husband did it, and it wasn't about a faulty furnace, you can be sure. But Director Bates is a definite 'possible.' "

"Why's that?" Mike asked.

"Well, first, we all heard Leroy threaten to turn state's evidence on what's been happening here. Second, Bates knew you had the archery set, and third, he has experience with them."

When they had finished the complete list of suspects, the "possible" and "unlikely" categories had between them ten staff

204

members and five residents. Most of the residents were in the "no way" list. Many were bedridden, many had dementia, and most could not have handled the bow.

"Okay," Carrie said, "now what?"

"Well," Marvin said, "we have to interview the ones on the 'possible' list for sure."

"Bring them in and give them the third degree," Mike said.

"No," Marvin said. "That would just make most of them mad at us and scare off the real murderer. We have to be more subtle."

"What do you suggest?" Carrie asked.

"We can divide up the list of possible suspects, engage them one at a time in casual conversation, talk about the murder. Everybody's talking about it anyway. See if they reveal anything and find out if they know anything about archery. I'll start with Mr. Peters."

"But we already agreed that he couldn't have done it," Carrie said referring to her lists. "He's on the 'no way' list."

"But he knew about the archery set. I want to find out if he told anyone. I'll go see him now. Then I'll meet you for supper. We can figure out who does what then."

They all left Marvin's room and went their own ways. Marvin walked down to Mr. Peters's room and knocked.

"Come in, Mr. Bradley."

Marvin went in the small room and moved a pile of clothing aside on the sofa to make a place to sit. "How'd you know it was me?"

"Everybody has their own way of walking and their own knock. What's up?"

Mr. Peters was sitting on his bed. The radio was playing, and he rocked from side to side listening to it. He reached over and turned it off.

"Mike showed you his archery set. Did you tell anyone about it?"

Marvin watched the blind man for any physical reactions that might suggest he knew something relevant. There were none.

"I told Bill Whitley. He and I used to hunt together during bow season. He never would shoot anything, though. Once he had an eight-point buck standing in a clearing about fifty feet away from us. He just lowered his bow and watched the buck until it ran off into the brush."

"Couldn't kill anything, huh?"

"He is a good and kind man. Best friend I ever had. He is my replacement for Bruno some days. Leads me to where I want to go. We didn't used to be able to communicate, much, though. He can't talk, and I can't read notes. So I would talk and he would listen. I'd talk about what I'd heard and he'd indicate yes and no by tapping my arm. Then we signed up for a course in sign language so he can talk to me now. It works really well."

"How does that work if you can't see?"

"I hold his hand while he fingerspells. It's not fast but it's easy." Mr. Peters put one of his hands in the other and demonstrated.

"Was Mr. Whitley good with the bow?"

"I don't know. I never saw him use it. I don't think he ever took an arrow out of the quiver."

"How many times did you go hunting?"

"At least once a year back in the day."

"How about you? Were you good with it?"

"I was pretty good. Yes, I was."

Marvin approached the next question with caution. "Could you use one now? Being blind and all."

"My hearing is pretty sharp. In the outdoors, though, we don't have good directional hearing. I can guess at what I'm hearing and how far away, but which direction isn't always that clear."

"How about indoors?"

"That's easier. If you know where you are, you can interpret the sound bouncing off the walls and make a good guess."

He swayed from side to side as blind people often do. "I think I know where you're going with this, Mr. Bradley, and I can appreciate you trying to help your grandson. I didn't kill Leroy. I doubt that I could have gotten the bow and arrow without waking Mr. Charles. But even if I could, I wouldn't take the chance of hurting someone else."

"Who else might you have hurt?"

"Leroy often went into the empty wing with a woman late at night. I've heard that. I don't sleep well. I wouldn't want to hurt Nurse Helen or Loretta."

"Have you told anyone else about that?"

"No. None of my business."

Having established that Mr. Peters might have been able to handle the murder weapon, Marvin now asked about motive. "Would you have shot Leroy if you could?"

"After what happened to Bill's cat, and me thinking that's what happened to Bruno, too, the answer is yes. If I could have. But I didn't."

"Did the cops question you?"

Peters laughed. "Briefly. They figured a blind man couldn't have done it. They questioned Bill, too. I was there. But when he couldn't talk, they figured he was senile. He let them believe it. By the time they got to us, they were tired from questioning so many blithering old people that they were ready to pin it on anyone else."

"And so they did. You say you don't sleep well and your hearing is good. Did you hear anything the night Leroy was killed?"

Arnie Peters hesitated. He rocked from side to side a bit.

Then he said, "Nothing that would shed light on what you want to know, Mr. Bradley. Nothing like that at all."

"But anything you heard might help even if it doesn't seem relevant to you."

Peters shook his head, reached over, and turned the radio on again, indicating that the conversation was over.

Marvin went out into the hallway and stopped at Whitley's room. He wasn't there. Marvin went in to leave him a note asking Whitley to come see him. Tabitha, Whitley's kitten, was asleep on the bed. She came awake when Marvin went in. He reached down to pet her, and she hissed and scratched his hand. Marvin pulled his hand back. He wrote the note and left it on the desk. Then he went to his own room to wash his injury.

He was in his bathroom washing the scratch with antiseptic soap when Whitley tapped on his doorframe. Marvin bandaged his hand to stop the bleeding. The blood thinner he took to prevent another stroke kept his blood from clotting properly.

"Come in, Mr. Whitley. Sit down, please."

Whitley sat in the recliner and Marvin sat on the bed. Whitley had his notepad and pencil with him.

"Mr. Peters told me about the sign language. I think I'd like to learn that, too, so you can talk to me without the notepad."

Whitley smiled and scribbled a note:

I can teach you. Only use finger spelling.

"What's finger spelling?"

Each letter has a sign.

"That should be easy enough. Only twenty-six signs to learn."

Ten numbers.

"Oh, yeah. Anyway I want to talk about Mike's archery set. Did you know he had it?"

Whitley nodded.

"Did you ever get to see it when Mike was showing it around?"

Whitley shook his head no.

"Okay. I'm trying to assemble a list of people here who know archery and knew about Mike's bow and arrows. Not that I'm trying to accuse anyone of anything. Just helping the lawyer by showing that more people than my grandson would have had access to the set, could have used it, and didn't like Leroy. Please don't take this the wrong way."

Marvin didn't like deceiving Whitley about his intentions, but desperate times call for desperate measures.

Whitley smiled and scribbled:

Add me to list. Anything to help.

"You used to go bow hunting with Mr. Peters?"

Whitley nodded and wrote:

Never shot anything but targets. Your hand?

"It's nothing. It got scratched."

Tabitha? She doesn't like tall men.

Whitley left, and Marvin's cell phone rang. Lawyer Epstein was calling.

"Freddie was indicted this morning. The judge set bail at one hundred thousand dollars. A ten percent bond will get him out."

"Don't need a bond. I can put up my house. The county assessed it to be at least that and it's paid for. Can you arrange the paperwork?"

"You understand, Mr. Bradley, if Freddie skips town, you'll lose your house?"

"I understand, Mr. Epstein. I trust him more than anyone in the world. Now, can you do the paperwork?"

"Can do, Mr. Bradley. My law clerk will bring the papers over later today. Sign them so the clerk can take them to the courthouse and file them right away. Freddie will be out by this evening, tomorrow morning at the latest."

"You can do it that fast?"

"It's a small town, Mr. Bradley. Everybody knows everybody. I'll call the judge right away, and he'll have it all set up by the time the papers arrive."

CHAPTER 37

At supper, Marvin, Mike, and Carrie sat together as usual. The fare tonight was spaghetti and meatballs with garlic bread on the side. Mike rolled his spaghetti up on his fork and looked at it.

"I don't know whether to eat it or go fishing with it," he said.

"Eat it," Carrie said. "No self-respecting fish would bite on it."

"And these meatballs. Billiards, anyone?"

"Don't forget the garlic bread. Now I know why vampires don't like garlic."

"When's the trial?" Mike asked.

"I haven't heard," Marvin said. "Freddie is out on bail and spends all his time with Lawyer Epstein working on his defense."

"I should help them with the case," Mike said. "I know a lot about courtroom procedure."

"Here it comes," Carrie said. "From what?"

"*Perry Mason, Law & Order, Anatomy of a Murder.* You name it, I saw it."

"Good grief."

"Okay, you two," Marvin said. "There's serious stuff to discuss. I talked to Mr. Peters and Mr. Whitley this afternoon."

"Mr. Whitley couldn't kill anybody," Carrie said. "He's too nice. He got this adorable kitten to replace Toby. No cat-lover could commit murder."

"Adorable?" Marvin said. "See these scratches?" He held up

his hand and pulled the bandage back. "The kitten did it. Hissed at me and scratched me when I went in."

"It probably doesn't like you," Mike said. "I get along with it just fine. Curls up in my lap, purrs, and goes to sleep. But that's because I'm a cat whisperer."

"Is that from when you worked for a veterinarian?" Carrie asked.

"No."

"Then who did you used to work for to learn about cats?"

"Nobody. It just comes natural. Why would you ask that?"

"Just a wild guess." She shook her head.

"Anyway," Marvin said, "Whitley admitted that he knows archery and knew Mike had the set."

"So, what's next?" Carrie asked. "Do we start grilling all our suspects?"

"Let's try our interrogation strategy on Mrs. Collins over there. See if we come up with anything. She's on the 'possible' list. Listen in while I talk to her."

He slid his chair over next to Elsie Collins at the next table. She was a "possible" because she was ambulatory and seemed to have all her faculties about her. No one knew why she was in a nursing home in the first place. But she wasn't very popular and ate most of her meals alone.

Marvin said, "Mrs. Collins—"

"That's Miss Collins," she said. "But call me Elsie." She batted her dark false eyelashes at him.

"I'm sorry, Elsie, of course." Marvin recalled reading her admissions records. She was indeed an old maid. "We've been talking about the murder of Leroy Parker."

"Who hasn't?" said Elsie.

"Why do you suppose the killer used a bow and arrow? You never hear of that happening."

Elsie gave him a peculiar look as if she couldn't understand why he'd ask such a question. "Well, let's see, Mr. Bradley. It's quiet, it's lethal, and there was one within reach. Other than that I can't imagine."

"But who knew it was in there in Mr. Charles's room?"

"I thought everybody knew."

"Did you know?" Marvin asked.

"No. But nobody ever tells me anything. But everybody else knew. I don't know why they leave me out of everything."

Marvin looked over at Mike and Carrie. Mike held his hand over his mouth, was looking away, and his shoulders were bobbing up and down. Marvin suppressed his own need to laugh. "Well, we've been kicking this around. If you wanted to do away with someone, and a bow and arrow was handy, would you use it?"

"Probably not. I'm more the chain saw kind. Or a hatchet or machete. Lizzie Borden . . . not Maid Marian." She started to giggle hysterically.

Mike made a muffled snort. Marvin looked over. Carrie was shushing Mike.

"Did you hear anything that night?" Marvin asked.

"Goodness, gracious, no. I was dead to the world. If I don't get at least eight hours of sleep every night, it shows in my face and my natural beauty is affected."

Mike made a stifled choking noise and fought to keep from laughing out loud. When Elsie looked over at him, he broke into a fit of phony coughing to cover the laughter.

"Are you okay, Mr. Charles?" Elsie asked.

"Oh, he's fine," Carrie said and pounded Mike's back.

"It's my bronical tubes," Mike said.

"That's bronchial, Mike," Carrie said.

"Whatever."

"Thank you, Elsie," Marvin said. He slid his chair back to the table with Mike and Carrie.

"You heard that. Did we learn anything?"

"We learned why she's still an old maid," Mike said.

"Why?" said Carrie. "Because she must've used a hatchet on her boyfriends?"

Mike snorted. "No. Because she looks like a circus puppet and has a voice like BBs on a cookie sheet. And we always wondered what she's doing in a nursing home. Now we know."

"Why?" Carrie asked.

"Because the loony bin wouldn't take her."

"Did we learn anything about our interrogation approach is what I meant," Marvin said.

"It doesn't work."

"Why not, Mike?"

"Because most of the residents here are as goofy as that one." He shook his head from side to side.

"What about staff?"

Mike put his arms on the table, leaned forward, and got serious. "I don't think it was staff, Marvin. None of them has the backbone to do something like murder. I think it was a resident getting even for the abuse. I'm serious about that. Let's not waste our time on staff."

"You might be right, Mike. Except for Bates and Loretta."

"But neither one of them would open up to us. Particularly if they're feeling guilty. If it was one of them, we'll have to learn it some other way."

Just then a young man came into the dining hall carrying an armful of envelopes. He went from table to table handing them out. He came over to their table.

"What are your names, please?"

"Who wants to know?" Mike said.

"I work for the clerk of the court. I have subpoenas. You can either tell me who you are, or I can get someone on the staff to identify you. So unless you think you can outrun me, which I doubt, you will be served today."

Mike said, "Whatever you serve us can't be any worse than the slop the kitchen serves us."

Marvin said, "I'm Bradley, this is Mr. Charles, and the lady is Mrs. Fenway."

The young man gave them each an envelope with their name on it and then he moved on to the next table.

Marvin opened his envelope. "We've been summoned to appear in court in Freddie's trial. As witnesses for the prosecution."

"They sure don't waste time," Mike said.

Chapter 38

The trial was due to start two weeks later. Lawyer Epstein had asked for an early trial date. He told them he had his strategy mapped out and didn't want the process to take any longer than it had to.

Freddie visited Marvin when he could, but he was busy working with Epstein. He didn't discuss much of the case with Marvin and his friends except to say that he was confident he'd be found not guilty. But the district attorney, Harvey Billings, was just as confident he'd get a conviction. At least that's what he said on the evening news.

Billings had deposed all the residents who had been in the dining room the day Freddie threatened to kill Leroy. He had them brought into the dayroom one at a time.

Epstein had instructed Marvin and the others to answer only the questions that Billings asked and not volunteer any information, particularly about the files Marvin had collected from the main computer.

"We don't want to tip our hand," he said.

In the deposition, Billings asked Marvin only one question.

"Did you hear your grandson threaten to kill the deceased?"

"I did."

That was it. Carrie and Mike reported that Billings asked them the same question and nothing else. Marvin told Epstein later, "If that's all he asks us, I don't know how we can be of any help."

"He'll ask more than that. So will I on cross-examination. Don't worry."

"Is this trial going to get a lot of media attention?" Marvin asked.

"The judge ruled in favor of a pretrial motion by the press to allow TV cameras in the courtroom. You'll all be TV stars."

Mike said, "Maybe we'll get our own reality show. I can see it now. Old Fogey Survivor. Anyone still awake at the end of the contest wins a year's supply of Metamucil."

CHAPTER 39

On the morning of the trial, the shuttle bus picked up all the residents who were to testify and any others who wanted to attend the trial as spectators. During the ride, the talk was all about the trial.

"Mr. Bradley," asked one of the ladies, "how is it looking for your grandson?"

"Well, he's in good hands. Lawyer Epstein seems to know what he's doing. He said the prosecution doesn't have a strong case."

"I wish we were on the jury," she said. "We'd let him off the hook."

"I wish you were, too."

They drove past the street where Marvin's house was. He watched out the window to get a glimpse of his house two blocks away.

Another lady said, "But they're going to ask us all whether we heard your grandson threaten Mr. Parker's life. And we did. What should we do?"

Marvin turned away from the bus's window and faced them. "Tell the truth. We aren't denying that."

A little lady in the back asked, "Did they tell you what we're having for lunch?"

Marvin smiled. "No, ma'am, they didn't. But I'm sure it will be good."

"I understand that lawyers and judges eat pretty good. Maybe we'll get what they get."

The bus pulled up in front of the courthouse and stopped. The driver opened the doors for those who could walk, and then came around to the side to operate the wheelchair lift. One by one, the elderly people got off the bus and went into the courthouse.

It took a while for all of them to get through the metal detector at the building's entrance. The ones in wheelchairs had to sit in a wooden chair that two beefy guards lifted and carried through. Carrie was the first in line. When they lifted her out of the wheelchair, she looked at one of them and said, "Easy with that hand, big fellow. Maybe a little lower?"

The whole room laughed. The guard blushed. Huffing and puffing, they wedged her through the metal detector, and the alarm went off. They looked around wondering how they were going to search this heavy, one-legged woman. Then Mike called out, "Hey, copper, it might work better if you took your gun off."

The guard blushed again. They both had to remove not only their guns, but their badges and utility belts, too.

Then Mike said, "They're disarmed. Let's rush 'em."

More laughter. It took a while to get all the folks with wheelchairs, walkers, and canes through the metal detector. Many of the residents had to be scanned with the wand because they had metal implants in their legs and arms. Elsie Collins went through, and her jewelry set off the alarm.

"Take off your jewelry, please," the guard said.

"Aren't you going to do a full body scan?" she asked.

They eventually all got past the security checkpoint and filed into the courtroom one by one. Those not in wheelchairs took seats in the gallery's rows of hardwood benches. The wheelchair occupants sat side by side at the back of the room.

Court convened, the clerk declared court to be in session,

and the judge entered from his chambers and took the bench. He was in his early forties, clean shaven and with short hair and a receding hairline. His name was Judge Roy Stauffer. He declared the court in session.

"Bring in the jury," he said. The jury filed in and took their seats in the jury box. The clerk swore in the jury and read the charges.

Marvin looked the jury up and down to see if he knew any of them. He didn't. The jury selection process would have eliminated anyone with close ties to the defendant.

He looked at each juror, hoping to see the kinds of people who would be sympathetic to the problems and challenges of the elderly. No one on the jury was much past sixty as near as he could tell. The ratio of men to women was about equal. They were all dressed as if to go to church, so he couldn't tell much about them individually from their appearances, whether they were employed, whether any of them were professional people, laborers, white collar, blue collar, homemakers, store clerks, anything. He found nothing in how the jurors looked that was encouraging. Or discouraging.

After preliminary motions by both sides, Epstein addressed the court.

"Your honor, we have a number of elderly people here under subpoena. Many of them have health and personal issues and are not able to sit and wait for long periods of time. In their depositions, they were all asked the same question, did they hear the defendant threaten the deceased. Rather than put them through all that, I propose to stipulate, with qualifications, that my client did indeed make such a threat. If the prosecution has no objections, of course."

Billings stood and faced the court. "That will depend upon the qualifications."

"We will stipulate that Mr. Bradley, the defendant, told Mr.

Parker, the deceased, that if Mr. Parker did harm to Mr. Bradley's grandfather, then Mr. Bradley, the defendant, would kill Mr. Parker. Since all these witnesses are here to testify only to that, I suggest we save time and their comfort by sending them home."

"Does the prosecution agree?" Judge Stauffer asked.

"We do, your honor," Billings said, "with these exceptions. I will call to the witness stand the defendant's grandfather, Mr. Marvin Bradley, a resident, Mr. Mike Charles, and another resident, Mrs. Carrie Fenway."

"I don't see the need for that," Epstein said. "Their answer to the question will be the same as the others."

"I have other questions to ask them," Billings said.

"Objection, your honor? The defense has no knowledge of other evidence that these witnesses might bring to bear on the prosecution's case."

"They have knowledge specific to the defendant's motive, your honor. They not only know that the defendant threatened the deceased, but we have reason to believe that they know why."

"My objection stands, your honor. The prosecution did not apprise us of this strategy."

The judge looked back and forth at the two lawyers. Then he said, "Will the three witnesses just named please stand so I can see you."

Marvin and Mike stood holding onto the back of the bench in front of them.

"Where's the third one?" the judge asked.

"I'm here," Carrie said. "I'd stand if I could."

"Very well. Are the three of you willing and able to sit here while the trial proceeds until it's time for your testimony?"

"Maybe if we can go to the bathroom from time to time," Mike answered.

"That will be allowed."

Carrie said, "They told us lunch would be served. If that's true, I want to stay. Besides, it's warmer in here than it is at the nursing home."

"Very well. I'm going to overrule your objection, Mr. Epstein. Later, if you need a continuance to deal with any unexpected evidence, I'll be lenient. Now let's take a break while the others who want to leave are taken out of the courtroom."

A voice from the back said, "What about lunch?"

"You can all stay for lunch if you want," the judge said, smiling. "Court's in recess for ten minutes." He stood and went into his chambers. Marvin and Mike came over to Epstein.

"What do you suppose Billings is going to ask us?" Marvin asked.

"Don't worry about it. I wanted it to go this way. I want you to testify so I can ask you about things that I hope Billings doesn't know. But I wanted Billings to think I was against it. If he hadn't asked that you stay, I would have."

"What's the strategy?" Mike asked.

"Reasonable doubt. Just answer all the questions honestly, his and mine, and don't worry about any of them. It might seem like I'm casting suspicion onto you. But that's nothing to worry about. It's part of my defense strategy."

After ten minutes, the clerk declared the court in session and the judge returned to the bench.

"I see most of you stayed," he said. "I don't know whether that speaks well for our food or ill for the nursing home's kitchen. Mr. Billings, you may proceed with your opening statement."

Billings took the floor.

"Ladies and gentlemen of the jury, the prosecution intends to prove that on the morning of January twenty-four, this year, the defendant, Mr. Frederick Marvin Bradley, slipped unseen onto

the premises of the Orchard Hills Nursing Home, took a bow
and arrow from the room of one of the residents, and used it to
murder Mr. Leroy Parker. We will prove that he had access to
the weapon, that earlier that day he had threatened Mr. Parker's
life, and that his fingerprints and only his fingerprints were on
the bow in question, the murder weapon."

He returned to his seat with a smug, superior look on his
face. The judge then called on Lawyer Epstein, who took the
floor.

"Ladies and gentlemen of the jury. Welcome to the courtroom.
I hope you enjoy lunch today as provided by the court. I know
all these elderly spectators will."

The gallery laughed.

"Let me begin by telling you that every single fact that Mr.
Billings just told you is true."

A few gasps came from the gallery.

"That's right. The facts are true. But not the prosecution's
conclusion. Only the facts. My client, Mr. Bradley was there
that night, he had access to the murder weapon, he even held it
in his hand, and he did indeed have words with the deceased
earlier that same day during which he told Mr. Parker in no
uncertain terms that if Mr. Parker harmed my client's grandfather, my client would kill him. All those things are true."

He paused for dramatic effect. The jury and spectators looked
at one another. Then he continued.

"Mr. Billings, in a rare moment of lucid vision, got most of it
right. Got that? Mr. Billings is an honest man. He would not
tell you something he knew to be false. And he will not during
the conduct of these proceedings. Neither will I."

He waited for what he had said to sink in.

"That's right, he got it right. All except for one thing. He is
mistaken when he concludes that the evidence he brings before
you proves beyond a reasonable doubt that my client killed Mr.

Parker. Mind you, he believes it. He would not say it if he didn't believe it. But he is mistaken. My client did not kill Mr. Parker."

Another pause. Lawyer Epstein paced the length of the jury box.

"You see, first, all the evidence that the prosecution will produce is circumstantial. That means the events Mr. Billings will place in evidence did indeed happen, but they don't prove anything. He has no eye-witness testimony and no compelling forensic evidence to connect my client to this crime. Furthermore, Mr. Bradley is not the only likely suspect in this matter."

He looked from one juror to the next. Every eye in the room was on him now, and no one made a sound.

"We will produce evidence that proves that virtually all the residents at Orchard Hills Nursing Home and many of the staff had motivation to see Mr. Parker removed from their lives and that many of them had the means and the opportunity.

"The police chose Mr. Bradley from this large list of likely suspects because of one piece of evidence. His fingerprints were on the bow. We will not only explain that to your satisfaction, but we will also prove that those fingerprints could not have been left during its use in shooting anyone or anything."

He paced up and down in front of the jury.

"Your responsibility here is justice. The prosecution must prove their case beyond any reasonable doubt. We, the defense, don't have to prove anything. Our whole case is based on the fact that the prosecution will not prove anything other than that the defendant could have and might have done the crime. They will not prove that he did it, and, in the absence of such proof, you must acquit him and send him home. It's called 'reasonable doubt,' and we use it to prevent zealous prosecutors from convicting innocent defendants. 'Reasonable doubt.' Keep that in mind throughout these proceedings."

He walked over to his desk, put his hands on the top, and gazed at Freddie.

"It's a good thing that we are not required to prove that the defendant did not do it because we can't. So, what we will do is prove that a nursing home full of people could and might have just as likely killed Leroy Parker."

He walked to his table, picked up a bottle of water, and drank from it. Then he returned to his position in front of the jury.

"Ladies and gentlemen of the jury, please take a look at the gallery of spectators we have here. What would you say is the average age out there? Eighty-five? Older? Those people are the forgotten, neglected treasures of society. They are, however, if we are lucky enough to live that long, your future, my future, the judge's future and, yes, even the prosecuting attorney's future. We should respect, honor, and venerate them for what they represent. We should care for them and keep them well and comfortable in their final years. Our parents took care of us, many of us for over twenty years as we grew to adulthood. We owe them at least that much in return when the end of their lives approaches."

He waited while the jury looked at the old folks in the gallery.

"But do we? No. Instead, we shuffle them off to nursing homes and transfer our responsibility to others, to professional health care workers, people whose very job is to care for our unwanted, inconvenient old people. Then we forget about them as we go about our own daily lives, tending to our own business, enjoying ourselves, reaping the results of the lifetimes of love and hard work that these old people put in solely for our benefit."

He took another drink of water, then continued.

"What am I getting at? Just this. Leroy Parker was one of those trusted professionals in whose care we place our old people. But he didn't care for them. We will prove that he abused them, threatened them, and stole from them. And someone killed him for it, which some would say was just deserts for an evil person, would say that the act was performed in service to this gallery of old people, would say that he needed to be removed from a position in which he could frighten, torture, and even kill the helpless old folks under his care."

He waited for a moment while the jury and spectators took full measure of what he had just said.

"The law doesn't allow citizens to administer such remedies, even when they are just, and sometimes even necessary, when no other option is available. The law doesn't permit it. Even so, someone unlawfully shot Leroy Parker with a bow and arrow. And most of the people in that gallery had motive, means, and opportunity, as much or more so than the defendant."

When he had finished, the gallery broke out in applause, whistling, cheering. Judge Stauffer gaveled the courtroom to order.

"If it wasn't time to break for lunch, I'd clear the courtroom," he said. "But I don't expect many of you to hang around after that so it won't be necessary. Court recessed until one thirty."

CHAPTER 40

Everyone filed out of the courtroom. Marvin said, "Who's up for going to a restaurant?"

"They're feeding us here," Mike said. "Why pay for a restaurant?"

"Because we don't get out that often. My treat."

"What? Did you get a rebate from Medicare?"

"No, I picked up some dough when I went to the house. Come on. Who wants a steak? There's a steakhouse across the street. We can discuss the trial there without a lot of other people around."

"Count me in," Mike said.

"Me, too," Carrie said. "What about Freddie and Lawyer Epstein?"

"They'll have lunch in the courthouse. They have things to talk over privately."

"Are we invited?" asked Mr. Peters. "Bill's my eyes and I'm his voice, so we come as a package deal."

Whitley grinned and nodded.

"Of course you're invited," Marvin said.

They made their way across the street and went into the steakhouse. A waiter seated them at a table for five and said, "Hi. I'm Brian. I'll be your server today."

"Hi, Brian. I'm Mike. I'll be your customer today."

"Hi, Mike. Can I get you folks something from the bar?"

"Do I get a cocktail, too?" Carrie asked.

"If you want, but don't forget, you have to testify."

"Oh, yeah, darn it. Diet cola, please. Did you remember your teeth?"

Marvin flashed her his toothy smile.

"Can I borrow them when you're done with them?" Mike asked.

Everybody broke into laughter, and the waiter laughed so hard he spilled water on Mr. Peters.

"What was that, what was that?" said the blind man. "Did I wet myself without knowing it?"

The laughter got louder, and the waiter walked away.

"I think Brian just wet himself," Mike said.

They laughed again. When they were finally under control, Brian came back and took their drink orders.

"What did you think of Lawyer Epstein's opening statement?" Carrie addressed her question to the group. Everyone except Marvin gave it a big okay.

Then Marvin spoke. "I didn't like it."

"Why not?" they asked.

"He obviously intends to get Freddie off on a strategy of reasonable doubt, and I don't like that."

"What's the difference?" Mike said. "He'll be off."

"I want him cleared beyond any doubt, reasonable or otherwise."

Brian returned with their drinks and said, "Now don't anybody say any more funny things until I get these drinks served. I don't want to spill anything else."

He gave them their drinks, took their food orders, and returned to the kitchen.

Mr. Whitley tugged on Mr. Peters's sleeve. Mr. Peters took his hand and said, "Bill wants to speak."

"Tell him to take his meds," Mike said. "Maybe he will in a year or two."

Nobody laughed and Carrie said, "Mike, stop it. What is it, Mr. Whitley?"

Peters held Whitley's hand while he fingerspelled. Peters spoke the words slowly.

"Could Freddie be convicted?"

Marvin said, "Lawyer Epstein doesn't think so. But he told Freddie you can't ever tell what a jury will do. We'll have to watch and see how the trial goes."

"He ought to just get the guilty party to stand up in court and confess like on *Perry Mason*," Mike said. "That would get Freddie off scot-free. But nobody ever listens to me."

After a while, Brian returned with the plates of food. He served them one at a time.

"Man, this is great," Mike said. "I wonder what the old people are eating today."

"Warmed-over ravioli," Carrie said.

They ate without saying much more, enjoying the feast.

Then Mike started in. "You know, this steak is great. If God meant for man to be vegetarians, He wouldn't have made animals out of meat."

About then Brian stopped by the table to check on them. "Is everything okay?"

"My elbow hurts," Mike said.

"Oh, I'm sorry, sir. Did you hit it on something here?"

"No, they operated on it last year."

"I don't understand, sir. What does that have to do with here?"

"Nothing. You asked if everything was okay. My elbow hurts."

Brian looked a little confused. He walked away.

"You just can't help yourself, can you?" Carrie said.

When they were finished eating lunch, Brian came back.

"Any dessert? Coffee?"

They all asked for coffee.

229

"Five coffees, coming up. Remember, my name is Brian if you want anything else."

Mike said, "What's your name if we don't want anything else?"

Brian just looked at him, then went to get the coffee. Carrie shook her head.

When Brian brought the coffee he said, "Separate checks?"

Mike said, "Put it on one check and give it to that guy over there." He pointed to a stranger sitting at a table across the room.

Marvin said, "One check. I'll take it."

Brian gave him the check and stood by.

"Can't I help you with that, Marvin?" Mike said.

"You can pay the tip if you want."

"Sure. Will two dollars be enough?"

Brian looked at the ceiling.

"Forget it, Mike. I've got it," Marvin said.

He took a hundred dollar bill and a ten out of his wallet and gave it and the check to Brian. "Keep the rest," he said.

"Thank you, sir. Thank you very much."

Brian helped Mike out of the chair.

"Have a good one," he said.

"I used to," Mike said and pulled himself up. Carrie punched him in the arm, and he almost fell over.

They got their coats, left the restaurant, and headed back to the courthouse.

CHAPTER 41

The bailiff announced that court was in session. Judge Stauffer came in and called the courtroom to order. The jury returned from the jury room and took their seats. This was it. Testimony was about to begin.

"Mr. Billings," Judge Stauffer said, "call your first witness."

Billings called Loretta Swann. The bailiff swore her in, and she took a seat in the witness stand.

Billings greeted her and said, "Miss Swann, please tell us in your own words what happened on the morning of January twenty-four."

Loretta had a concerned look on her face, her eyebrows lowered, her mouth tightened, her eyes darting about the courtroom, but she managed to answer. "I went to the vacant wing at about five in the morning. I found Leroy, Mr. Parker, lying on the floor with something stuck in his back. I called the medical department, and the night nurse came and said Leroy was dead. Then we called the police."

"Prior to that time, did you witness an argument between the deceased and the defendant?"

Loretta squared away her shoulders and said, "Yes. In the dining hall. Mr. Bradley, the defendant, said he'd kill Leroy, er, Mr. Parker."

"Thank you, Miss Swann. Your witness."

Lawyer Epstein began his cross-examination. "Miss Swann, why were you at the nursing home at five in the morning on

231

January twenty-four?"

Loretta hesitated. "I was falling behind in my filing. I came in early."

Epstein went straight to the chase. "Why were you in the vacant wing at that time?"

She was ready for him. "I needed supplies. That's where we keep them."

"Miss Swann, what was your relationship with Mr. Parker?"

Loretta fidgeted around. "We were friends and co-workers."

"Were you in a romantic relationship with Mr. Parker?"

"No, I was not."

"And had you not recently discovered that he was cheating on you?"

"How dare you? That isn't true!"

"And I suggest that maybe you were there in the empty wing with Mr. Charles's bow and arrow in order to kill Mr. Parker. Isn't that true?"

"No, it is not!"

"No further questions. Thank you."

Loretta left the witness stand and stomped across the hardwood floor, eyes down, shoulders forward. She brushed past the uniformed guard at the back of the room and pushed the tall swinging doors open with a loud bang.

Billings then called Detective Murray.

"Detective Murray, please tell us in your own words about the events of the morning of January twenty-four."

Murray testified that he had responded to an early morning call about a dead body at the nursing home.

"I found the body of Mr. Parker laying face down on the hallway floor with an arrow in his back."

He then testified that Loretta and Bates had pointed out Mike Charles as the owner of the archery set and told him about an argument between Leroy and Mike, Marvin, and Carrie.

"They also told me that Mr. Parker had been accosted in the dining hall the previous day by Mr. Frederick Bradley, the defendant."

He then testified that the fingerprints on the bow matched Freddie's, and they arrested him.

In cross-examination, Lawyer Epstein asked Detective Murray, "Prior to arresting the defendant, did you consider other suspects for this crime?"

"No sir, not once all the evidence was in."

"Did you ask the defendant why he was there that night?"

"Yes, he said that Mr. Parker had tried to harm his grandfather."

"Did you question anyone else as a potential suspect?"

"Well, yes, I did. Before I knew about the fingerprints."

"Whom did you question?"

"I questioned Mr. Mike Charles."

"Why did you question him?"

"The murder weapon belonged to him. We found it in his room."

"And why did you eliminate Mr. Charles as a suspect?"

"He's eighty-five years old, walks with a walker, and isn't strong enough to pull the bow."

"Given that, why did you bother questioning him in the first place?"

"We were told he had a falling out with the deceased."

"A falling out, eh? What was the nature of this falling out?"

"It wasn't clear, but after a run-in with Mr. Charles, Mr. Parker needed medical attention. The nurse told us he had several injuries and was temporarily blinded."

"And Mr. Charles did all that?"

"Apparently."

, "So, Detective Murray, you are telling us, are you not, that this small, frail, elderly gentleman who needs a walker to get around did all that to a man half his age and twice his size but that you eliminated him as a suspect because you don't think he was strong enough?"

"Yes."

The crowd muffled their laughter. The judge smiled, too.

Lawyer Epstein asked, "Did you question any other suspects?"

The detective said that he had questioned Nurse Helen's husband about his altercation with Leroy and that he found nothing about it to make him a suspect.

"Didn't you learn that Leroy was romantically involved with Crenshaw's wife, who is a nurse at the home?"

"No. No one told me about that."

"Did you question anyone else of interest?"

"If you mean did I have viable suspects other than the defendant, no."

Under Epstein's questioning, Murray testified how he learned about Marvin's nighttime encounter with Leroy and the shotgun and about Leroy's threat to expose Bates.

Murray told that he had learned of Leroy's threats to Bates about not taking the rap alone.

"Now, let me summarize what we've learned here so far. According to your testimony, you had six viable suspects."

Lawyer Epstein held up his fingers one at a time to enumerate the suspects.

"You had Miss Swann, who was jealous because the deceased was cheating on her. You had Mr. Charles, who had been in a scuffle with the deceased. You had Mr. Crenshaw, whose wife was involved with the deceased. You had Mr. Bates, who was worried about whatever the deceased was about to say. You had my client's grandfather, whose life the deceased had threatened and who had actually taken a shotgun to the deceased. A shotgun! And finally, you had my client, the defendant, who was concerned about his grandfather's safety and that of the other elderly residents. All these people had means, motive, and opportunity, yet you chose to consider only one of them, the defendant, as a viable suspect. Is that about it?"

Mike leaned over to Marvin and whispered, "Next he'll have the jury believing the judge did it."

The bailiff shushed them.

Detective Murray answered, "That's about it, Mr. Epstein. The defendant is the only one out of all those people who threatened to kill Mr. Parker and then left fingerprints on the murder weapon. That's usually enough for me."

"Thank you, Detective Murray. No further questions."

The judge called for a break. When court was in session again, the prosecutor called to the stand Dr. Winslow Atkins, the medical examiner, who testified about the morning in question.

"I took the body back to the lab, removed the arrow, and checked it for fingerprints. There were none."

"Later, did the police bring an archery set to you?"

"Yes. It was a quiver, a bow, and several arrows identical to the one I removed from the deceased's back."

"Did you test the archery set for fingerprints?"

"Yes, there was one set of prints on the bow. No others. They were later matched to the prints of the defendant's right hand."

"What did your examination of the body reveal?"

"Cuts and bruises all over his body. And, oh yes, he had urine on his shirt."

"Urine? What kind of urine?"

"We sent it to the lab. It was feline urine."

Billings sat down and Lawyer Epstein took the floor.

"Dr. Atkins, why do you suppose the arrow had no prints but the bow did? Doesn't that strike you as being unusual?"

"Not really. I don't know what's usual and what's unusual.

This is my first case of murder by bow and arrow."

"But if you had to guess, what would it be, given your status as an expert?"

"I just collect and report the evidence, Mr. Epstein. I don't make suppositions or draw conclusions. I leave that to you lawyers."

"Would you help us with a small demonstration, Dr. Atkins?"

"If I can."

Epstein took the bow from the evidence table and placed it on the floor in front of the witness stand.

"If you would please be so kind, step around and stand by the bow."

Dr. Atkins left the witness stand and stood there.

"Now, sir, please bend over and pick up the bow."

Dr. Atkins reached down and picked up the bow with his right hand.

"Now, where you are holding the bow in your right hand, is that about where you found the defendant's fingerprints?"

"Maybe an inch or two either way."

"Now, if you will, please pretend to shoot an arrow from the bow as if you had one."

Dr. Atkins moved the bow to his left hand.

"No, Dr. Atkins, please keep the bow in your right hand."

"But I'm right-handed. I'd hold the bow with my left and pull the string with my right."

"Yes, of course. You are right-handed. Do you know whether the defendant is right-handed?"

"No."

"Well, should we assume that since the prints on the bow were of his right hand that he is left-handed?"

"I suppose so."

"He is right-handed, like you, Dr. Atkins. But holding the bow in your right hand, please pull the string with your left."

Dr. Atkins held the bow with his right and lifted it in to shooting position.

"No, Dr. Atkins. Hold the bow in a way that would leave the prints you found."

"I can't do that and pull the string," Dr. Atkins said.

"Of course you can't, sir. Neither could the defendant. Please return to the witness stand."

When Dr. Atkins was back in the witness stand, Epstein asked him, "Dr. Atkins, given what we just did together, and thank you for your assistance, what do you think the fingerprints you found on the bow prove?"

"That the defendant held the bow in his right hand."

"Exactly. That sometime before the police found it in Mr. Charles's room, he held it. Is there any forensic evidence that he shot it?"

"No, sir."

"Thank you, Dr. Atkins. No further questions."

Court recessed for the day. Mike and Marvin approached Lawyer Epstein. Mike asked, "When will you reveal the real killer in court?" Mike asked.

Epstein smiled. "I don't think it will come to that."

Mike turned away and clumped his walker toward the exit. "This isn't how Perry Mason would have handled it," he said.

They boarded the bus, and Carrie said from the wheelchair lift, "I could have had that cocktail after all. I wasn't called up yet."

CHAPTER 42

When court convened the following morning, Billings called Carrie Fenway. She wheeled up to the witness stand and parked in front of it. The bailiff swore her in and said she could remain in her wheelchair. He undid the witness microphone from its holder and handed it to her.

Billings began his examination. "Mrs. Fenway, did you hear the defendant threaten Mr. Parker?"

"I'd call it more of a promise than a threat."

"Are you aware of an incident in which Mr. Parker was injured by Mr. Charles?"

"Aware? I was there."

"You were there? What was your role in the incident?"

"I had the hat pin."

The crowd laughed and the judge hit the gavel on his desk to quiet them down.

"Was the defendant's grandfather there, too?"

"Yes. He had a hickory cane and whacked Leroy with it."

More laughter.

"And what did Mr. Charles do?"

"He had the cattle prod. And the hand soap."

At this point the crowd laughed so hard that the judge pounded the gavel and called a five-minute recess. When they reconvened, Billings asked his last question.

"Would you say that given all that happened to Mr. Parker, that he had it in for the three of you and that the defendant felt

238

a need to protect you?"

"Objection, your honor. Calls for speculation."

"Sustained."

"I have no further questions."

Epstein came forward. "Mrs. Fenway, I understand that you like to keep lists of things."

"Yes, I do."

"During the days following the murder, did you make any lists?"

Carrie sat up with pride. "Yes. I made a list of all the people who could have murdered Leroy."

"And how many people were on that list?"

"After we eliminated a bunch of names, there were maybe six, seven names. Should I get it out?" She began to fumble in her purse, bumping the microphone into the arms of her wheelchair and making noises in the PA system.

"No, ma'am, that's not necessary. Did you offer to give the list to the police?"

"I never got the chance. They'd already arrested Marvin's grandson."

"Thank you, Mrs. Fenway. No further questions."

Billings took over again. "The state calls Mr. Marvin Bradley to the stand."

Marvin patted Carrie on the shoulder when they passed one another going to and from the witness stand. "Nice job, Carrie," he said.

Marvin was sworn in and took the witness stand. Billings said, "Your honor, I'd like to treat Mr. Bradley as a hostile witness."

Marvin said, "Why don't you wait and see if I'm going to be hostile?"

"Mr. Bradley," Judge Stauffer said, "It only means that the prosecutor can ask you leading questions."

"Well, I guess I don't mind that. But I'm not hostile. Ask away."

"We've heard mention here about a shotgun that belongs to you. Please tell the court in your own words about it."

"Well, it's a double-barreled twelve-gauge, break action, breech loader with a twenty-one-inch barrel, what they call a 'riot gun.' "

"Well, thank you for the description, but I was more interested in how you got it."

"I bought it in town at the hardware store."

"No sir, how did you get it to the nursing home?"

"My neighbor brought it to me."

"Why did you want a shotgun?"

"For protection from Leroy Parker."

"So you had reason to believe that Mr. Parker, the deceased, wanted to harm you?"

"That's right. He told me so."

"Did your grandson know that Mr. Parker had threatened you?"

"Yes."

"Thank you, sir. No further questions."

Lawyer Epstein took over.

"Mr. Bradley, did you have occasion to use the shotgun?"

"You mean shoot it?"

"No, did you use it to protect yourself?"

"Leroy came to kill me one night in my room. I chased him off with the shotgun."

"Do you know why Leroy came to kill you?"

"Because I was part of the team that set out to expose him and Director Bates in their scheme to kill off the resident population."

"Lies! Lies!" Oliver Bates yelled, standing up and shaking his fist. "Those are lies!"

"Shut up and sit down, Ollie!" Mike yelled out. The other residents began yelling, too.

The judge pounded the gavel. "Order! Order! Bailiff, seat that spectator. If he interrupts the proceedings again, take him into custody. Continue, Mr. Epstein."

"Those are serious charges, Mr. Bradley. How did you intend to prove them?"

"I have files of documents and videos that we've been collecting, including a video of Leroy coming to get me."

"Where are these files?"

"On my laptop."

"And where did you get them?"

"We made the videos ourselves with my camcorder. I got the documents from the computer."

At that bit of news, Oliver Bates got up from his seat and hurried out of the courtroom. He was gone before the next question was asked.

"So, it's safe to say that enough evidence exists to have had Mr. Parker arrested?"

"More than enough."

"And Mr. Bates?"

"Him, too. If you're going to arrest him, you better hurry. He just skedaddled out of here."

"Did your grandson know that the evidence would implicate Mr. Parker and Mr. Bates?"

"He did. He helped me correlate the data."

"So he would have no reason to murder anybody?"

"None at all."

"Thank you, Mr. Bradley. No further questions."

After a short recess the DA called Mike Charles. Mike came up to the witness stand and stood in front, gripping his walker while the bailiff swore him in. He went around to the side of the stand, let go of the walker, and rotated himself up into the witness chair by holding on to the rails. He adjusted the position of the microphone to put it close to him and blew into it several times, saying, "Testing, one, two," between each puff. Then, satisfied that everyone could hear him, he said into the microphone, "Okay, I'm ready."

Billings began the questioning. "Mr. Charles, it's been said here that you and your friends attacked and harmed Mr. Leroy Parker, the deceased. Is that true?"

"More or less."

"Why did you do that?"

"He caught me videotaping him hitting one of the old people. Leroy had been hitting them and I was trying to get evidence. I got it on video, and Leroy came after me."

"Tell us what happened next."

Mike sat forward and bounced up and down. "Well, he chased the three of us into the men's room."

"Who are the three of you?"

"Mr. Bradley, Mrs. Fenway, and me."

"Were Mrs. Fenway and Mr. Bradley involved in collecting your evidence?"

Mike spread his arms. "We were all trying to prove that Leroy was the one doing it."

Billings frowned. "Doing what? Leroy was the one doing what?"

"Hitting the old people! Weren't you right here when I just told you? Judge, don't we have a DA with a better memory?"

Judge Stauffer suppressed a smile. "No, Mr. Charles. Mr. Billings is all we have. Now please just answer the questions and hold the opinions for later. Proceed, Mr. Billings."

"Mr. Charles, what happened in the men's room after you and your friends went in there to hide?"

"We didn't go in to hide." Mike seemed exasperated. "Did I say we went in to hide? Judge, aren't you sure there isn't a law clerk here or a janitor or somebody with a better memory?"

"Just answer the question, Mr. Charles."

Mike made a pouring motion. "Well, I poured hand soap on the floor, and Leroy slipped in it and fell on his butt. Whop! I shocked him with my cattle prod. Marvin hit him on the head with his cane, and Carrie stuck him in the butt with her hat pin. You should've heard him holler."

The gallery laughed. The judge pounded the gavel and called for order.

"Mr. Charles, the police did not find a cattle prod when they searched the nursing home. Where is it?"

"Right there." Mike pointed to his walker standing on the floor next to the witness stand. "It's Velcro'd on."

"It's been there all along? You brought a cattle prod into the courtroom?"

Mike looked up at Judge Stauffer. "Judge, you need to look into your security here. They aren't too swift."

Judge Stauffer smiled. "I'll do that, Mr. Charles. Now please continue with your testimony."

"Well sir, we got out of there."

"Out of where?" Billings asked.

"Out of the bathroom! Where do you think? You know, young fellow, they have herbs and potions that improve your memory. We have them at the nursing home if you want some. Ginkgo and ginseng are real good for that."

"Mr. Charles, please tell us what happened next." Billings seemed to be losing his patience.

"We ran down the hall, and Leroy came after us. Well, we didn't actually run. We can't. Marvin uses a cane, and Carrie is in a wheelchair. I have a wheelchair, too, but mostly I use that walker right there. Unless I'm in a hurry. I didn't know I was going to be in a hurry that day, so I didn't have my wheelchair."

"Mr. Charles . . ."

"Sorry. Leroy can't run either. Well, he can't now 'cause he's dead. I mean he couldn't then because of what all we did to him. That and those ugly cowboy boots—"

"Sir . . ."

"Oops. Sorry. We split up, and Marvin and Carrie went somewhere, and I went in my room and set the booby trap."

"What booby trap?"

"I had it all ready to go. The others didn't know about it. I had a scrub bucket full of rocks and some nuts and bolts that I took from the tool shed and the bus garage. You know, they ought to clean that place up. It's a mess. Junk all over the place. And the bus. Now there's a real bucket of bolts. Needs a tune-up. If you ask me, it's the bus driver's job, but he doesn't do anything but drive the bus." He turned to the judge. "You know, Judge, there's a lot of folks on the county payroll who are shirking their duties."

Billings put his head in his hands. Epstein was laughing into his hand. Judge Stauffer said, "Mr. Charles, please try to stay on course and tell us about the bucket of bolts."

"Well, it's yellow. I think it used to be a school bus."

"No, Mr. Charles, the bucket with nuts, bolts, and rocks."

"Oh, yeah. I forgot. Sorry. I should take more of those herbs, myself." He looked around the room and laughed. "Anyway, I had nuts and bolts and rocks from the garden. I had all that in the bucket. I knew Leroy would be coming in there, so I opened the door a crack, stood on a chair, and put that bucket of bolts on the top of the door leaning against the wall."

"Wait a minute, Mr. Charles. We've heard testimony that you don't have the strength to pull a bow, yet you can lift a bucket of heavy items off the floor and onto the top of a door?"

"Adrenalin, sonny. You never know what you can do until you find yourself in danger. They have specials about that on the Health Channel. Or is it the History Channel?"

"Just proceed with your story."

"It isn't a story, son, it's the truth. Stories are when you make things up. I'm under oath, and I take that seriously."

"Very well. Please continue with your account of the events surrounding the bucket of bolts."

"The bus?"

"No, Mr. Charles, the real bucket. The one with nuts, bolts, and rocks. The one on your door."

"Oh, that. How do you know about that?"

Billings raised his voice. "You were telling us about it. You went in your room, stood on a chair, and put the bucket on top of the door. What happened next?"

"I got back away from the door. Leroy came busting in, and the bucket fell on his head. That put him down for a while."

More laughter. More gavel.

"What happened next?"

"I jumped over him and got him again with the cattle prod. Then me and Carrie and Marvin took off. Well, he came after us again. Sometime during the chase, he fell down the cellar stairs."

"How did that happen?"

"I'm not sure. It might have been the trip wire. He sure was accident-prone."

The crowd laughed even louder. The judge rapped.

"And what happened after the deceased fell down the cellar stairs?"

"It didn't stop him. Well, the stairs didn't stop him. The shelf of canned goods stopped him. But we hit the hallway again. He came up and after us, so we tricked him into Mr. Peters's room. Then, when the bulbs went off, it blinded the sonofa—, er, Leroy. That stopped him."

"Bulbs?"

"Flashbulbs. I keep all my flashbulbs in Mr. Peters's room."

"Why do you keep them there?"

"Because they don't provide us a place to keep our flash-bulbs."

"But why in Mr. Peters's room? Why not your room?"

"Because Mr. Peters is blind and they won't bother him when they go off."

"How did they go off?"

"Leroy turned on the switch."

"What switch?"

"The light switch. What switch do you think? I'm telling you, Judge, you better replace this guy."

At this point the gallery laughed uncontrollably. Judge Stauffer pounded the gavel.

"I will not have these outbursts," he said when everything got quiet. "Although the humor in the situation is not lost on me, we must have order. Now please control yourselves so I don't have to clear the courtroom. Ask your next question, Mr. Billings."

"Given all that you did to Mr. Parker, what did he do in retaliation?"

"Nothing for a while. I think he went and took a nap."

"Didn't he confront the three of you in the dining hall?"

"Oh, yeah. He told us he'd get us for that."

"Did the defendant learn about that threat?"

"I guess so. He came to see us and gave Leroy what for."

"Now, Mr. Charles, let's talk about your bow and arrow. Why did you have a bow and arrow in your room?"

"I already told you. They don't give us any other place to keep our stuff."

"Why a bow and arrow?"

"The same reason I have a cattle prod and flashbulbs. Protection."

"Where do you keep the bow and arrow?"

"Arrows, sonny, arrows. Not arrow. There's more than one. I keep them in my room leaning against the wall in the chair just inside my door."

"Could the bow and arrow, er, arrows be seen by anyone passing by?"

"No. Not anyone."

"Why not?"

"Mr. Peters is blind. He can't see anything. Neither, at the time, could Leroy very well. You know, what with the flashbulbs and all."

Billings sighed. "But anyone else passing by your room could see the bow and arrows out in plain sight."

"I suppose so."

"Thank you. Now let's talk about your employment history. According to your application at the nursing home, you've had about fifty different employers, all in different kinds of businesses, and all for very short periods of time."

Mike puffed up with pride. "I'm what you call a jack of all trades."

"Don't you consider it odd that a man would have so many different jobs in his lifetime?"

"Since I did, I don't think it's odd. What do you think?"

"Can't you hold down a job?"

"Doesn't seem to be a problem now that I'm retired."

Judge Stauffer interrupted. "Let's break for lunch. Court recessed until one P.M."

CHAPTER 43

After lunch, the judge called Mike back to the witness stand. Billings resumed his examination. "Mr. Charles, during the lunch break, I got a phone call from one of your former colleagues who saw you on television this morning, someone in Washington, DC, who has some interesting information about you."

"Where in Washington?" Mike asked, a tremor in his voice.

"Well, actually it's the Virginia suburbs." Billings voice got quieter and he spoke slowly. "Langley, Virginia. I assume you know where that is."

Mike's jaw took on a firm set and he spoke with clenched teeth. "Who was it?"

"I'm sorry. He didn't want his name mentioned in open court."

Mike got very still and stared at Billings for a moment. Billings went to speak further, and Mike held his hand up to silence him. Billings stopped short and seemed surprised at being cut off that way. Then Mike got a grim, hardened look on his face, turned to the judge, and said, "Chambers?"

"What's that, Mr. Charles?"

"Chambers, your honor. I need to speak to you in your chambers."

"What about?"

"We'll take that up in there. Until then, I have nothing further to say."

"I can compel you to testify, Mr. Charles."

"No, sir, you can't. You can tell me to testify, but you can't compel me to. There's a lot more at stake here than you and these lawyers realize, and I don't intend to discuss it in open court until I've discussed it with you in private. You can find me in contempt and lock me up if you want. I don't mind. I understand the food at the jail is better than the slop we get. And in jail I'd be safe. And warm."

The judge took a moment to consider what Mike had just said. "Maybe that won't be necessary, Mr. Charles. Bailiff, take the jury out. Lawyers, approach."

The lawyers went up to the bench. Marvin turned his new hearing aids up to full volume so he could hear what they said.

"Mr. Billings, what is the point of your current line of questioning?" the judge asked.

"Your honor, the caller suggested that prior to Mr. Charles's retirement, he worked for the government, that all his so-called employments were cover assignments, and that he was somehow involved in domestic intelligence activities."

"What is the relevance of such uncorroborated and anonymous speculation in this trial, Mr. Billings?"

"I intend to show that Mr. Charles, along with the defendant, the defendant's grandfather, and Mrs. Fenway conspired to murder Mr. Parker. That Mr. Charles, being a retired intelligence agent, facilitated it by making all the plans, by disabling the victim, and by providing the murder weapon, and that they recruited the defendant because none of them could handle the bow. We'll look into charging the three of them when this trial is over."

"That is quite a stretch, Mr. Billings. Mr. Epstein, again, aren't you going to object?"

"No, your honor. If I did, you might sustain the objection, and then I'd miss enjoying the show and watching Mr. Billings make a complete and utter fool of himself."

"Very well," the judge said, shaking his head. "Stand back."

The lawyers returned to their tables.

"Would the two attorneys please accompany Mr. Charles and me into my chambers?"

"No, your honor," Mike said. "Not them. Just you and me."

"That's highly irregular, Mr. Charles." He sat back against the wall, folded his hands in front of him, and waited a moment. Then, "But why not? Nothing else in this trial has been conventional. Come along, Mr. Charles. Court is in recess until we get this matter settled."

The judge retired to his chambers, and Mike followed behind with his walker.

Marvin and Carrie went to the defendant's table to talk with Lawyer Epstein and Freddie.

"What's that all about?" Marvin asked.

"I don't know," Epstein said. "I guess we'll find out when they return. But why would the judge do that? It's judicial misconduct and could be grounds for a mistrial. It'll certainly help if we have to appeal, however, so I have no complaints."

About then Mr. Whitley and Mr. Peters approached them. They had been in the gallery observing the trial. Mr. Whitley led Mr. Peters along by the arm. Mr. Peters whispered something to Epstein that the others couldn't hear. Epstein said, "Okay, sir, we can meet when court recesses today."

About then, the judge and Mike emerged from the judge's chambers. Court was declared in session and the judge addressed the court.

"Mr. Charles's testimony is over and he is dismissed. Bailiff, call the jury back in."

The jury filed back in and took their seats. The judge said, "Mr. Billings, call your next witness."

Billings said, "Your honor, Mr. Charles's testimony was to

form the basis for the balance of our case. Since we are not to complete his examination, and since Mr. Epstein will not be allowed to cross-examine him, I have no other choice. The prosecution rests."

Epstein walked to the podium.

"Your honor, I move for dismissal of all charges on the grounds that the prosecution has failed to meet its burden of proof."

"Motion denied. Court recessed until tomorrow morning when the defense can present its case."

CHAPTER 44

That night at supper, Mike was quiet. Marvin and Carrie tried to get him to tell them what went on in the judge's chambers.

"No. You're better off not knowing."

Marvin said, "My laptop and camcorder are missing from my room. And my shotgun, too."

"Three guesses who took them," Carrie said.

"Who?" the other two asked together.

"Bates. Who else? Did you see the look on his face when you testified that you had all those documents and videos? And how he scooted out right away? He wanted to get them before we came back."

"What good would that do him?" Marvin asked. "Lawyer Epstein and Freddie have copies."

"Yeah," Mike said. "But he doesn't know that. He probably thinks you had the only copy. And you can bet the main computer has been cleaned off by now, too."

"Look at him sitting over there watching us," Carrie said. "He must think he put one over on us."

Bates sat at his usual table with Loretta, but his attention was on the table where Marvin, Mike, and Carrie sat.

"I'd like to get the laptop back," Marvin said. "It's Freddie's. But it's probably locked in Bates's office."

"We'll get it," Mike said. "And the camcorder. I'll pick the lock to his office tonight."

"You can do that?" Carrie asked.

"Sure. I used to work for—"

"A locksmith?" Marvin and Carrie said together.

"You might put it that way," Mike answered with a smile. "Do you still have all those tools in your room, Marvin?"

"Yeah."

"I'll need a small flat-headed screwdriver and a heavy-duty paper clip. And a flashlight and pliers."

"I got 'em," Marvin said.

"Good. Let's meet about midnight at Loretta's desk. The office staff should have gone home by then."

Carrie changed the subject. "What do you suppose Mr. Whitley and Mr. Peters wanted to talk to Lawyer Epstein about?"

"I don't know," Marvin said. "They're sitting over there."

"I guess we have to wait," Mike said.

"I hope it's something good for our side," Carrie said.

Just then, Bates got up from his table and hurried out of the dining hall.

"I have something to do," Mike said. "I'll see you two at midnight."

CHAPTER 45

Marvin had fallen asleep on his bed, still dressed from the day in court. He awoke to a tap on his door. Carrie sat in the doorway in her wheelchair.

"You ready to go get your stuff back?" she asked.

He sat up and rubbed his eyes. "Where's Mike?"

"I don't know. He said he'd meet us there."

Marvin pulled on his leather jacket, gathered the tools Mike needed, and joined Carrie in the dark hallway. The fluorescent lights were turned off, and the wall light fixtures were turned down to their lowest settings. Marvin and Carrie made their way toward the administrative offices. When they got there, Mike was sitting at Loretta's desk waiting for them.

"Ready to go in?" he asked.

"Let's go," Marvin said.

Mike got up and clumped his way with his walker over to the door to Director Bates's office. He handed the flashlight to Carrie. "Hold this and point it right at the lock," he told her.

"You want it on?" she asked.

He shot her a stern look, and she giggled and turned on the flashlight.

Marvin gave Mike the tools and then stood looking over his shoulder. Mike inserted the blade of the small screwdriver into the key opening and put gentle pressure on it in the counter-clockwise direction. Then he inserted the tip of the paperclip, which he had bent upward with the pliers, into the lock and began pulling it back and forth, keeping a steady pressure on the screwdriver. After about ten seconds, the lock turned and the door opened.

"Shh," he said. They crept into the office. "Don't turn on the lights."

He took the flashlight from Carrie and swept the office with its beam. There on the desk were Marvin's laptop and camcorder.

"Jackpot!" Mike said. "Get them and let's go."

"What about my shotgun?"

"Bates took it with him."

"Did you see him?"

"Yep."

Marvin got the laptop and camcorder from the desk and turned to leave.

"Hold it right there!" a voice said from out of the darkness.

They stopped and looked toward the door. The overhead light went on, and Director Bates stood in the doorway with the shotgun in one hand pointed at them and his other hand on the light switch. Marvin pressed the Record button on the camcorder and set it on the desk aimed at Bates.

"Where do you three think you're going with that?" Bates said.

"To the cops," Marvin said. "Now put that shotgun down before I take it away from you." Marvin was nervous but he wasn't going to let Bates see it.

"You're not taking anything away from anyone, Bradley. But I'm about to shoot three burglars in the dark."

"You've got two barrels, Bates. There's three of us. We'll get you." Marvin raised his cane and moved closer to Bates, putting himself between the shotgun and Carrie. Bates backed up, looking around the room.

Mike was standing next to Bates, and as Bates stepped

backwards, Mike made a quick movement. That fast, Mike had his cattle prod in his hand. He swept the prod upwards and hit the bottom of the shotgun barrel. The gun went off and sprayed rock salt onto Marvin's shoulder. It stung his cheek, and he jerked off to one side. Mike poked Bates in the midsection with the business end of the cattle prod. Bates screamed, backed away, and pointed the shotgun at Mike. "At least I'll get you, you crippled little piece of—"

An arm in a white uniform came from behind Bates out of the dark and went around his neck. The other hand pulled the barrel of the shotgun upwards. Rhonda, Mrs. Simpson's nurse, stood behind Bates, holding him off.

He struggled, and she tightened her grip. "Let go of the shotgun, fatso," she said.

Bates released the shotgun and Rhonda leaned it against the wall. Then she pushed Bates to his desk and bent him over it, pinning him down with her arm.

"What the heck is going on here?" she asked. "I heard a shot."

"Police! Everybody stay where you are!" The new voice came from out in the hallway. Detective Murray stepped into the room, a pistol in his hand. He looked the situation over and said, "Who's doing the shooting and why is that man pinned down?"

"Bates came to visit his mother-in-law," Rhonda said. "He had a pillow and a shotgun. When he saw me, he left. Mr. Bradley had warned me about him, so I followed him down here and heard a shot. Then I came in and grabbed him."

"Is Mrs. Simpson alone?" Marvin asked.

"No, her daughter is there. She's been coming in at night."

Murray holstered his pistol and moved toward Bates.

"You can let him go," he said. He pulled Bates's arms behind his back and put handcuffs on him. Then he looked at Marvin, Carrie, and Mike.

"What the heck are you three trying to do? Don't you know you could've been killed?"

"Not likely, Detective," Marvin said. "It's loaded with rock salt. Wouldn't kill a mouse. Look here." He indicated the shoulder of his leather jacket. "It didn't even penetrate. Why are you here, anyway?"

"Mr. Charles called. He said Bates was probably going to try to kill you three and his mother-in-law."

"How did you know that, Mike?" Marvin asked.

"I followed him from the dining hall," Mike said. "He came here and stayed until a short time ago. I hid in the dark out in the reception area. Then he left with the shotgun. I couldn't keep up with him and stay back far enough that he wouldn't see me, but I figured he was going to his mother-in-law's room. You sure got here in a hurry, Detective."

"I was in the squad room when you called. I came here right away and went to Mrs. Simpson's suite. Her daughter said that Bates had just come for a visit. Neither she nor her mother could figure why he was visiting so late at night and why he was bringing her another pillow. Hearing that, I headed down here."

"We're glad you believed Mike, Detective Murray," Carrie said. "A lot of what we've been saying has been ignored around here."

"After what happened in court today, I'll believe anything. I'm grateful to you three for what you've done. You too, ma'am, I don't know your name."

"Rhonda." She turned to go back upstairs. "I better get back on duty. Mrs. Montana will be wanting to go home. I'll tell her what happened. Let me know if you need a witness in this dirt-bag's trial, Detective."

Bates stayed in place face-down on the desk, whimpering with his hands cuffed behind him.

"Thanks, Nurse Rhonda," Carrie called out. "Thanks very much."

Marvin said, "Would you like a video of what happened here tonight, Detective?"

"You've got one? That would help us convict this guy."

"Give me a minute to upload it to my laptop. For my files." Marvin took the DVD from the camcorder and copied the video. Then he gave the original to the detective. "Lawyer Epstein has all the other stuff. You can get it from him."

"Thank you, Mr. Bradley," Murray said. "Billings is going to love this. It might make up for the shellacking the three of you gave him in court."

"It isn't over yet," Marvin said. "We still have to get Freddie off."

"If he's innocent. I hope so. The three of you go to bed now. You've had quite a night. I'll see you tomorrow in court. Are you going?"

"We wouldn't miss it," Carrie said.

CHAPTER 46

The next morning on the bus, the conversation buzzed about the case.

"What do you think the jury thinks about all this so far?"

"Did the DA prove his case?"

"What will Lawyer Epstein present as a defense?"

When the bus pulled up to the courthouse, they got out and went in. The guards had streamlined the procedure for getting them through the metal detector and into the courtroom and there weren't nearly as many spectators as there had been the previous days. They were inside in only a few minutes.

Marvin, Carrie, and Mike took their usual seats in the gallery. Mike yawned a lot, Marvin had dark circles under his eyes, and Carrie closed her eyes and dozed in and out. The previous night's adventure had taken its toll.

Mr. Whitley and Mr. Peters sat in the front row. Lawyer Epstein opened the defense's case.

"The defense calls Mr. Arnold Peters to the stand."

Billings leaped up. "Objection, your honor," he said. "Mr. Peters isn't on the defense's witness list."

"Your honor, we have new evidence that we just learned about," Epstein said, "and Mr. Peters's testimony is essential to our defense. Here is an amended witness list to include him and Mr. Whitley."

"This is just a ploy to impress the jury, your honor. The defense brings in a surprise witness with new testimony in the eleventh hour."

"Overruled," said the judge. "Mr. Peters will take the stand."

When Peters was sworn in and seated in the witness stand, Epstein began his questioning.

"Mr. Peters, please tell the court what you remember about the morning of January twenty-four."

"Well, sir, I was in my room. On that particular night I had my door open. I heard a scuffling down the hall. Then Leroy Parker went by."

"How could you tell it was Parker?"

"Well, sonny, everybody has their own way of walking. When you've been blind this many years your other senses take over. I heard him walking and I knew it was him."

"What did you hear next, Mr. Peters?"

"I heard Mr. Whitley come out of his room and down the hall. He stopped at Mr. Charles's room, then came by going in the same direction as Mr. Parker. A few minutes later he came back, stopped at Mr. Charles's room again, and returned to his own room."

"You can tell all that just by hearing it?"

"I can."

"So, on the evening of the murder, you heard Mr. Whitley follow Mr. Parker toward where the murder took place. Is that true?"

"Yes."

"And you heard him stop at Mr. Charles's room on the way."

"Coming and going."

"Did you hear anyone else out there that night?"

"No."

"Not even the defendant?"

"No. But he could've been there later. I went to sleep."

"Thank you, Mr. Peters. Your witness, Mr. Billings."

The judge said, "Mr. Billings, since this is a surprise witness, do you need time to prepare for cross-examination?"

"No, your honor. I'm ready now. Mr. Peters, you say you could distinguish who was in the hall based only on the sound of their footsteps?"

"That's right."

"And you expect the court to believe that?"

"I don't expect anything, sonny. I told you how it is. I don't give a hoot what you believe."

Epstein got out of his chair. "Your honor, I do care whether the jury believes Mr. Peters. Perhaps we can arrange a demonstration."

"Yes, Mr. Epstein," the judge said. "I'd like to see that myself. What kind of demonstration do you have in mind?"

"Mr. Peters knows everyone in the gallery. Let's pick one or two and have them walk around. Let Mr. Peters identify them from the sounds of their footsteps."

"Your honor," said Billings. "How do we know this isn't a setup? How do we know Mr. Peters doesn't already know who Mr. Epstein will choose?"

"Well," said Epstein, "In that case, Mr. Billings can do the choosing. Unless he doesn't trust himself."

"I'll allow it," Judge Stauffer said. "Mr. Billings, make your choice."

"Very well, your honor, how about that lady right there?" He pointed at Carrie. "Ma'am, would you please walk over here?"

"No, I won't," Carrie said.

"You honor, please direct the lady to walk over here."

Epstein said, "She's in a wheelchair, your honor, and is missing a leg. Mr. Billings should at least have the good sense to pick someone who can walk."

"Well, I didn't know. Sorry. Let's try a different one."

"Let's. But don't give us an edge, Mr. Billings. You let it slip that you picked a lady."

"Sorry again," Billings said with a sigh. "Would everyone in the gallery who can walk unassisted please raise your hands?"

Several hands went up. Billings pointed at Elsie Collins. "Please walk over here," he said to Elsie.

Elsie slid across the bench and strutted around the room.

"Mr. Peters, who is that?"

"It's Elsie Collins. Can't you hear her jewelry jangling?"

Billings said, "Are you Elsie Collins?"

"The one and only."

"Mrs. Collins, thank you, and please take your seat."

"It's Miss Collins, young man," Elsie said and returned to her seat.

"Let's do another one, someone without jewelry," Billings said, and he pointed to Mr. Whitley. "Would you please walk up here and back?" he said.

Whitley got up and walked toward the center of the room and back.

"It's Bill Whitley," Peters said. "Hi, Bill. How'm I doing?"

Whitely smiled and nodded as if to say, "You're doing fine, Arnie. Just fine." Peters couldn't see the gesture, but everyone could tell that he got the message.

The judge said, "That's enough of a demonstration. Mr. Billings. I think we got the point. Please ask your next question."

"Mr. Peters, why didn't you come forward with this information before now? Are you sure it's not something you cooked up just to get the defendant off the hook?"

"I didn't come forward before now because I didn't think you were smart enough to convict Mr. Bradley's grandson, Mr. Billings. Everybody says you're dumber than a box of rocks, and yesterday Mr. Charles proved it. But when it looked like you might have the upper hand and might actually convict an innocent man, I decided to tell what I heard."

"And implicate your friend in this crime?"

"He doesn't mind. He said it would be okay."

"I see. So the two of you conspired to subvert justice and set free a guilty man. I have no further questions of this witness."

Epstein proceeded. "The defense calls Mr. William Whitley to the stand. And we'll need Mr. Peters to stay up here, if it pleases the court."

"Your honor, really," Billings said. "What's this all about?"

"Your honor, Mr. Whitley is a stroke survivor and cannot speak. We need Mr. Peters to interpret. They communicate with sign language."

"But, your honor," Billings said. "Mr. Peters is blind. How can he read sign language?"

"They do it hand-to-hand," Epstein said. "Mr. Peters holds Mr. Whitley's hand while Mr. Whitley fingerspells."

"And how do we know that what Mr. Peters says is what Mr. Whitley fingerspells?"

"Well, I suppose if the translation is inaccurate, Mr. Whitley will let us know somehow."

The judge said, "I'll allow it. Mr. Peters stay where you are. Mr. Whitley, please come forward and be sworn in. Mr. Peters, you are still under oath. Ladies and gentlemen of the jury, the witness will fingerspell his testimony and his translator, Mr. Peters, will speak the witness's words."

Whitley came to the stand and stood next to Peters. He put his hand into Peters's hand. The bailiff swore him in.

Epstein said, "Mr. Whitley, please tell the court what happened on the morning of January twenty-four of this year."

Whitley began to fingerspell, and Peters spoke the words slowly. The courtroom was still and silent. The jury paid rapt attention to the small man's reading of the large man's words.

"I was getting ready for bed when Leroy Parker came into my room. He pushed me down on the bed and grabbed Tabitha, my new kitten. He had killed my other cat, and he was go-

Al Stevens

ing to kill Tabitha, too."

"You were sure of that?" Epstein said.

"He said so. He said, 'This one is headed for the Dumpster,' and he walked out with it. I couldn't let him kill my kitten. I followed him out to jump him if I could catch him. I didn't have much of a chance of stopping him, him being younger and stronger, but I couldn't walk fast enough to even try."

Whitely took a moment to pause for a breather. Then he put his hand back in Peters's hand.

"I passed Mr. Charles's room and remembered the archery set. It was leaning against the wall in a chair just inside the door. I used to be pretty good with archery, so I grabbed the bow and an arrow and headed toward where Leroy went."

"How did you know which way he went?"

"I could hear Tabitha crying. She was so scared. I was scared, too, but I had to do it. Leroy turned a corner into the vacant wing, and I made it to the corner. When I got there, I saw him at the end of the corridor. His back was to me, and he was holding Tabitha up with one hand and had his other hand around Tabitha's neck."

He stopped again.

"Do you need a moment, Mr. Whitley?" Epstein said.

"No. I put the arrow in the bow, pulled the bow back, and let it fly. Leroy fell to the floor. I went to where he was laying and picked up Tabitha. She was scared but okay. And that's about it."

Mike leaned over to Marvin and Carrie and whispered. "See, didn't I tell you? Just like on *Perry Mason*. It's never one of the ones you think it is, and the guilty party always confesses in court. But does anybody listen to me?"

The bailiff shushed him.

Epstein asked, "Mr. Whitley, did you think to call nine-one-one?"

"No. He was dead. The arrow went right through his heart."

"How come you didn't leave fingerprints on the bow and arrow?"

Whitley fingerspelled and Peters spoke. "I wiped the arrow with my handkerchief from where it went in Leroy's back up to the feathers. Then I wiped down the bow and held it with a clean part of the handkerchief. I took it back to Mr. Charles's room and left it on the floor inside his doorway. I flushed the handkerchief down the toilet in my room. It had blood spots. You know. DNA."

"Mr. Whitley, given all that you've told us, I suppose it was a traumatic experience."

"I have no regrets, Mr. Epstein. The man was evil. He killed not only Toby but Mr. Peters's dog and Mrs. Meade, too. And who knows who else? And he wasn't done killing. He had to be stopped. The only regret I have is that my friends had to be put through all this. And the effect on Tabitha."

"What effect?"

"She doesn't like tall men, now. Has a fit when one comes around."

Marvin nudged Mike and pointed to the scratch on his hand, now mostly healed.

"Thank you, Mr. Whitley. I have no further questions."

Billings took the floor. "That's a quite a story you've concocted for us, Mr. Whitley. How do we know you could have done it? Are you an archery sharpshooter?"

Whitley said through Peters, "I am. Put an apple on your head and we can have us another courtroom demonstration."

The courtroom burst into laughter. The judge gaveled them to silence.

Billings said, "Mr. Whitley, I am having difficulty understanding why you would come forward now when you were in the clear before. You weren't even a suspect. If you did it, why tell us now? You will be arrested, tried, and convicted. You'll spend years in prison."

"No, Mr. Billings, I won't."

"And why not?"

"According to my doctor, I have maybe six months, maybe less."

Having just spoken these words for his friend, Mr. Peters broke away and began sobbing. "I'm sorry," he said, "I didn't know that." Other people in the courtroom were weeping, too. Mike blew his nose with a loud honk, and the bailiff glared at him.

Billings then said, "So, given that you haven't much time left and nothing much to lose, you're willing to take the rap for your friend's grandson?"

Mr. Peters regained control and took Mr. Whitley's hand again. "Mr. Billings, I killed Leroy Parker because he was going to kill my kitten. That's all you need to know. I have nothing further to say."

"And neither does anyone else," Judge Stauffer said. "The witness has rights. I should have stopped him before this. Until he is represented by counsel, this court will hear no more of his testimony."

Epstein began, "Your honor—"

"Never mind," the judge said. "I'm way ahead of you. I am hereby entering a directed verdict of not guilty for the defendant in this case. Does the prosecution have any objections?"

"No, your honor," Billings said. "Not in light of this confession."

"Your honor," Epstein said, "the defendant works in the defense industry with a security clearance. Having an arrest and indictment on his record can compromise his ability to continue in his job. The defense moves that his record be expunged."

"So ordered. Bailiff, release the defendant into his own

custody. The jury is discharged. Mr. Bradley, you are free to go. Case dismissed. Court adjourned."

CHAPTER 47

Two days after the trial ended, a small group of people gathered in the nursing home dining hall at supper time. Freddie was the guest of honor. Marvin, Carrie, Mike, Lawyer Epstein, Mr. Peters, and Mr. Whitley were there. Charlie Danvers had come up to get the shotgun and tools and take them back to town, so Marvin had asked him to join in, too.

They pulled two tables together so everyone could sit together at their victory celebration. The temperature was at a comfortable level for the first time that winter. And the food was edible again. The server brought trays with plates of broiled chicken, steaming vegetables, and piles of mashed potatoes and gravy. Even she seemed happier today, smiling at everyone and saying, "Enjoy your dinner."

"It's nice to have it warm in here," Carrie said.

"Well," Mike said, "my guess is that the new guy found out what happens to a maintenance man who lets it get too cold." There was laughter all around.

The rest of the chatter was about the trial. Marvin asked Epstein, "Are they going to charge Mr. Whitley with anything?"

"No. Billings met with Detective Murray and me after the trial. They asked me to represent Mr. Whitley's interests."

"And you got him off," Mike said.

"This is an election year. The judge and Billings are seeking re-election. Freddie's trial got a lot of national media attention. Cable television, the evening news, everybody covered it. It's a great human interest story, and nothing else was going on in the world at the time."

"My daughter watched it," Carrie said. "They called to tell me."

"They don't want the country watching them prosecute an elderly man with a terminal illness who was protecting his beloved kitten. They worry that it would make them look bad to voters. And I would certainly see that it did. You're in the clear, Mr. Whitley."

Mr. Whitley looked all around, smiled, and nodded.

"He says thanks," Mr. Peters said.

"Tell him he's welcome," Mike said.

"He can hear, Mike," Carrie said. "Tell him yourself."

"What about Ollie?" Mike asked.

"You mean Bates?" Epstein said. "He's in for the long haul. I gave Billings the files and videos you collected. He about turned handsprings over it. This will be a high-profile case for him. Practically guarantee his re-election. You can all expect to testify."

"Are they going to charge Loretta?" Marvin asked.

"She got a lawyer and cut a deal. No charges in exchange for her testimony against Bates."

"His goose is cooked," Mike said. "Hot dang, I wonder if we'll meet that blonde lady who hosts the court shows on cable. She's one hot tomato."

"No," Carrie said, "and you're too old to be drooling over the women on TV."

"What? I should drool over the women here? Fat chance."

"Wouldn't Billings need to have had a warrant in order to use the documents?" Marvin asked. "After all, I stole them off the home's main computer."

"Murray had a warrant, which he got based on your testimony. The cops took the computer when they arrested Bates, and he hadn't erased anything yet. The package you prepared just told them what documents to look for. The videos were yours, so they don't need a warrant for them."

"What about the people Bates worked for?" Marvin asked.

"He'll probably roll over on them all. Mrs. Simpson has retained me to represent her in an action to break their lease, which should be no problem. This thing will have repercussions all over the state when the media get hold of it."

"When families realize what that investment company has been up to," Marvin said.

"I'm also handling Mrs. Simpson's daughter's divorce. You mentioned that the heat is up, and the food is definitely better. The judge issued a court order for the state to take over operation of the home until all this gets cleared up. I'm told that most of the original staff will be offered their jobs back."

They all cheered.

Mike asked, "Who's going to take care of Tabitha when, well, uh, you know?" He looked at Whitley.

Carrie shot Mike a stern look, but Whitley grinned and pointed to Carrie, who said, "That's right. Tabitha will come to live with me. That'll keep the tall men out of my room. Now if I can only figure out what to do about the short ones." She made a face at Mike, who stuck his tongue out at her. "Hot tomatoes indeed," she said.

"Settle down, children," Marvin said.

Carrie said, "Nurse Helen came to see me last night."

"What about?" Marvin asked.

"She wanted my advice. It's a sad thing. Her husband has been beating her. It's why she got involved with Leroy in the first place. She wanted to know what she ought to do."

"Why did she ask you?" Mike asked.

"She had read my psych profile and knew that I went through the same thing years ago."

"You?" Marvin said. "You were a battered wife?"

"Oh, yeah. Big time. I have the scars to prove it. And no, Mike, you can't see them."

"But you never told us."

"We all have our secrets, Marvin, the details that we keep to ourselves. Like what we learned about Mike yesterday. Think about what all he's never told us. And probably never will."

They all looked at Mike, who looked away and avoided their stares.

Carrie continued. "I have things I don't want people to know, Mike has things he doesn't want people to know. What about you, Marvin? Any skeletons in your closet?"

"Nah. My life is an open book."

Charlie Danvers spoke up for the first time. "Don't you believe it, folks. Marvin has a notable past. And I only wish he would let people know about it. You'd be proud."

"Dummy up, Charlie," Marvin said.

"Tell us, Charlie, tell us," Carrie said, pleading.

Charlie shook his head. "Ask Marvin."

"Don't ask Marvin," Marvin said.

"So, what advice did you give Nurse Helen?" Mike asked.

"I told her to leave the guy. They have no kids, and there's no reason she should stay in that kind of a situation."

"Is that what you did, Carrie?" Mike asked.

"I threw the bum out. That's ancient history, though. I told Helen she needs to be more selective about men. Whatever her husband did, it was nothing compared to Leroy Parker."

"That's good advice," Epstein said. "Did you tell her you happen to know a good divorce attorney?"

They all laughed and Carrie said, "I should've. Anyway, I don't want to hijack this festive celebration, but I have wonderful news. My son-in-law called today. I'm going to be a grandmother. Ann is pregnant."

"Who does he suspect?" Mike asked.

Everyone laughed again and Epstein said, "That's great news, Carrie. You're all a remarkable bunch of people, an inspiration to the younger generation. I am proud to know you and to have been a small part of your crusade to put a stop to what was going on here. You are all heroes."

"Well," Carrie said, "I think we should acknowledge the real heroes here. Marvin for spearheading and engineering the downfall of the new regime, and our boy, Mike. What can I say? Look at all he did. Booby traps, videos, picked the lock, and even knocked the shotgun out of Bates's hand. And the way he handled that Billings in court."

"No big deal," Mike said. "Don't make a fuss."

"We brought you a reward, Mike. Marvin got it for us." She reached in her tote bag, took out a dusty Mason jar of strawberry preserves, and handed it to Mike. He took it and grinned.

"There's plenty more where that came from," Marvin said.

Carrie said. "Mike, I hate to admit it, but you are amazing. It's a side of you we never saw. How in the world do you know how to do all those things?"

Mike looked around the table at his friends. He gripped the jar of preserves with both hands, tapped it on the table, leaned forward, and smiled. "Didn't you hear the prosecutor?" the little man said. His eyes sparkled and his eyelids crinkled mischievously. "I used to work for the CIA."

ABOUT THE AUTHOR

Al Stevens is a retired author of computer books and an entertainer. For fifteen years he was a senior contributing editor and columnist for *Dr. Dobb's Journal,* a leading magazine for computer programmers. He lives with his wife, Judy, and a menagerie of cats on Florida's Space Coast, where he writes by day and plays piano, string bass, and saxophone by night.